Deadly Cargo

Hal Archer

To my fellow writer friends Gary, Adam, and Nick. I've treasured our regular meetings over coffee and words. May we share many more years of camaraderie.

After you finish reading this book, look for the link in the back to signup for the Hal Archer Readers' Group email list and be the first to hear of new releases and sales. To say thanks, I'll send you a download link to get a free copy of the Jake Mudd novella, Tangled Peril.

Also, look at the end of this book for the preview of Forced Vengeance, Jake Mudd Adventures Book Two. You'll find the first three chapters there, along with a link to get the book.

CHAPTER ONE

Adrenaline kept Jake's thoughts away from his broken ribs and cracked hip bone. The Faklu motivated him to get off his ass and move clear of the beast's charge.

He scrambled to his feet and leapt out of the clearing for cover.

The monster halted its charge, but not until it had moved well past the spot where Jake had been.

Jake realized he couldn't outrun or outmuscle the creature, so he climbed a tree.

All this for some credits and the generous gratitude of a rescued slave girl. Not sure they're worth it. Well, she was.

The Faklu, barreling through the weaker trees, charged him again. It lowered its shoulders as it neared the tree Jake was on, striking the base of the trunk with its bony hairless forehead. The tree cracked, then shattered. Splintering limbs cast off in all directions, forming thickets of rough-hewn spears on the ground and in the canopy. They lodged into the adjacent trees like arrows.

Jake held part of the upper half of the tree as it fell, separated from its base. The top of the tree, Jake still clinging to it, caught its ends on two adjacent trees, leaving him gripping the branch, suspended ten feet above the Faklu.

The creature grunted and snorted. Jake smelled the noxious mist as it rose to his face. He grew dizzy as the cloud filled the air around him. He gagged at the taste of the discharge, like blood and sewage, if he had to guess. The creature swung its head from side to side, searching for the morsel that had been left for it to eat. With thick tight muscles on the back of its neck, it was unable to raise its gaze to see Jake hanging overhead.

Jake looked to another branch he could jump to, if only he could get a little momentum first. He swung his body back and forth. Before he made the jump, he heard a loud crack. He and the large branch he held plummeted toward the Faklu.

Jake turned his body mid-air, as best he could, guiding the speared tip of the branch to strike the beast. The wood, with his weight bearing down on it, drove into the neck of the creature. He fell onto the Faklu, slamming into its neck beside the planted tree top. The beast dropped to its belly, and its chin crashed to the ground. The thump sent Jake tumbling off his kill and into the dirt.

He lay on his back breathing heavy.

Adrenaline leaked away. Sharp pains took its place.

Broken ribs. A cracked hip bone.

Sarah's gonna love saying I told you so.

CHAPTER TWO

The field drives faded, fixing the distorted ship in space a minute outside the projected orbital distance, and as the soothing hum of the drives ceased Jake woke from his typical in-flight nap. If anyone on the planet's surface happened to be watching his arrival, they'd see the faded red nine-foot-high lettering on the side of the class 4 Tarian cargo vessel. GDS — Galactic Delivery Service. Twenty-three hundred eighty-two feet in length, his beloved Sarah remained a reliable companion despite the trouble she'd endured on his behalf over the twelve years they'd been together. The blast marks on the outer hull. A few asteroid dings here and there, from the times Jake and Sarah argued over manual versus auto-pilot mode. The new panels crudely welded on in a hurry to get her off the ground and off-planet just before an aerial bombardment. A bombardment which may have had something to do with Jake's friendliness toward the betrothed of a local warlord on Geida Gamma. Bumps in the road.

Jake felt the lingering aches from his injuries

suffered during the run-in with the Faklu. The med bay
in his ship had done its job, but his body needed longer
to forget the incident.

"Glad to see you were able to sleep." Sarah turned
on the lights directly over Jake's face. She flipped them
on to full brightness, not dim like he always asked her
to do.

"Is that really necessary?" He squinted and raised
his right hand to shield his brown, blood-shot eyes. The
light washed out his tousled brown hair and his tanned,
stubble covered jaw, making him look paler than he
was.

"I'm just programmed. Remember?" Her voice was
normally pleasant, one that might belong to a confident
healthy twenty or thirty-something woman, even a little
sexy at times. Right then she just sounded pissed.

"That was two days ago," he said, as he reached
with his left hand to press the button, killing the lights
she had turned on. "I said I was sorry. Besides, you
took it the wrong way. It was supposed to be a
compliment."

He swung his legs off the bed rack and sat up. She
turned the bright lights back on. He shook his head.

"So," Sarah sounded calmer, "we're here. Daedalon."

"Great. Thanks for driving," Jake said. He patted the
bed rack with his hand. She felt it, as she felt
everything in the interior of the ship. AI-linked meta
materials throughout.

"You know you can count on me." Her tone was soft.
It seemed the spat was over.

"Like no other." He stood and headed to the bridge to

get his first direct look at the planet, a new stop on his delivery route. "I trust you've already staged the cargo for Daedalon?"

"Of course, Jake. All the documentation has been transmitted to the appropriate systems on the surface too. You're clear to deploy the surface shuttle with the cargo whenever you're ready."

"Thanks, darlin'."

* * *

Though all the logistics and documentation were handled by Sarah and her AI counterparts on the various planetary drop sites, galactic regulations still demanded all cargo deliveries be overseen by whichever person held the cargo delivery license, be they human, like Jake, or any of the other twenty-six races party to the Galactic Shipping Treaty. No AI, ship or otherwise had ever been granted a license, not even one as sophisticated as Sarah. Thanks to his familiarity with a few black-market channels, Jake's license was anonymized, but valid. He preferred it that way to keep trouble from following him around the galaxy. And so, after taking in the sight of the red planet Daedalon for a moment through the shielded window on the bridge, he went to the prep deck outside the cargo hull to suit up for departure to the surface.

* * *

"Don't you want to eat something before you head down?" She spoke to him as he dressed.

"I'm sure I can grab a bite once I'm down there. We've got what, three days until our next scheduled delivery?"

"Technically," she said. "So, you're not coming right back?"

"It's a new planet, darlin'. You know I've got to look around. I won't be longer than a day or two."

"And what am I supposed to do in the meantime?"

"I'll call you," he said.

He pressed a flat square on the wall beside the bench he sat on. The silver metal opened, folding down. Then a single tray extended, pushed out by some hidden smooth hydraulic action. Jake took the pistol from the form-fitting depression in the tray. He held down a black button on the side of the weapon with his thumb until a green light lit up on the top of the blaster. He let go of the button. The light went off. He stood and holstered the gun on his right hip, zipped up his dark brown leather flight jacket and grabbed his overnight bag before heading into the cargo bay toward the shuttle.

"No sense in saying be careful," Sarah said. Not a question. She knew better.

"Two days, tops."

Jake walked across the cargo bay to the shuttle, passing scores of stacked cargo containers, some waist high, others small enough for him to hand carry. As he neared the shuttle door he pressed a transmitter on his belt. The exterior lights around the base of the shuttle switched on, a blue glow. A whirring motor sound built up, not loud but still powerful sounding. Two jets of air shot out a few inches either side of the shuttle door. Then it opened and lowered, again with hydraulics, the tubes visible this time. The door's top edge moved down until it rested on the floor of the cargo bay, forming a ramp.

He stepped onto the inclined platform, then turned to face the open cargo bay. "By the way, what's the drop?"

"Couldn't tell you," Sarah said, her voice echoing slightly in the cavernous room. "It's a secure package. The receiver has the code."

"Great." He shook his head. "I hate surprises. With luck, they'll take it and save the cargo inspection until I'm gone. Last sealed package, if you'll recall, stirred up an uninvited welcoming party."

"That's why this one's bringing in a million marks," she said. "I negotiated it for you while you were sleeping."

"Yep," he said, "probably heading into a party on this one too."

Still, it'll go a long way to keep the General away from Sarah.

"Oh, one more thing."

"Yeah?"

"They didn't want to do the credit transfer digitally. They want to give you a marker chip in person upon delivery."

"You tell me this now?"

"What?" she said. "You're a tough guy. I'm sure you'll be fine."

"You're a peach."

"See you in two days," she said. "If I don't hear from you in three, I'll start interviewing for your replacement."

"Two days. And you work for me, remember?"

Jake turned back to the shuttle ramp opening and walked into the ship. The platform raised up and sealed. A minute later the large door of the cargo bay opened, revealing the red-orange cloudy atmosphere of the planet, twenty-four thousand miles below. A blue glow built up under the shuttle. Then it lifted, turned, and flew out the opening into space and down toward the rendezvous point on Daedalon.

CHAPTER THREE

Jake switched off the link with Sarah once the shuttle cleared her cargo bay door. Any offense she might have taken at that action had been addressed years ago. It was routine now. He preferred to handle the landing and the on-planet delivery alone. Besides, he had his hand-held comm device clipped to his belt. Of course, he had enough sense to keep it switched off most of the time.

Twelve years aboard her, as used to each other as they were, called for a couple of days off now and then. Eventually the pattern settled into his solo landings and deliveries, with the rare exception of when the delivery was too large for the cargo shuttle. Then both would head down to offload the cargo from her, but that entailed more difficulty since she was designed for space, not atmospheres and surface landings. He preferred the smaller cargo deliveries, for some time alone and the chance to explore on his own.

Ten years of frontier mercenary work before he got into cargo delivery never quite got out of his system. A day or two roaming the back alleys of an out-of-the-way planet usually sated his more adventurous urges, at least enough so he didn't mind when he headed back up to the sterile and orderly environment of her interior. Plus, she had some of the best crisis med tech available. And that had come in handy on more than one occasion, though she always interrogated him while he sat in the med pod getting stitched up.

Never had that during the merc wars, Jake often thought as she pulled him back from the reaper. Then he'd wonder if he was getting soft in his old age. "You're only forty-three," Sarah would remind him. "If you'd stop being an idiot, you may live to actually see old age."

He pulled up the rendezvous point on the shuttle computer, then hailed them. "This is G.D.S. inbound with cargo for Halcion Station. Do you copy? Over."

No response. He continued his descent.

"Halcion Station, this is GDS. I am inbound to your destination with cargo. Over."

A few beeps came through the speaker. Then static. After a second, it cleared.

"Oh, sorry," a young woman's voice sounded through the speaker. "I had to switch this thing on. I'm not usually the one that handles this."

Jake heard some shuffling, like she was moving something, sounded like her chair. Then she spoke again.

"Yes. This is Halcion. You're clear to land. Sending the coordinates now."

He glanced at the screen to the left of the shuttle

controls. The coordinates appeared.

"Coordinates received. I'm bringing her in. How's the weather down there?"

"Uh, fine I guess," the woman said. "I'm afraid my father's not here to receive you as he wanted, but I will let you in once you land. Maybe you could wait for him to sign for the cargo."

"Works for me," Jake said. The woman sounded like she might not be bad company, if her voice was any indication.

"Great. I'll flag you in once you land."

"If traffic's light, I'll be there in ten minutes," he said.

"What? Traffic?"

"Never mind. See you soon."

Jake hit a switch to close the channel. Then he punched a few codes into the controls, starting a surface scan of twenty square miles around Halcion Station. A moment later, the display to his right showed a color-coded topographical map. Spots of red, orange, yellow, and green.

"Not too crowded, are you?"

He pressed a button on the panel and energetic mostly melodious music came through several speakers embedded all around him in the walls of the craft. A few minutes later he piloted the shuttle through three layers of orange-red clouds. Then he corrected the ship's trajectory to line up with Halcion Station, as shown on the screen by a blinking blue light. Another minute and the structures in the area around Halcion Station, shown as colored icons on his screen, came into view. He noticed they weren't at all uniform in construction. Some were small and looked to be an assemblage of scavenged materials. A few were larger, about three times the size of the smaller ones. The larger ones had polished metal roofs and white walls, looked like plaster or white stone. The area was crisscrossed with wide lines running between the buildings and in the area just beyond them. As he descended, changing the angle of his view, he could tell the lines were trenches. They looked like roads dug down into the ground and they were deep.

The air was still, though it was the shuttle's instruments that told him that. He saw no vegetation of any kind on the planet, at least where he was headed. The ground offered only dirt and rock and sand, all the way to the horizon in every direction. No water in sight either. Hills surrounded the settlement, and beyond those, five miles out, mountains. Some of the tallest he'd seen.

"Why the hell would anyone live here?"

The shuttle screen marked Halcion Station with a crosshair. He turned the craft to line up with the flat stretch of dirt just behind the station. Halcion was one of the larger buildings, the same white walls he could now see were stone. Big rectangular blocks stacked three high, then the metal roof on top. Fixed to the roof, a satellite dish and an antennae array. No vehicles outside. Not around that building or any of the buildings.

Jake took the shuttle down to land. The dust kicked up a red cloud. He couldn't see the ground for the last sixty feet. The thud jolted him in his chair, even with the landing shocks doing their job. He figured he miscalculated the ground by about fifteen feet. Not the worst landing of his career. Still, he was thankful there weren't people outside to see what he'd done.

Then he saw a woman standing beside an open door of the Halcion Station building. She had one arm high above her head, waving it back and forth. Jake cut the engines and stepped to the shuttle door just as it was opening and lowering to make the ramp. He left his go bag in the shuttle next to his pilot chair, but not before pulling the atmospheric meter from it. With the shuttle door down, he held the gauge out to get a quick reading.

All planets on the delivery route were pre-cleared for atmosphere, but Jake figured it better to find out himself instead of relying on the research of the Galactic Shipping Regulatory Agency. He heard of a few planets that bought their way into the system despite failing minimal atmospheric safety standards. Getting air toxicity sickness would put him out of work for months, and his one-man company, G.D.S., still had loan payments to make for Sarah. That's what he called the payoffs he regularly made to anyone that might be able to keep the General and his men at bay.

"Breathable."

He shoved the meter into his jacket pocket, then he stepped down the ramp and out of the shuttle. He gave a wave back to the woman at the door to the station, some thirty feet away, through a haze of freshly disturbed dust. She waited for him.

Walking away from the shuttle, he pressed the

transmitter on his belt, shutting the ramp door. He made a survey as he walked toward her. Her voice had been spot on. She looked in her late twenties. Fit. Long brown hair. A refreshing change from the usual sort that he met on cargo drops, slave girls aside. Her clothing might have been a uniform. She had tan pants, form fitting, and a shirt that crossed in the front at a diagonal, two sides forming a triangular neckline. There were emblems on the shoulders, though he couldn't make out what they were.

The red cloud his shuttle kicked up on landing hadn't settled. As he stepped in front of the woman, a hot wind blew across the yard behind him, throwing the red sand and grit against his back, and then all around the two of them. Before he could greet her, the wind howled and the red sand stung his face. Without saying anything, she stepped through the doorway and signaled for him to follow her inside, which he did.

Once inside, he noticed that it wasn't the red sand in the air that made her skin look reddish. That was its color. A muted rust sort of red. Not a sunburn, at least it didn't look like one. It looked more like her pigment. He wasn't surprised. He'd seen many non-human races over the years. But he was curious, he hadn't seen her kind before. Aside from her skin, she looked human, at least what he could see of her. He wondered if he'd have a chance to check the rest out later. *What sort of woman makes it in a harsh place like this. Must be something inside her.* Then he thought about the cargo and the fact that he'd soon be handling a much-needed million-credit chip. Priorities.

"Do you have the code, or do we need to wait for your father?" Jake asked.

"He has it, but he should be here soon. Where's the package?"

"On the shuttle." Jake looked for signs of distress in her face. A small precautionary test. "In my experience, it's best to meet the point of contact for the delivery before bringing in the cargo. Especially for secure goods."

She walked to the other side of the room, past a table with three chairs, to a waist-high cabinet. She opened the door to the cabinet.

"You don't look like you're any trouble though," he said.

"If you say so." She winked at him. "Why don't you bring the package in, I'll make you a drink while we wait. It shouldn't be long."

"Sure. If he'll be here soon, I guess." He hoped her father wouldn't be there any time soon.

He walked back to the door and opened it. A quick look outside. "At least the wind's down. Should be just a minute." He stepped out and hit the transmitter on his belt to open the shuttle door.

A minute later he returned holding a small silver box by the handle on its top. He shut the door to the station just as the wind started up again.

"I'm Nadira, by the way," she said as she walked to the table and placed two simple metal cups on it.

Jake moved to the table and took a seat opposite her. He placed the case on the table and put his hand on the cup, but didn't drink. "Thanks."

She sat and took a sip from her cup.

He maintained an air of ease, but he noticed the door behind her at the back of the room, not the one he had entered but another, was open just a few inches. When he'd been in the room the first time, the door was closed. He was certain. Situational awareness saved him for ten years in the merc wars. A habit doesn't fade after that kind of history.

"So," he said, "what's the drink?"

"They call it Daedalon wine," she said. "It's distilled from one of the indigenous root plants in the area and fermented. It's my favorite."

"You're not from here?"

She didn't answer right away. A glance at the table. A sip from her cup. "Not originally," she said. "My father and I came here when I was a child."

Jake kept note of the door behind her as he reached under the table and flipped open the strap that was across the grip of his pistol.

"Try it," she said.

"What?"

She nodded toward the cup in front of him.

"Sorry," he said, "I should have told you. I should stay away from alcohol. I had a bit of a rough night, and I don't think my stomach could handle it right now."

"Oh."

He noticed she let slip a frown for a split second before recovering her pleasant demeanor.

"No offense," he said.

"No, of course." She got up from her chair and took his glass and hers and walked to the counter where she'd poured the drink.

Jake watched her, and the door, and he moved his hand onto the grip of his pistol.

He noticed her reach into her pocket, fiddling with something.

Damn secure packages.

CHAPTER FOUR

He preferred not to have to shoot her. He thought it might be worth getting to know her. Sure, she had red skin, but she was a beauty, and not every planet he stopped on turned out so well.

Before he could give the dilemma more thought, the door across the room flew open, and a large gray-skinned man burst in with a weapon drawn. Jake stood and stepped to the side, and at the same time flung the table up on its edge from underneath, shoving it toward the man. It was enough of a maneuver that the blast missed Jake.

Jake aimed his pistol, already drawn by now, and fired back. His shot, even taken while moving, pierced the man through his left shoulder. Unfortunately, his assailant held his weapon in his right hand, and the energy bolt from Jake's gun didn't deter him. If anything, the man gained ferocity. Dressed in a uniform like Nadira's, the attacker advanced a couple of strides toward Jake and took aim again. But he hesitated.

Jake noticed something in the man's gaze, the way

he looked at Nadira.

Jake stood beside her. Out of the corner of his eye, he saw her raise a pistol toward his head.

He made a quick decision to trust his instinct about what he saw. He ducked her gun and swiveled around behind her. Then he reached up and knocked her weapon from her hand. He wrapped his arm across her chest, holding her in front of himself.

"Do it!" she screamed to the man fifteen feet away, his gun still trained on Jake.

The man floated the barrel of his weapon, trying to get a clear shot at Jake. But he didn't shoot.

Jake, easily overpowering Nadira, held her so that her body blocked his. She elbowed him, but he didn't loosen his grip.

"Drop your weapon," he said, fixing his aim. A courtesy. He knew from the grimace the man wore that he wouldn't give up.

Jake watched the events of the next second unfold, as if in slow motion. The man's eyes narrowed. His brow furrowed. His jaw clenched.

Then, the cue Jake waited to see. The man's tension disappeared.

Jake, still holding Nadira, dodged to the side, keeping her tight against himself, out of the line of fire, answering to a deep instinct.

He heard the charge of the blaster bolt surge past his ear. Unlike Jake, the heavy gray man didn't dodge. Jake's aim found dead center. Aptly named. The man dropped to the floor.

Jake took his arm away from Nadira, but turned his

blaster on her.

"Waiting for your father, eh?"

She said nothing in response. Her eyes darted, then settled on her weapon on the ground behind him.

"I'd rather you didn't," he said. He kicked her pistol farther behind him. "This is why I don't like secure packages."

With his weapon still trained on her, he stepped over to the silver case on the floor. He knelt and picked it up.

"If you don't have the code for the case," he said, "and he's not going to be any help—" he pointed his gun at the dead man, and then back to her "—then this delivery is turning out to be a problem."

"I must have what's in that case."

"I'm sorry. If you weren't paying attention for the last couple of minutes. I don't think that's going to happen. Here's the thing. I've been shot at plenty of times. What doesn't happen, though, is a delivery failure. Not my drops. So, you're getting real close to ruining my day."

"What are you going to do?" She worked a tear up. Maybe it was real.

"I'm going to ask you one time, why did you two try to gun me down for the case and what did you do with the Halcion Station person or persons? Unless they're all dead, I'm making this delivery."

"They're not dead," she said. "At least, I don't think so. Though, they may be by now. They were taken."

He stepped over to the table he'd toppled and stood it back up. Then he pushed a chair next to it. "Sit down and explain, and maybe I won't shoot you."

She sat. He picked up her weapon and stuck it

between his belt and pants. Then he sat opposite her.

"We're desperate," she said.

"Keep talking."

"The contents of that case are our only chance to stop the Cracians. They hunt our people, the Waudure. Some of us survived by running and hiding. But then they started the hunts."

"What's in the case?"

"I don't know. My father wouldn't tell me."

She wiped the tear. Looked real enough. He motioned for her to continue.

"Years ago, we were brought to this planet against our will to work their mines. When the mines dried up, they didn't need us anymore, but they didn't want to share the planet's resources with our people. Sending us home was too costly, they said." She paused and seemed to be feeling the events again. "There was so much death."

Her breath took on a staccato rhythm. He caught himself noticing how the light played with the rust brown color of her eyes through the contour of another tear in the making.

"I'm not saying I believe one thing you're telling me." He holstered his pistol, "But I'll play along for now. I've got a payment to collect, and you're going to help me get it."

"Thank you."

"Where's the marker chip for this delivery? Something that valuable doesn't just disappear."

She cast her eyes downward, but he still saw the tear fall. "The Cracians have it, along with my father, but far from here."

"So, how can I find these Cracians?"

She looked to the man on the floor. "He was one of them."

Jake got up and stepped over to the body. With his right boot, he nudged the man's face, turning it upward, to take a closer look.

Not a rookie, he thought. A scar on his left brow. His skin lacked Nadira's red tone. In fact, it looked drained of color entirely.

Maybe just his kind's look.

Years of strain and concern was etched on the Cracian's face. Now, Jake thought, they served as an epitaph to a stranger.

Jake knelt and felt for a pocket, anything that would give him a clue about the man, about the Cracians. Nothing. He picked up the man's weapon, but the grip felt awkward. He dropped it onto the man's chest.

"Your partner isn't being cooperative." Jake turned back to Nadira. "How far are the others?"

"He's not my partner. And I told you it's far from here."

"You told him to shoot me."

"I had no choice! They have my father."

"You sounded pretty convincing when he had me under the gun."

"I had to keep him fooled. I agreed to help him get the case in exchange for my father's life. I might've shown him more interest than I really felt, but I had to."

"That's the problem. You're easy to believe."

"They're expecting us to return by nightfall," she said.

"Our transport pod is just outside. They'd see your ship coming, and their defenses are too strong. The pod's the only way to get inside their base."

"So, what's in the case?"

"I already told you, I don't know."

Jake walked back to the table and leaned over it, bracing himself with his hands on the table top. He came in close and looked at Nadira's brown eyes. Her breathing was audible, and it warmed the air in front of him.

Too easy to believe.

She looked at him, but said nothing.

"So, we hop into the pod you and the dead guy came here in. Then we head straight into enemy territory, with just a couple of blasters. And once there, we rescue your father, I get my payment marker, and somebody takes this damn package off my hands. And all without the Cracians capturing or killing us, or you shooting me in the back. Is that the plan?"

"I know, it sounds crazy."

Jake soaked in her gaze and breathed in her words. He gave a slight nod, and an exhale that said why the hell not.

"Works for me. I have some time to kill. Just don't cross me again. I've had a rough week."

Nadira reached across the table and grabbed his hands. "Thank you!"

He slid his hands out from under hers and stood upright. "Show me the pod. And you need to tell me more about the Cracians. How many are we talking about?"

"Thousands, but I know a way to where they're keeping my father that will get us past their defenses." She stood. "It's a long journey there. We must hurry. The pod's this way."

"Two blasters. Thousands. If you're leading me into a trap, darlin', we're not going on a second date."

"No trap, but I can't promise it'll be easy."

"It never is. I'm going to grab some gear and send my shuttle back up for safe keeping. Give me a few minutes."

"Of course."

Jake stopped at the door before he headed back out to his shuttle. "You know we're going to need a better plan, right?"

She threw every bit of allure and desperation she had into her eyes. "I just need your help."

He left her and went back to his shuttle to retrieve his go bag. When he got there, he called up to Sarah.

"I didn't expect to hear from you this soon," she said through the transmitter in the shuttle.

"There's been a snag down here."

"Nothing you can't handle, I hope."

"That remains to be seen. I'm sending the shuttle back up to you for now. Send it back down in a couple of days. Same coordinates. If I don't call in then, give me another day or two before you celebrate."

"So, push the next delivery out a few days?"

"It can't be helped. Besides, with the money we'll get on this one, we could take a month or two off without worrying about it."

"You're the boss. What's the problem, anyway?"

"It's complicated. They've got my payment marker, so I'm going to retrieve it."

"There's a girl involved, isn't there?"

"Just business, darlin'. I'm sending the shuttle back up in a few minutes."

"Ok. But don't die down there."

"Not my plan."

CHAPTER FIVE

"Can we trust her?" The slender man with reddish skin addressed Kharn with his head bowed, eyes averted. The man wore a uniform, gray and unassuming, a single insignia on the right lapel of his buttoned coat. A circle containing a section of a DNA double helix spread apart at one end, each diverging strand merging into the surrounding circle, the insignia marked him as a member of Crassus Kharn's science service.

Roles were assigned to all in Kharn's grand experiment, the society he'd built on Daedalon after leaving the Cracian home world under threat of execution. On Daedalon, Cracians, and those Waudure that stayed loyal to him, became scientists, soldiers, or one of a small group of administrators that served Kharn. The system was necessary, Kharn had decided, to advance his cause — the rise of Cracians to their collective destiny.

Kharn had fought with the Planetary Council on Cracia for years, struggling to convince them of the potential of the Cracian people, and their place among the more advanced civilizations in the galaxy. Tired of waiting for his plans to be implemented, he ignored the Council's rulings and began to form his own society within that which already existed on Cracia. His actions were deemed treasonous, and he was given a choice between death or exile.

Long before the Council passed judgement upon him, Kharn had quietly prepared behind the scenes. When their judgement came, he had already secured vast resources off planet through untraceable channels. Though he wanted the rise of his people to begin on their home world, he was prepared to do his magnificent work elsewhere. The so-called rulers of his world were too short sighted to embrace his superior vision.

"Time will tell," Kharn said. A foot taller than the other man, and with broad shoulders, he held his hands behind his back near his waist, long bony fingers interlaced. He wore a uniform like the other man's, but darker, which contrasted with his light gray skin. He stood facing the large indestructible crystalline glass window that afforded him a view of the wall of mountains on the horizon, the border keeping the creatures of the Untamed Lands outside the plateau he'd claimed long ago to build the base, the womb for his new civilization.

His science officer slowly looked up at him, seeing from the position of Kharn's boots that his emperor faced away from him. "And...if the resistance—"

Kharn spun around and shouted at the man, "Do you

doubt me?"

The science officer lowered his gaze. "Never, Great Kharn."

Kharn eased his tone. "Good. The people of the Untamed Lands are simple un-evolved creatures. All they might dream of contriving, I have already accounted for. It is unfortunate that many of them left the honorable place I bestowed upon them. It has slowed our progress, but more laborers are coming. I have seen to that."

"Of course, my lord."

"We will expand our operations then. The current situation will be resolved soon enough. My new friend sent us a gift. Your daughter is on her way now to retrieve it for us."

"You sent Nadira?"

"She is loyal."

"Yes, my lord."

"And she loves her father, I'm sure." Kharn turned back to the mountains in the distance. Bands of reddish-orange and gray clouds stretched above the peaks. "Now, leave me."

The man bowed before stepping backward to the door and leaving.

CHAPTER SIX

Jake stepped back through the door of Halcion Station. Nadira stood in the middle of the room, staring at the dead Cracian. Jake slung his bag over his shoulder and pushed the bulk of it around to his back as he walked into the room.

"You OK?"

She didn't take her eyes off the body. "He would've shot me to get to you."

"I know."

"You weren't using me as a shield after all."

"Not my style."

She turned to face Jake. "Thank you."

He walked to her, but then past her. "If you are shot today, I'm going to be the one to do it. So, don't worry." He spoke in stride, not looking at her, as he headed for the door at the back of the room.

She stood there without a retort.

He stopped in front of the open door the Cracian had come through. "We're going to your pod, right?"

"Uh, yes," she said. Then she glanced at the body

once more before catching up to Jake. "You have the case?"

Jake patted his go bag.

He let her step in front of him, then he followed her.

They passed through two more rooms, one with lockers on two walls and a couple of benches, the other a smaller room with a single table in the middle and chairs in around it. No decor. No life. Just a couple of empty rooms in a now unmanned outpost on a far-out planet with its own particular set of problems.

She opened a door at the back of the room. On the other side, a set of stairs carved from the stone and dirt of the ground led down fifteen feet into one of the channels Jake saw on his landing approach. The pod sat a few feet past the bottom of the stairs.

"So, we're rolling our way there?" Jake said.

"The seats inside don't roll. Gyroscopes. But yes."

Nadira stepped over to the ten-foot-diameter metal sphere. Originally silver or the metallic gray of steel, the ball wore an uneven coat of caked red dust and dirt accented with discoloration from scrapes all around and a large gouge near the bottom. That spot, packed with grit, held a mix of browns and reds, with flecks of white. From where Jake stood, the ball appeared windowless.

"Looks like it's seen better days," he said.

She glanced back at him. "So do you."

She's good.

He moved closer, behind her. She raised her right hand, touching the sphere. A seam in the ball appeared as a panel moved out. She stepped backward, and

Jake did as well to avoid blocking her movement. She turned her head away from the pod.

Jake watched her cup her hand against her face next to her mouth and eyes. He craned for a look in front of her at the raised panel on the pod. A loud whoosh sounded as the pod blew out a strong jet of air through the opening all around the panel. The ejected air whipped up a red cloud of dust that rolled over her shoulder and into his face.

He blinked and rubbed his eyes while he coughed the dust out of his mouth.

She chuckled.

The panel lowered to the ground.

"Thanks for the warning," he said.

"Ok. I did that on purpose." She smiled at him before turning and entering the pod through the opening. Jake followed, lowering his head to clear the opening.

Inside, the two took their seats. Jake put her confiscated gun into his bag. Then he shoved it down beside his seat, away from her. He left his own blaster holstered on his side, shifting in his seat until he found a comfortable spot.

The interior of the pod made good use of the ten-foot diameter of the sphere. Two seats took up most of the space, but the curved walls made the area feel more spacious than it otherwise would have seemed. There was a window after all, large, covering a third of the circumference of the sphere. The two seats faced it. Below the bottom edge of the window were the controls for the pod. A single panel, seven buttons and a couple of levers, the sort with horizontal grips that move along a single arc forward and backward.

Jake noticed the sphere had a seam on either side of the window. He peered under his seat, then at one of the seams.

"The sides of the outer sphere rotate," Nadira said. "The middle doesn't."

"That's good."

"So, when do I get my blaster back?"

"When I become more concerned with someone other than you shooting me."

"You mean like a thousand Cracians when you try to take the payment marker from them without giving them the case?"

"Who says I'm not going to give them the case?"

"You'll help me rescue my father, won't you?"

"Just drive. We can deal with all that when we get there, and you can fill me in on their base and where your father is being held on the way."

Nadira pressed a button on the panel in front of them, and the pod door behind them closed.

The view out the window in front of them was of the earthen trench in which they and the pod rested. No turns visible, except at the end, though Jake couldn't tell for sure. The trench extended to the limit of his vision. The high walls of the ravine shifted in color as the wind blew the clouds overhead, moving the shadows and spots of light around on the dirt.

She reached to one of the two levers. "You don't get queasy, do you?"

"I think I'll manage."

She pushed the lever all the way forward, full throttle.

The sphere moved at such a rate that the walls of the trench shifted into a reddish-brown blur. There was no acceleration. It went from stop to full speed. Jake put his hand over his stomach. Nadira chuckled.

"I'm fine," he said.

"Good," she said, "but it's the turns that'll get you. Hang on."

He cocked his head toward her and glared at her with wide eyes.

The sphere sped toward the trench wall ahead, then, without any loss of speed, shot off to the left. Jake groped at his side for something to hold on to. He didn't find anything on the sphere to grip, so he clenched his bag.

"You gotta be kidding."

The pod raced ahead. He groaned for a second, then checked himself, glancing over at her to see if she noticed.

"Another turn," she said.

After a minute of this routine, she pulled the lever back halfway and the pod slowed. It still moved quite fast, but Jake's stomach settled.

She looked at him and grinned.

"I'm glad that was fun for you," he said.

"Thanks. Took me half a year to get used to it. It doesn't bother the Cracians. They designed the pod system."

"So, tell me about them," he said. "Who's their leader, and how long have your people been fighting them?"

"Hiding from them is more like it. We haven't had the

means to fight them. There are too many of them, and my people aren't trained or equipped to take them on."

"But there's a resistance developing, right?"

"Some of us escaped capture in the last round of raids. A hundred or so. We've tried to do what we can to stop Kharn. But a lot of those that escaped just kept running. They moved to the Untamed Lands, where the Cracians won't follow them. They joined the others there."

"Kharn?"

"Their leader."

"But you and your father didn't keep running. Why?"

"We thought we could stop them. We just needed more time. My father is a brilliant man, and he knows about their technology. He worked with them, developing it in exchange for leniency for our people. He secured a guarantee from Crassus Kharn. But then, when he found out what he was building, my father refused to help any more. Then the mines dried up. And the hunts started."

"What were they building?"

"My father never told me."

"And the mines?"

"Resources for their research, I guess. I heard the mining needs changed over time."

"What about the others that escaped, the ones that didn't run to the Untamed Lands? Maybe they can help us."

"I'm taking you to them now."

CHAPTER SEVEN

Jake learned from Nadira about the Cracians as the two of them hurtled through the channels dug into the dry Daedalon soil. She told him of the weapons the Cracians used on her people in the hunts. Not just the blasters and rifles, but creatures. After she described them, Jake called them hounds.

Four-legged creatures, as tall as a man, the hounds, or crag beasts, were native to Daedalon. They came from the Untamed Lands, but after settling on the planet, the Cracians captured a few the beasts. Once they broke the animals of their wild ways, they trained them and conditioned them to follow orders. They became creatures of war. The more peaceful Waudure used them for travel and protection.

"So, the Cracians aren't native to Daedalon either?" Jake asked.

"No," she said. "Though they pretend they are. They were here before us, and they told us this was their planet. But after my father started working inside their base he learned more about them. They colonized this world to mine it."

"What were they mining?"

"They call the ore, drast. Our people call it lenura."

"What do they want with it?"

"We're not sure. The last time I could ask my father about it, he told me they're storing it underneath their base, in a natural cavern. But that was long ago.

"And those we're going to meet," Jake said, "you think they'll be willing to help us rescue your father?"

"Yes. They came here with my father and me, to Daedalon, I mean."

"You said the Cracians captured your people and brought them here?"

"That's right. All of us arrived here on the same ship. The ones we're going to see worked with my father."

The pod made another turn, but since they still were moving at half speed Jake's stomach took less offense.

"What kind of work?"

"Engineering projects, and research. Propulsion systems and those types of things."

"Could your father's work with the Cracians have something to do with one of those projects?"

"I don't know. It was all very secret. But I think it was something else."

The view down the trench darkened to near black.

Jake looked up through the large window on the front of the pod. The sky, barely visible, seemed to be moving. "What's going on? A storm?"

"They happen every day at dusk and dawn. It's why these trenches were constructed. Nothing that isn't bolted down can withstand the winds and the sand.

The storms cover a good part of the planet's surface."

"Good thing I sent my shuttle back up."

Nadira tapped one of the buttons on the panel in front of her. Lights on the front of the pod came on. They illuminated the sheets of dust that rained down as the winds above the trench carried large volumes of the loose surface soil across the opening to the channel. Pings accented the heavy static noise coming through the pod's metal walls as the sphere shot through the wild cloud filling the trench.

"We're almost there," she said.

The pod approached an intersection with three pathways. She moved the other lever and pressed a couple of buttons. The sphere took them down the left opening.

As they sped down the trench, she pressed and held a button on the panel. "It's Nadi. Move the gate." She released the button. Static came through a speaker in the pod.

The sphere sped on. Jake saw the end of the trench ahead. A dead end. No turns. No opening. Just a wall of dirt.

"It's Nadi. Open the gate unless you want a wrecked pod blocking your door."

Static.

"I don't see a door," Jake said. "You want to slow this thing down?"

She didn't slow the pod. She pressed the button again. "Someone answer. I'm not stopping. The storm's getting too big out here."

"The gate's open, Nadi. Sorry. You caught me at

dinner. Had food in my mouth."

The sphere moved to within a few hundred feet of the dirt wall at the end of the trench.

She pressed the button. "Jafir? You always have food in your mouth. Stand clear."

"Clear."

Jake pointed to the dead end and looked at Nadira.

She let the pod speed on. He gripped his bag again and cocked his head down a little, as if that would help him deal with the impact.

The pod shot into the wall at the end of the trench. Red sand blotted out the view through the window, but the pod didn't stop. A moment later, the sand slipped off the outside of the window.

Jake released his grip on his bag.

The pod slowed and then stopped. He looked around out the window. They had passed through a thick sheet of pouring sand. Now the pod sat inside a rectangular cavernous room. Metal lined the floors, ceiling, and walls.

Nadira pressed three buttons in sequence. The lights on the exterior of the pod went off and the sphere's hum, which Jake hadn't noticed before, quieted and then fell silent. She got out of her seat as the panel door behind them opened. He grabbed his pack and slung it over his shoulder as he stepped out of the pod behind her.

Nadira stepped clear of the pod as a pile of sand and dirt slipped off the top of the sphere landing on Jake's shoulder. He shrugged and flicked the rest off himself with his hand.

Nadira headed down the room, moving the left side to walk a path marked by a painted line on the floor. "Follow me."

Jake noticed two more transport pods ahead, parked. He felt the chill of the room, then he noticed the other difference in the air compared to what he felt outside Halcion Station. Moisture.

He spoke to Nadira, who continued walking down the painted path in front of him. "Why's the air different here? The temperature drop. The humidity. The storm?"

"No. These caverns are sealed, locked off from the storm and the air outside. I'll show you. Just follow me."

They walked for another minute, still in the same massive room. Nothing in it but the two of them and the three transport pods behind them. They reached the end and stopped in front of a recess in the metal of the wall at the back of the bay, or docking station, or garage. Whatever they called it. A painted rectangle outlined the recess in the wall.

"Now what?" Jake asked, as they stood there facing the wall, no handle or doorbell to be seen.

"Just stand still."

He stood still, feeling the comforting weight of his blaster holstered at his side.

Nothing happened.

"Yeah," he said, "your guy's on the ball again, I see."

"Just try not to lay your charm on so thick when you meet them. OK?"

"So, now I'm charming?"

The recessed panel on the wall in front of them slid

to the left. A man stood on the other side of the opening. His cheeks bulged. He chewed for a second, then swallowed. Jake spotted the other half of the sandwich in the man's left hand, which rested down at his side.

"Hey, Nadi. Who's your friend? Not a Cracian, I can see. At least you aren't that stupid. You know you're not supposed to bring anyone here."

"Where is he, Jafir?" She stepped past him and walked into the small room. She walked by the few chairs and a large metal crate serving as a coffee table. She went to a computer display embedded in the wall at the other side of the room.

"He doesn't want to talk to you," Jafir said. "He told me to see what you want and then to tell you no."

Jake grinned at hearing someone else giving Nadira a tough time. He stepped past Jafir, grabbing the other half of his sandwich from him.

Jafir turned and reached for Jake, who had already stepped away from him. "Hey, that's mine!"

Jake mumbled something that sounded a little like 'hungry', though his speech came out garbled with his mouth full. He'd taken it in a single bite.

Jafir tailed Jake as he walked over to Nadira, but let the argument die out. Jake figured the guy realized he came up a foot shorter and sixty pounds lighter.

Jake stepped behind Nadira as she was swiping her finger down the side of the display screen on the wall.

"So, what's going on?"

"Give me a minute. I'm just trying to get him down here."

The screen flickered, and static came through a speaker. Then the screen cleared to an image of another reddish-skinned man, but he looked to be larger, stronger, like he could handle himself. He wore a dark blue jacket. He appeared much more formidable than the man that gave Jake a sandwich. Jake wondered if the two of them would get along, or if he'd have to test the man's mettle at some point.

"Hello, Nadi," the man said. "I didn't think I would see you again any time soon."

"It wasn't my fault, Rekla" she said. "We've been through all this before, but we don't have time for it now."

"Why is that?" he said.

"We're going in," she said, "after my father."

"You know that's suicide?"

"No. I don't know that. I have to get him back, and he's going to help me." She nodded to Jake who stood just behind her left shoulder.

"And who's he?" Rekla asked.

Nadira glanced at Jake again. "The delivery guy."

Rekla's face soured. "Why does he care?"

"He's got his reasons. We have an agreement."

Rekla looked at Jake. "Is this so?"

Jake stepped around Nadira. "I'm just going to get what's mine. And to finish the job I came to Daedalon to do."

Nadira spoke up again. "So, are you going to help us?"

Rekla looked to her, and to Jake, then back to her. "You know I will. But he's your baggage."

"I'm nobody's baggage," Jake said. "If you go with us, fine. But don't end up on the wrong side if a shootout starts."

"Fair enough," Rekla said. "The others and I will meet you in the prep room in a few minutes. Feel free to grab something from the kitchen on your way."

The screen went blank.

Nadira turned to face Jake.

"So, where's the kitchen?" he said.

She rolled her eyes, then walked to the hallway across the room.

CHAPTER EIGHT

Kharn gripped the man's throat. The Cracian administrator had just informed his emperor that the package was not yet on its way back. The man's eyes teared and his face grew pale. He made small clicks and gurgles with his throat as Kharn squeezed.

"You assured me your man had the package in hand," Kharn said.

The administrator's knees buckled, dropping his body downward, but Kharn held him still.

"Your services have proven unworthy." He released the man's throat, letting him collapse to the floor.

He turned away from him and stepped to a table nearby. He lifted a decanter and poured himself a drink. "Remove that."

Two guards who had been standing motionless and silent by the door hurried to retrieve the administrator, who still lived, but couldn't get up unassisted. They lifted him and carried him from the room.

Kharn took a sip of his drink.

He walked over to the controls to the left of his large

viewing window, glancing at the mountain vista as he passed by. He tapped a square on the surface of the panel.

"Sir?" The voice from the speaker was a woman's, spoken with a crispness, but there was an undercurrent of static.

"Any word from our agents?" He took another sip of his drink.

"We've received word from Jafir."

"And why wasn't I informed before now? My orders were to be notified at once."

"The contact only came in a while ago. The transmission was scrambled. The storms, as usual. We just finished clearing it up."

"And?"

"You were right. She's contacted Rekla for help. She has it."

"Good."

"What shall I tell them?"

Kharn stood for a moment before answering.

"Tell them to get the package, at any cost."

"And Nadira?"

"At any cost."

"But sir, her father, we need him to finish it."

"Leave him to me. Just bring me the package."

"Understood, sir. One more thing."

"What is it?"

"She has someone with her, a man. He may be trouble."

"Rekla can deal with him. Bring me the package."

Kharn pressed the square on the panel again. The

speaker clicked and went silent.

CHAPTER NINE

Jake and Nadira entered the prep room, Jafir followed them. It was the smallest room they'd been in. A long metal table in the center took up most of the room, leaving just enough space around it for everyone to get to their chairs. Four people had taken their seats, two women and two men. One of those four was the man Nadira talked to on the display. Jake, Nadira, and Jafir took their seats.

"How did you get out?" Rekla asked.

Nadira glanced around the table. "I had a plan, Rekla. It almost worked.

"Why didn't it?"

She looked at Jake.

"Don't blame me," Jake said. "You tell a guy to shoot me, I'm not going to stand around asking questions."

"A Cracian," Nadira said. "The plan went bad, but actually," she looked at Jake, "he saved me."

"Not good," Rekla said. "Now they'll be after you. And you lead them here. I thought you knew better than that."

"You, of all people, have no right to judge me. Besides, we're not waiting for them. We're taking the fight to them."

Jake leaned into the conversation. "I'm not one to shy away from a fight, if someone's insisting on it. But my plan is to go in and get what I'm due, then get out of there. Having a gun battle with a thousand Cracians, and only a few of you on my side is something even I can recognize is not the best idea."

"You're right," Nadira said. "We will try to go in quietly. But the fact is, we may get in undetected, but getting out will be a little more difficult. My father is under heavy guard. It's not likely his disappearance will go unnoticed for long."

"Look," Rekla said, "we decided not to go to the Untamed Lands because we got tired of running. And now," he looked around the table, "we're tired of hiding. We'll help you get your father out as quietly as possible. But I have no desire to live out the rest of my life hiding in caverns."

A couple of the others at the table spoke up. "Agreed." "Truth."

Nadira reached into her pants pocket and pulled out a small metal disc, the size of the tip of her thumb. She placed it on the table. "These are the plans for their base. My father passed them to me before they took him away."

"Right then," Rekla said. "You've looked them over?"

"I have."

"Show us where they're keeping him, then we'll gear up."

"We should move in before the storm dies down," Nadira said. "We should be able to get there undetected that way."

"Will the trenches take us all the way there?" Jake asked.

"Almost," she said. "There's a quarter-mile perimeter around the base. We'll go on foot from that point in. A mountain range protects one side of the plateau. The rest is mostly flat land, but no trenches get close to the base.

Jake glanced up. "And the storm?"

"I didn't say it would be easy."

Rekla got up from his seat and walked over to Nadira. He held out his hand. She gave the disc to him. He stepped over to a display screen on the wall, like the one in the other room. He inserted the disc into a slot below the screen. A blueprint of the Cracian base appeared. Still facing the screen, he dipped his chin downward and said something, touching a device on his collar. Jake couldn't hear what he said.

Rekla moved to the side, so everyone could see the display. "Ok. Show us where we're going."

He backed away from the screen some more, taking a spot at the corner of the room.

Odd.

A loud boom sounded. The wall behind them exploded. The steel casing that covered the rock and dirt wall ripped back and scattered on the floor behind them. The lights flickered. Chunks of debris flew across the room.

A hand-sized piece of the wall struck the man seated

beside Rekla's empty chair. The rock busted his head, leaving a gash that quickly filled with blood. The man collapsed backward against his chair, then dipped to the side and fell to the floor.

The two women seated with their backs to the wall that exploded were sprawled across the table. Jake saw how bits of grit from the wall flew into both their backs. Scattershot. He instinctively dove away from the wall as it erupted. On his way to the floor, he scooped Nadira into his right arm, taking her down with him. A piece of debris grazed his shoulder, but it only cut shallow.

The dust settled after a moment. Jake heard coughing. Nadira moaned, but he knew he'd shielded her from most of the blast and debris. "Are you OK?" he asked her.

"Yes. The others?"

Jake stood up to assess the damage. Two bodies sprawled across the table. Motionless. Wounds on their necks removed any doubt. He stepped around Nadira, who was kneeling on the ground, dazed. He assessed the man that had been sitting next to Rekla's spot. No question about him either. His story had ended. Rekla leaned against the wall next to the display screen. He was bent over with his hand on his knee. A bit of shock, maybe. No severe wounds visible. Distance from the blast.

Lucky timing.

"Three down for good," Jake said. He turned to see how Jafir faired. "Where is he?"

Nadira rose to her feet and glanced around at the

carnage. "Jafir?" She cupped her hand over her mouth at the sight of the two women draped over the table and of the man on the floor, his head resting in a pool of his own blood. "Rekla, where's Jafir?"

Rekla pushed off from his knee and walked toward her. He looked around the room. "He's not here."

Debris littered the floor, but not enough to hide another body.

Rekla touched Nadira's shoulder as he passed her. "I'll check the next room." Then he turned to Jake. "Thank you for shielding her from the blast." He looked at Jake's right shoulder, a tear in his shirt, the cut bleeding, but only a trickle. "We have some medical supplies. I'll get them for you. He glanced at the man on the floor and the two women on the table. "Too late for them, I'm afraid."

Jake nodded to him.

Rekla left the room to check for Jafir.

"Nadira," Jake said. "We need to move. This doesn't add up."

"What do you mean?"

"The damn wall just blew in and Rekla is going to fetch medical supplies for this?" Jake glanced at his shoulder. "Too calm. We may still be in danger."

"Yes."

"Maybe an accident. Spark in the wrong area. Who knows? But I bet somebody detonated that wall. Come on."

Jake took her hand to lead her out of the room. She let him.

CHAPTER TEN

Jake and Nadira left the destruction and death of the prep room seeking answers. They walked into the other room. Empty.

"Where's your friend?" he asked.

"Not my friend."

They checked the next room too.

"No sign of Jafir either. How well do you know these guys?"

"Well enough."

"Sounded like you and Rekla have some bad blood."

"We had a falling out, but that was a long time ago."

Jake flicked open the strap across the grip of his blaster. "Stay close to me until we figure out what's going on."

"It must've been an accident. This facility is secure and we're the only ones who know of its existence. I'm certain."

"In that case." Jake pulled his blaster from its holster, then he took out Nadira's weapon. "He started to hand it to her. "Try not to shoot me."

"You don't think?" She reached for it, but he pulled it back before she grasped it.

"That's exactly what I think. One or both set that blast. Too convenient that Rekla stood at the far side of the room, out of range. And sandwich boy probably slipped out just before the blast." He tucked her blaster back under his belt. "But I think I'll hang on to this for now."

"I'd rather have it handy," Nadira said, "but I get it."

They passed through the kitchen and a couple more rooms. No one in sight.

"That's it," she said. "The only area left is the landing bay."

"The pods."

They hurried back to the massive room they had arrived in. The three transport pods sat parked as before.

Jake led, his blaster held in front of his chest, at the ready. Nadira followed him. She kept behind him, but poised to react to any threat.

Jake tipped his head back toward her, but kept his eyes forward. "Stay near the wall until we get closer."

She nodded.

A hundred feet to the first transport pod, he raised his hand and gestured toward the sphere. A man's leg jutted out around the pod's edge. Someone at the far side of the sphere, doing something to the vehicle.

"Come on," he said to Nadira. He sprinted toward the man, using the pod as cover. The noise from his footfalls carried through the metal-lined room and the man from behind the pod stepped into view, a gun in hand.

The blasts from the man's weapon zipped past Jake and Nadira, missing by a couple of feet. They couldn't make out the gunman's face. But Jake recognized the scrawny build. "Jafir. That little bastard. Glad I took his sandwich."

He returned fire, still running to get to the sphere to block Jafir's line of fire.

Outmatched, Jafir bolted. He ran away from them, toward the next pod down the bay.

Jake and Nadira veered their run to chase him down. Jafir was fast. He was opening a gap between him and his pursuers.

As they neared the first pod, where Jafir had tampered with something, Jake saw him glance back at them. Jafir slowed his run enough to pull a device from his pocket. The first pod exploded. A flash. A wave of heat. The air smacked Jake and Nadira hard, taking them off their feet. Jake questioned the blackness filling the room as he flew backwards. Everything went quiet. Dark.

CHAPTER ELEVEN

Jake felt the cold from the metal floor against his cheek, a stark contrast to the heat radiating from the wound on the side of his head. Both sensations reminded him he was still alive. He also felt bits of grit caked to his skin, on his face, his arms — debris from the blast. His nose drew in the lingering vapors of burned components from the pod, polymers of some kind. He opened his eyes.

Nadira lay a few feet in front of him, head to one side, her eyes closed. He would have thought she was only sleeping were it not for the trickle of blood dripping down her forehead. He reached his hand out to her, diverting the slow red stream before it reached her eye.

She stirred slightly at his touch.

"Nadira?" He folded his reddened finger and used the back of his hand to caress her face.

She opened her eyes. "I guess we didn't stop them."

He smiled at her. "What gave you that idea?"

They got to their feet, unsteady at first. After a moment, the shock from the blast wore off.

He looked to where the pod had been, while she glanced around to get a handle on what happened.

"I guess we won't be leaving the same way we came," he said, nodding to the two piles of debris, all that was left of two transport pods. The third one was missing.

Nadira held her hand out to Jake. "I'd feel better with a weapon. I was as much a target as you were."

Jake hesitated. Then he pulled it out of his belt and handed it to her.

She took it and holstered it. Then she turned to see the destroyed pods. "I can't believe he did that."

"They were working together." Jake holstered his blaster too, then stepped over to her to glance at the wound on her head. "You're lucky. It's not too bad." He ripped a piece off the bottom of his shirt and used it to dab the blood from the cut on her head. "This is your planet. Any chance we get out of here on foot?"

"Halcion Station is the only place within walking distance of here." She looked around the room, then sighed. "But I suppose that's where you want to be going now."

"Why the hell would I want to do that?"

Nadira looked confused. "I just figured all this would be too much trouble for you. You just came here for a delivery. This is my problem, and it looks like I may not be able to do anything for my father after all."

"You don't know me that well," Jake said, "but one thing you can count on is that I keep my word. I'm going to make my delivery, and I will help you rescue your father."

"Thank you."

Jake pulled his comm device off his belt. "We can get the shuttle back down here." He flipped it on. "Sarah."

Silence.

"Sarah, we're going to need the shuttle."

No response.

"Could be the rock," Nadira said. "We're pretty deep."

"That's never been an issue before."

"Storms then. The ones in the upper atmosphere get highly energized. Sometimes I can't even get through on a connection down here."

"That's just perfect. Seemed like it was going to be such a good day this morning."

He clipped the comm device back to his belt. Then he looked at Nadira. He realized her problems were bigger than his.

"Ok," he said. "Maybe that's the worst of our troubles. Let's get going."

She nodded, and her eyes showed a renewed sense of purpose. "We should gather supplies."

"Lead the way."

She headed back to the other rooms. He followed.

As they rummaged through the kitchen, they gathered food packets and a few other items, Nadira turned to Jake. "I take you at your word, Jake, and I'm thankful. But why go through so much for a cargo delivery?"

He un-slung his pack from his back and shoved a stack of food packets inside it, next to the package for delivery. "I need the payoff on this one. When I heard the price on offer, I couldn't believe it. It's the kind of money that can solve a guy's problems for quite a while."

Sometimes a guy needs to do something because… it just feels right.

"We were desperate. I know you can't just give it to me," she said while staring at the case in his bag.

Jake cinched up his pack. "I had no idea of the circumstances. But the terms were clear, and the credits from this job are going to save the life of someone very dear to me, at least for a while."

He grimaced and turned away from her. She could tell he was pulling back from the topic.

"If we can find a way to get into their base and get to my father, you'll get your payment."

"I wouldn't mind killing those two for trying to blow us up, while we're at it."

They left the kitchen once they packed all the supplies they could find. After glancing in the other rooms one more time, they headed back to the transport pod bay. As Jake and Nadira entered the bay, they heard something.

Bang. Bang. Thud.

The sound came from the middle of the room, from the floor near where the transport pods had been.

They glanced at each other.

"The maintenance pits," she said, "The sound is coming from one of them."

They jogged toward the sound. About twenty feet from the second pile of rubble, they came to a metal grate on the floor. Three feet wide, four feet long. A recessed handle.

Bang. Bang. The metal plate thumped a little with each sound.

A muffled sound rose through the grate. A man. No words. Just a murmur.

"There shouldn't be anyone else here," Nadira said.

"He sounds gagged." Jake leaned over and gripped the handle. "They must've locked him in." He looked at Nadira, before pulling on the handle. "Keep your guard up."

She drew her blaster and nodded.

He lifted the grate, and tossed it aside.

"I don't understand." Nadira let her gun droop a little as she stared at the man at the bottom of the maintenance pit.

"Cracian, right?" Jake said.

The man stood in the hole, his hands and feet bound with rope. His forehead was bruised. Rags stuffed in his mouth. His eyes bulged at the sight of Jake and Nadira, and her blaster, which still pointed in his direction. He didn't murmur again, but the sucking sound through his nostrils was audible. It quickened, and he cowered even while lying on the ground.

"How?" Nadira said.

Jake touched the top of her pistol, pushing it down farther. "I'm the tourist, remember? Why don't we hold off on shooting him, in case he has a few answers for us?"

She regained her composure. "Right. Yes." Holstering her weapon, she gestured to Jake. "Maybe you should take his gag out."

"Suppose so." He jumped down next to the Cracian. "Just so you know, doesn't matter much to me if she does end up shooting you. So, I suggest you cooperate. Last thing I need right now is for you to try something. Agreed?"

The man nodded.

Jake reached over and pulled the bunched-up rags from the man's mouth. The Cracian gasped and coughed for a second, then he swallowed to clear his throat. "Thank you," he said.

Keeping his eyes on the man, Jake pointed his thumb up at Nadira. "She's going to ask you a few things. You're going to answer. Got it?"

The man nodded.

"Untie him."

"What?" Jake said. "We don't need to untie him yet. Just ask him what you want to know."

"I said untie him. Now!" Her tone carried unrestrained emotion.

Jake looked back and up to see Nadira holding her blaster at her side. She was smiling.

"You've gotta be kidding," Jake said.

Nadira took a deep breath and exhaled, looking relieved. She holstered her weapon. "Do it."

He looked at the Cracian. The man was smiling too. He held his bound hands up to Jake.

Jake shook his head and glanced back to Nadira. "Your partner? Do you even know whose side you're on?"

"I'm on the right side," she said, "and so is he. Now

untie him. We're wasting time."

"Not until you tell me what's going on," Jake said.

"He's Cracian, yes," Nadira said. "But he's not one of them. I mean, he's not with Kharn."

Jake looked at the man, and then back to Nadira. "Not good enough."

"We met long ago," she said. "He's proven himself countless times. I trust him. And…"

"And what?"

"And we need his help. Why would they have tied him up if he was working with Kharn? Please get him out of those."

So, she has a heart in there.

Jake took a moment to consider the situation. "That may make sense, but I'm beginning to wonder about this planet."

She spoke to the bound man. "He's OK. We'll get you out of there."

Jake turned to the man and began untying the ropes from his ankles and wrists. Then he glanced at Nadira. "You realize you're not going to get a second date now?"

"Shut up," she said. "Tay, how did you get here? This wasn't the plan."

The man stood up and stepped back from Jake before climbing out. Then he held out his right arm to Nadira. "Bond, not birth."

She placed her right arm over his. "Bond, not birth."

"Your father is close to completing his work," Tay said. "I tried to stop them, but I was discovered, and I couldn't fight them on my own."

"What are you saying?" Nadira asked.

Jake was standing in the maintenance pit, his face a mixed expression, pissed off, yet oddly entertained.

"Rekla and Jafir," Tay said, "they're working for Crassus Kharn."

Jake interjected, "The one's we came to for help. I'm not sure you know how this is supposed to work."

Nadira shook her hand at Jake. "Shut up!"

"I didn't like the look of your buddy, Rekla from the start," Jake said. "I have a sense for these things."

"Bastards." Nadira huffed, then she pulled out her blaster and shot at the opposite wall. The energy bolt crashed into it and sent sparks flying. The impact left a hole a few inches across and as deep in the metal.

"I came to warn you," Tay said, "but someone must've tipped them off that I knew. They were waiting for me."

Nadira placed her arm on Tay's shoulder. "We'll get to my father." She looked at Jake. "He has what we need to stop Kharn."

Tay turned and looked down at Jake, who had unslung his pack and was eating one of the food packets. "How?"

"He's the delivery man," she said. "Give us the case."

Jake took another bite from the chewy brown bar sticking out of the wrapper in his hand.

Nadira repeated herself. "Please, Jake, give us the case."

Jake held up his forefinger, while he finished chewing. After he swallowed the bite, he cleared the inside of his mouth with his tongue. "Don't get me wrong, red. I think I'd refuse to give it to you even if I still had it." He moved his tongue over his teeth and across the inside of his lip again. "Problem is, your boy Rekla seems to have taken it after we were knocked out." Jake tilted his pack forward and pulled the top open for her to see. The bag held a dozen or more food packets. No case.

Nadira's face turned redder than usual. "No!"

Tay touched her arm. "We can stop them."

She looked at Tay, and calmed slightly.

"We must stop them," he said. "Kharn will use it if we don't."

Nadira looked at the piles of rubble that were the transport pods. "How can we even get there?"

"Same way I got here," Tay said. "You don't see my transport, do you?"

"Not the crags?" She looked uneasy at the realization.

"They're not that bad. And we can cut across near the mountains to make up time. Rekla and Jafir will have to stick to the trenches. They run through twenty outposts before they get to the Cracian base."

She took in and exhaled a deep breath. "You know you're crazy, right?"

"It's our only chance."

She turned back to the maintenance pit to deal with Jake, but he wasn't there.

"I'm right here, red." She and Tay turned around. Jake stood behind them with his blaster pointed at her. He held out his empty hand. "Maybe I gave your weapon back too soon. Maybe you're OK. I don't know, but things are beyond getting complicated. I'll need it, for now. I'd feel better, until things get sorted out."

She handed him her gun.

"Here's the deal," Jake said. "I'm getting out of here, but I'll be damned if I'm walking back to Halcion Station empty handed. When we get outside, I'm getting my shuttle back down here."

"If that works." Nadira nodded toward Jakes comm device. "Let's hope it was just the rock around us here that blocked the signal."

"Shuttle?" Tay asked.

"From his ship," Nadira said. "It's orbiting Daedalon."

Tay shook his head. "Not likely. It probably wasn't the rock that caused the problem. The high storms have the outer atmosphere too charged to get a signal out, I suspect. At least for hours, maybe days."

"You're kidding, right?" Jake said.

"I'm afraid not," Tay said. "I watch the skies. Haven't seen them build this way for a long time."

Well that's just peachy. Doing the right thing can be a pain in the ass.

"Fine. If that's the case, you two are gonna help me get into the Cracian base. If Rekla and the other guy do work for this Crassus Kharn, then Kharn owes me money. And I aim to collect." He looked at Nadira. "I'm not saying I have you figured out. But you could've shot me when you had the chance. So, I'm willing to bet that's not high on your list. Maybe, you're just desperate. But I'm not a fool. So, don't expect to get your weapon back any time soon. At least not until we get to the base. You two get me there and you can go your own way."

Nadira and Tay looked at each other.

"I rode in with a pack of crag beasts," Tay said to Nadira. "They can take all three of us there."

"It looks like we don't have much choice," she said.

"Right," Jake said. "But there's one more thing, before we go."

"What's that?" she asked.

He gestured his blaster at Tay. "He's Cracian. Is he really going to go against his own kind when it comes down to it?"

Tay spoke up. "Not all of us agree with Kharn's vision. I worked with Nadira's father. But while we cooperated and worked on Kharn's grand project for the planet so we could stay alive, we secretly have been looking for a way to stop him."

Nadira interjected. "We need what's in the case. It is the final piece. My father didn't tell me what he was building." She looked at Tay.

"Even I didn't understand it fully," Tay said, "but these last few weeks it became clear to me he can't be allowed to succeed."

Jake had serious doubts about what he was hearing. "Oh, yeah?"

Tay darted his eyes around but didn't let them settle on Jake. "It's hard to explain. It'd take too much time. We need to get going."

"Couple of gems." Jake waved his blaster, directing them to move. "Let's go see these crag beasts."

CHAPTER TWELVE

The three of them walked over the red dusty hill. The crag beasts came into view. Five of them. Tay continued toward them. Jake and Nadira stopped in their tracks at the sight of them. Each of the creatures stood five feet at the shoulders. They walked around on all fours.

Jake grabbed his comm device and tried reaching Sarah again. He couldn't reach her. "Gotta love this place." He clipped it to his belt.

Two of crag beasts were laying down still, but stood up as Tay approached. One of those two was larger than the other four. Tay walked up to that one. He held his arm out to the crag beast. The animal lowered its head slightly, and stepped forward until Tay's hand was touching it.

"I can see why you warned me about these creatures," Jake said.

The beasts were strong. Their skin stretched tight over their muscles. Their heads were large, and their jaws were heavy. Like machines, designed to crush and mangle whatever it bit.

Jake and Nadira walked closer. He saw the creature's yellow eyes had a membrane over them, like a film, mostly transparent, but with a slight tint.

A howling wind blew over the hill, past Jake and Nadira, and down to Tay and the beasts. Red sand filled the air. Jake protected his eyes from the grit with his arms.

Tay reached into the pocket of his pants. He pulled out a pair of black goggles and strapped them on.

The sand swirled.

Jake and Nadira moved closer to Tay. The beasts watched them. A few of the creatures snarled and growled, but they didn't move.

Jake noted the creatures ignored the grit pelting their face. The film on the animal's eyes kept the sand out. They didn't blink.

After a few more seconds, the wind died down and the dust settled.

"This one's their leader," Tay said. "He and I have ridden together many times. The others won't turn on you, unless he does."

"Comforting," Jake said.

Tay pointed to the mountains in the distance, beyond the vast plain they stood on. Jake noted the absence of any buildings or vegetation. Only the dryness of rock and dirt as far as they could see.

Nadira stepped closer to Jake. He covered the grip to his blaster with his hand. Her weapon, tucked safely in his belt on his opposite side.

"I haven't been able to trust anybody for a long time,"

she said. "I just wanted the case. It was wrong for me to demand it. I'm sorry."

He looked at her for a long moment. Then he turned his glance to the crag beasts. "Let's just get on these damn things and make it to that base." He walked away from her. Moving next to Tay, he said, "So, any advice?" He tilted his head toward the crag beasts.

Tay mounted the leader of the pack. "Hang on tight. And don't make them angry."

"Right." Jake's expression showed he was less than satisfied with the answer.

He chose one of the creatures and got on it. Nadira did the same.

The necks of the animals offered a mane of matted clumpy black hair, the only way to hold on to them. Jake grabbed it and blew out a few hard puffs until his nose and mouth dulled to the rancid stench of the creature.

Tay looked back, checking that the two were ready. Then he leaned over and whispered into the ear of his mount. The creature leapt forward, carrying him faster than Jake thought possible, even with the creature's impressive musculature.

Jake tipped backward, clenching the mane to avoid falling off, as his beast pursued the leader.

Nadira's mount, and the other two beasts, ran along side.

Jake soon discovered the smell and the extremely bumpy ride were not the only problems in traveling by crag beast. He heard a few snorts. A long stringy glob of glutinous sandy mucus flew up from the creature's snout, catching Jake's cheek and shoulder. He rolled his left hand in the mane to grab more hair. Then he released his right hand to wipe his face and flick the viscous snot away into the breeze.

They rode on for another thirty minutes. He cleared his face a few more times along the way.

After ascending a ridge, Tay slowed his mount. The others followed suit. The group stopped and gathered close.

Tay looked at Jake. "I should've warned you. That one has a nasty cold."

Jake fixed him with a hard stare. "Really? I never noticed," he said, trying unsuccessfully to flick the last cloying blob off his hand.

"Why are we stopping?" Nadira said. "We haven't much time."

"We have a choice." Tay pointed to the distance.

CHAPTER THIRTEEN

Straight ahead in the distance, on the horizon, a thick layer of reddish-brown clouds blanketed the sky, and hung low, close to the ground. Flashes of lightning lit up the massive storm front.

Jake knew if that was one of the two choices and Tay hadn't yet decided the path, the other choice must be something he didn't want to hear.

"We can ride toward the storm," Tay said. "There are caves in that direction. We should be able to get to them and take shelter before the storm reaches us. I've received word from a contact inside the Cracian base supportive of the resistance that the cave systems are the most direct route to the base."

Jake gazed in the direction of the caves, but couldn't see anything but a distant haze and dust. "Wouldn't they be guarded?"

"They've long been abandoned, I'm told," Tay said. "All but forgotten."

"And the other choice?" Nadira asked.

Tay turned his head to the left and pointed to a

grouping of rolling hills in the distance. "Beyond those, the Untamed Lands. If we move into them and follow that line of hills, we'll come to a passage in a mountain range. It'll take us out of there and put us within a few miles of the western border of the base. The storms won't reach us on that path, but it's twice the distance. It will add hours to our journey," he patted his crag beast, "even with their speed."

"Rekla will reach Kharn before then" Nadira said. "We must go through the storm."

"Agreed," Jake said.

Tay nodded. "The mountains are watched, too. I doubt we'd make it undetected." Then he whispered to his crag beast. The creature ran, carrying him in the direction of the storm. He rode the animal as if born to it.

Jake and Nadira did what they could to steady themselves as their mounts and the other crag beasts followed.

Sometime later, as they rode nearer the caves, Jake heard the howl of the swirling winds ahead. The lightning lit up the otherwise darkening sky and landscape. The boom and crackle with each strike pushed through his chest. He felt cold as they rode into the winds on the periphery of the storm. The torrents grew louder and stronger. He leaned forward against the crag beast to keep from falling off and glanced to his side. Nadira also leaned forward, fighting the storm.

Tay rode about ten feet in front of Jake. He pulled one hand from his crag beast's mane to gesture ahead. He pointed toward a formation of rocks about fifty feet high and a couple hundred feet across.

Jake saw Tay's mouth moving, and him yelling something. But the storm drowned out his words.

Jake thought he saw a figure on top of the rocks ahead. He guarded his eyes from the sand and wind with his hand, and looked again. No one was there now. *Cursed storm.*

The canopy of clouds rolled out in every direction. Darkness grew. Jake could only see his hands on the mane in front of him. He held on, trusting the crag beast would find its way.

A flash of light and a thunderous boom. For a split second, he saw Tay in front of him and Nadira at his side. Then blackness again. The dust pelted his face and hands. He leaned forward and down again, closing his eyes to save them.

He held on.

Flash. Everything lit up for a moment. Brighter than before. The lightning bolt shot down in front of Jake, striking Tay.

Jake's mount leapt to the side, avoiding the tumbling creature ahead. Jake's beast landed with him still on it. Then it ran a few more paces, before slowing to a halt. The sound of the wind faded to a muffled droning. They'd reached cover, the high rocks that housed the caves. The grit no longer wore on Jake's skin.

He felt Nadira and her crag beast beside him, her leg brushed against his as they crowded into the cover of the cave.

"Did he make it?" she asked.

Jake didn't need to answer. The storm, declaring its

victory, offered a dazzling display of lightning strikes, followed closely by deafening thunder. Tay's body lay on the ground next to his mount. They'd been struck down just outside the cave entrance. Tay's eyes were open, but without life. The flesh on his face and exposed chest, charred and torn.

Jake heard a whisper from Nadira. "Bond, not birth." He glanced at her and noticed a tear clearing a channel through the caked dust on her cheek. Another boom of thunder. Then blackness.

CHAPTER FOURTEEN

Jake unslung his bag from his shoulder and drew it open. He pulled out a small rectangular device and pressed the button on it. A light shone, bright enough to illuminate a ten-foot-wide circle inside the cave.

"We should wait out the storm," he said, looking at Nadira. Her left cheek showed a smudge pulled across it. She had wiped away her tear.

"May it pass quickly." She spoke with a tone of resentment for the storm, her eyes gazing out toward the dark that kept Tay's body.

"Sorry about your friend," Jake said.

She didn't look at him, but nodded.

Jake's crag beast made a low groaning noise. Its body jerked and twitched. He patted the neck of the creature beside the mane.

The other three crag beasts joined his mount in making the groaning sound. All four of the animals stared toward the body of their pack leader, dead ten feet in front of them, outside the cave. Jake noted how the creatures' vision seemed to pierce the darkness.

He remembered what Tay had said about them not turning on him or Nadira, so long as their leader didn't attack.

The sound from his mount went from a groaning to a growling. The creature turned its head from side to side, as if to look at Jake.

"We have another problem," he said.

"What?" Nadira continued to stare in the direction of Tay's body.

"Get off the crag beast, slowly. And step to the back of the cave." He dismounted while instructing her.

All four of the crag beasts growled and turned their attention to him and Nadira.

She got down from her mount and stepped toward him. He held out his arm in front of her.

"Move behind those rocks." He glanced to a cluster of large rocks behind them.

Nadira did as he suggested, taking cover behind a rocky mound on the cave floor that rose to the height of her chest. Jake, with his blaster held in front of him, stepped backward toward her. The four crag beasts, in an arc, matched his move and closed in on him.

He held his trigger finger, hoping the creatures would settle down on their own.

A crag beast attacked, jumping at him. He shot it as it flew toward him, jaws wide, its eyes fierce. Jake's blast hit the beast in the chest, blowing a hole open. Blood spilled out over the burnt flesh.

The creature landed on top of Jake, knocking him to the ground. His blaster fell out of his hand and ended up several feet away.

The crag beast suffered a mortal wound, but wasn't ready to give up the fight. It thrashed and pummeled Jake with its heavy paws. He dropped the light from his other hand. He held back its deadly mouth with all the strength his arms could summon. The beast was powerful, even as it bled closer to death. From its mass and the blows it delivered with its paws, Jake felt his energy draining, his breathing difficult.

Risking a bite from the creature's teeth, Jake let go of its head with one arm and thrust his fist into the wound he'd made with his blaster. The beast roared and convulsed. Jake opened his fist, still inside the beast's chest, and ripped out his hand, clawing and scraping what he could. He tore the wound wider as he did. The blood gushed, covering his arm.

The beast gave up the struggle. Jake pushed it off him as it slumped.

He scrambled to his feet and picked up his blaster. Raising his weapon toward the other crag beasts, he moved to the rocks for cover, as Nadira had done.

One of the three remaining creatures stepped forward, snarling. Jake steadied his exhausted arm, leaning it on the rock.

He shot the beast. His blast clipped its shoulder. It bled, but didn't slow. The animal lowered its head over its front paws, preparing to pounce. Before it sprung, the two beasts behind it attacked it. Caught off guard, it tumbled and the three creatures rolled into a vicious fight.

"They're deciding who's the new leader," Jake said.

"Do we let them fight it out?"

"Yes. Don't draw their attention. Let them kill each other, if we're lucky."

They watched for the next few seconds as the beasts bit and tore at each other. Blood squirted. Yelps and growls turned to snarls and the sounds of ripping flesh and chomping jaws and teeth.

"Look here." Nadira patted Jake's shoulder.

He turned to see a hole in the cave wall behind them. The opening looked just large enough for each of them to squeeze through, though a much tighter fit for Jake's muscular body. He nodded to her.

Feet first, she slipped through the hole into a larger cave on the other side. As Jake stepped toward the opening to follow her, the crag beasts settled their quarrel and turned their attention back to him. He made it most of the way through the hole before one of the creatures jumped at him. Jake shot its head with his blaster, as he pushed the rest of his body between the opening in the rocks.

The crag beast slammed into the stone, extending a paw through the hole, clawing. Jake rolled out of the way. The creature scraped and lunged against the rock, unable to get its body into the hole. The thuds, savage muscle against heavy stone, echoed through the cave. Chunks above the passageway broke off. The creature grew more determined.

Jake heard the wall between the two caves crack. More rock fell. Dust pushed into the back cave. It was dark. The shadow of the angry beast fought against what little light shone through.

Nadira coughed.

The beast persisted. Clawing. Pushing. Snarling.

Crack. More rocks fell. The opening narrowed.

Jake shot the creature.

A yelp. Then it slumped, dropping its head against the now smaller hole. A few rocks slid down the gravel and dirt that had piled up from the crag beast's efforts.

Muffled growls from the other side. A howl. Then silence. The dust drifted down, settling. The air cleared.

Jake and Nadira were still for a moment. Breathing. Resting. No light in the cave. No sounds but their own.

"Jake, we're trapped."

The sound of a couple of breaths. Jake felt the sting of his sweat passing over the scrapes on his face and arms.

"We're alive."

He unslung his pack and dug in it for his backup light. He pressed the button and the cave lit up.

He saw Nadira sitting against the cave wall with her arms wrapped in front of her knees, the caked dust and the smudge on her face cut by channels from a steady stream of tears.

He walked over to her. "Look on the bright side." He holstered his blaster. "The way things are going, you may not have to shoot me." He smiled.

She chuckled. Then she sniffed and wiped away the tears from her cheeks. "At least there's that."

He held out his hand to her. She took it, and he pulled her to her feet.

He glanced around the cave and took a few steps, noticing a slight movement in the air.

"Come over here," he said, moving to the rear of the

cave. He raised his other hand to the rock wall. "Here. Feel it."

She put her hand next to his. A cool current of air flowing out a wide crack in the rock.

Her eyes widened. She smiled. "Is it?"

"A way out." He handed her his light and reached into his pack. He pulled out a cylinder, five inches long, an inch in diameter, with a two-inch spike extended from one end. He pushed the spike into the crack, the rest of the device sticking out from the rock. Then he moved back from the wall. "You'd better stand over there." He pointed off to the side, away from the wall and beyond where he stood.

She moved where he suggested.

He drew his blaster from its holster and aimed at the device on the wall. A few seconds passed. He didn't fire. He stepped back another five feet, then took aim again and squeezed the trigger.

The blast struck the device he'd embedded.

Boom.

Rocks and dirt flew out toward him. He turned his face away from the spray. Most of the larger pieces missed him. He took a few bits to his arms. One to his cheek.

Hot air accompanied the flying debris. His skin dried as the gust blew over him. Then cool air, like before, but stronger.

Nadira waved her arm in front of her face to clear the dust. "Are you alright?"

Jake spit to clear some grit from his mouth. He stepped to the exploded wall. The cool air flowed against him, pouring through the large gap, three feet wide, where the crack had been. "Yes."

Nadira came over to him. "How far do you think it goes?" She held the light up.

They had a clear view ten feet into the tunnel. The same rock walls, top, bottom, and sides. But it looked too uniformly circular, tube-like, to be natural. Perhaps a river could cut something like it, Jake thought. *Maybe.* But then he saw the scrapes on the walls at the point where the light faded up ahead.

Someone made this. Or some thing.

He decided not to mention the scrapes, at least for now. Nadira either didn't notice them, or she pretended not to see them.

"I have no idea, but it's our best chance at getting out of here."

Nadira entered the tunnel, walking past him. "Come on. We're still going to the base. Maybe this will lead to a way out."

She must be done with her tears, Jake thought.

Nadira heading down the tunnel. She walked at a pace that lacked any hint of hesitation. Jake fixed his pack more snugly, then headed off after her.

He let her keep the lead for a few minutes, taking in the view. He also noticed how she glanced at the scrapes on the walls as they passed them. But she didn't mention them. He figured she didn't want to get bogged down worrying about what they were or that the tunnel wasn't natural. Interesting under different circumstances. All it meant for now was the tunnel lead somewhere, and Jake knew he'd better keep his holster flap open.

The tunnel turned this way, then that. And then went on for long stretches, remarkable in how straight it ran. The tubular nature of the walls became more distinct. While still entirely of rock, the walls took on a more polished finish, almost a sheen.

She looked back at him. "Hurry up. We're not out for a stroll."

Woman on a mission.

Jake admitted to himself that he was a sucker for a girl who could have tears one minute and blast her way out of danger the next. She was adding up well, so far.

The air in the cave grew damper. Shallow puddles appeared up ahead in the middle of the tunnel floor. The moisture in the air and on the walls, gave way to full-on wetness. Drops of water clung to the ceiling and occasionally fell, hitting Jake and Nadira as they walked.

The cool air and the water served to refresh them as they traveled the tunnel unimpeded for another thirty or forty minutes. They shared only a few words now and then about how much longer the cave might continue.

Jake, who had been walking beside Nadira for most of the last half hour, noticed he had to slow his pace to avoid pulling ahead of her on several occasions.

Nadira stopped walking. "I need a rest."

He stopped too. "Sure. That's fine."

The tunnel had widened at this point to fifteen feet from wall to wall. She walked over to the side of it and sat down, leaning against the curved rock.

He joined her, sitting beside her.

"Just a few minutes," she said. "We've been moving so much. And what happened with Rekla and the pods, and now Tay."

"I understand." He nodded to her. The fact she'd held it together this long surprised him.

She took in a deep breath, then let it out. "I just don't know if we're going to make it in time."

Jake measured the fading hope in her face. "I know it's not what you want to hear, but there's no way to know for sure if we'll get there first."

He saw the disappointment in her face.

"Still, whether we do or not," he continued, "I'm getting the job done."

"Yes. The case, and your payment. I know." She spoke with more than a note of disdain.

He placed his hand on her knee. "I gave you my word. Yes. I'll get payment on my delivery, one way or the other. But we'll find your father too."

"Why are you even helping me?"

"Maybe you're growing on me."

"Am I?"

"Besides, you didn't seem to be rooting for the crag beasts. Maybe I'm growing on you too."

She turned and looked at him. Then she placed her hand on his. "You really think we'll find him in time?"

"I can tell you this," he said. "So far, this delivery is going smoother than my last one did."

She laughed. "That's comforting, I guess."

They held each other's gaze for a moment. Then she slid her hand up his wrist and forearm, and grabbed his elbow. He leaned in.

"Don't you get lonely traveling from planet to planet?" she asked.

"I suppose I should. I do sometimes. My ship keeps me company."

"And whatever desperate woman you run into on each planet," she said, her tone teasing.

She kissed him.

Then she leaned back and put her hand on his chest, holding him at bay. "I don't really know anything about you."

Jake leaned back. "What do you want to know?"

"I'm not sure," she said. "How did you get into this line of work?"

"It's a long story. I didn't always do this." Jake gazed at the wall across from them.

He sat silent for a moment, thinking of Sarah.

"I'm listening."

"Many years ago, there was a time when traveling to another planet meant going into battle. Problem was, it wasn't always for a good reason or for the right people. It started out decent enough. Rescues of colonization crews. Overseeing peace negotiations between warring factions."

"Honorable."

"But then, the leader of the outfit I was with, a man we called the General, decided it was time to take on more profitable ventures. Those of us that went along with it did pretty well for quite a few years. Those that didn't ended up left behind on one mission or the other. I was on a straight road to dying a bad man. But then, something changed my mind. Someone, really."

"What was her name?"

"Sarah."

"The woman on your ship, right?

"No. That's my ship's name too."

"Huh?"

"It's complicated. Never mind."

"What happened then?"

"I couldn't let her be a part of that life. And I couldn't be that guy and be with her. So, I left it all behind. I promised myself I'd do something legitimate. We set out together for a new life.

"Where is she now?"

Jake was silent for a moment. *What am I doing?*

"I don't want to talk about it," he said, as he got up and stepped away from the wall.

He swung his pack around to his front and opened it. "How about we grab something to keep us going? And then, we need to do that. Keep moving, I mean."

"Yes. You're right." She stood up, dusted herself off.

He handed her a bottle. She took a drink, then handed it back to him. He gave her a food bar from his pack. They ate and took a few more drinks. Then they packed up.

"Alright, then," she said, "Let's go."

"Yes. We'd better. At least the storms can't get to us in here."

They walked in silence for another half hour, enjoying the relative safety of the cave.

CHAPTER FIFTEEN

"My dear, Eliana, you always know just what to do."

Kharn reclined in the padded lounge chair, while Eliana rubbed his neck and shoulders as she stood behind him.

His trusted companion since he found her among the first wave of laborers he brought to Daedalon, she had always been the exception to his contempt for the Waudure. Her body tipped the scales toward beauty sufficiently, but it was her unusual look that drew him to her among others with superior forms and curves. Her slightly larger than normal eyes, full lips, and elongated neck was rare if not completely absent in their race.

Eliana wasted no time maneuvering herself into his heart. The first time he had her brought to him for a private audience, a week after her arrival, she fed his interest in her. By instinct, she teased his appetites with a delicate and disorienting balance between submission and feigned dissatisfaction. Such play had worked on many a man by women with similar understanding of their gifts, but Kharn, for all his vision, fervor, and will to dominate, was particularly susceptible to such things. Eliana, forced from her home world like thousands of other Waudure, merely wanted to survive.

"We haven't had time together like this for quite a while," she said, still massaging his neck. Her hair hung down across her cheeks, and the tips of it danced on his head.

"I've been preoccupied, I admit." Kharn closed his eyes as she continued to work on him. "But all is coming together now."

"You always manage to accomplish what you set out to do," she said.

"Rekla," he opened his eyes, glancing up at her and gesturing with an arm, "the man we have near Halcion Station, he will arrive soon with something I need."

Eliana lowered her face down to his and kissed him just in front of his ear. "To continue your great work?"

"That is right."

"And the ones that have been causing your trouble?"

Kharn reached up and took hold of her wrists. "My power and influence extends well beyond these walls. We know where they are. I've seen to it that their interference will end soon, including that off-worlder. He's served his purpose."

Eliana slid her arms from his and then wrapped them around his shoulders and chest, leaning down and placing her head against his. "How did you persuade them?"

He reached up and stroked her hair.

"I've left that task to the creature of the caves."

CHAPTER SIXTEEN

The tunnel became cavernous, as the ceiling rose sharply to a height of at least fifty feet. The path took on an upward slope and the moisture in the air diminished, but those weren't the most interesting details Jake noticed as they walked. He stopped next to an inscription carved into the rock of the wall.

"Do you know what this means?" He sidestepped to allow Nadira an unobstructed view of the marking.

She moved closer. "No. Not entirely."

"What do you mean?"

"Well, it looks Cracian, but not exactly. The lines are similar, but I don't recognize it."

Jake ran his fingers across the cuts in the rock. "How well do you know Cracian? Maybe you never learned this version."

"All our people know the language." She cast her gaze down, shaking her head slightly. "They fed their language into us during our transit to the planet. Said it was to foster better understanding between our peoples. Turns out it was to make it easier to command us as we served them as slaves."

"And this means nothing?"

"It looks older, maybe. If I'm reading it right, it's some kind of warning or closure notice."

"That's encouraging. But, as you said, it's old. I wouldn't worry about it." He stepped back from the marking. "Let's keep going. There must be something up ahead."

"Wait. I recognize this here." She pointed to a few curved lines on the right side of the markings. "Death."

"Great warning sign. Come on." Jake took a few steps down the way between the larger rocks on the ground, then waited for her.

"What's that smell?" she said as she joined him.

"Don't know. But it's foul."

They continued up the sloping path. More gouges marred the walls. This time they ran in sets, three cuts into the rock on each side of the great rocky hollow. They arced downward, tracing a ten-foot expanse on each side of the cave.

Jake and Nadira stopped in their tracks.

"Death," she said.

Piled up on one side of the extended cave, bones. They looked humanoid but it was hard to tell. Broken and splintered and hundreds of them as they were.

But the worst of it. Not all the bones were old. Remnants of flesh. Some rotting. Some fresh. Blackening blood caked but not yet fully dried. Skin and sinew hanging from the shattered frames in bits and strands.

Nadira covered her mouth. "Oh. What kind of. . ."

"We don't have any choice but to go forward," Jake said as he drew his blaster. "If we're lucky, whatever creature did this isn't coming back anytime soon."

Nadira seemed shaken still. "I hope you're right."

Jake headed down the path first, mumbling to himself, "So do I."

After several minutes, the smell from the pile of bones faded. It was far behind them now, and they'd seen no other signs of the creature. Jake put his weapon away.

The slope of the cave continued upward. Jake felt the air warm.

He held his hand out in front of her. "Hold on."

She stopped. Then he switched off the light in his hand, but the subterranean world didn't completely darken.

"I thought so."

Forty or fifty feet ahead of them, the cavern turned sharply to the left. They could see the turn because of the soft glow of light coming in from around the bend.

"It must be the way out," Nadira said. She hurried past him, running to the light at the end of rocky expanse.

"Wait!"

He rushed to catch her. She was too far ahead. As they ran, each of their footsteps echoed off the rock walls.

When Nadira reached the turn, he saw a large shadow block the light that had shone on the wall from around the corner. Still speeding toward her, he watched her stumble as she halted her run. She fell, sliding on the loose rock on the ground. Her scream echoed all around him.

Then a thunderous roar drowned out her cry. A coarse howl declaring death to all. The shadow stretched across the wall, then disappeared as the monster itself came into view. Five times taller than a man.

Lit from the side by the daylight promise of escape coming into the cave, the monster cast a visage of ungodly horror. Untamed, for surely no one could harness such a beast, it's two large black eyes bore a look of primitive malice.

Jake shot the creature. The blast deflected off its scaled hide and struck the rock above it. A few pieces of stone began to fall.

Nadira scrambled away from the beast. She pushed with her feet and hands against the slippery gravel beneath her until her back touched the cave wall. It wasn't enough. The monster stepped toward her. It settled its feet on the rubble, until the loose rocks shattered beneath the creature's weight. The ground shook.

Jake shot repeatedly, while he moved to help Nadira to her feet. The blasts did nothing to the creature's impenetrable hide.

More rocks fell from the ceiling where the energy bolts from his weapon deflected. Most of the falling debris was no bigger than a fist, but a fissure in the ceiling had appeared from where the pieces dropped.

Jake and Nadira moved back from the huge beast, retreating several yards deeper into the cavern. The escape, so close by, still guarded by the monster.

"It's going to kill us," she said.

He aimed his weapon to shoot the fissure in the ceiling above the creature.

The creature turned to them. Jake glanced at its legs. Massive, but clumsy.

"Get ready to run for the opening behind it," he said.

"What?"

He put three shots from his blaster directly into the crack in the rock above the monster. It was enough. The stone gave way and a large piece of rock cleaved off, striking the creature, then falling to the floor of the cave.

"Ready," he said.

The beast drooped its shoulders and its body swayed. Then it shook its head and raised its gaze back toward Jake.

A roar. Hot putrid breath blew against Jake and Nadira. Wet.

Jake's ears rung.

The monster raised its leg to charge the two of them. With its first step, the creature planted its weight down on the edge of the large misshapen stone that had fallen. The rock tipped. The beast lost its footing.

As the creature fell forward, Jake grabbed Nadira's hand. "Now!" He pulled her as he jumped out of the way of the falling monster. They ran around the side of the creature.

A few steps from the opening to the cavern, the prone beast turned.

Jake pulled Nadira forward, and shoved her out of

the cave ahead of him. He leapt over a pile of rubble as the creature struck him from behind.

Jake flew out of the cave, coming down in a skid beside Nadira. He barely noticed his rough landing. The pain running across his back overwhelmed him. Heat. Throbbing.

His mind drifted for a moment. He thought how the pain was worse than the lashing he'd been subjected to on the planet Farias, when he'd been made a slave for three months before escaping.

The creature's roar bellowed out of the cave. The ground shook.

"Jake!" Nadira knelt beside him, grabbing his shoulder. Touching him to make sure he could still respond.

He groaned.

The ground shook again.

"It's coming." She pulled at his shoulder, but couldn't move him.

His brown leather jacket, ripped across his back at a diagonal from belt to shoulder blade. His flesh bore the same gash, but the creature's claw only drew a shallow path. It bled, but enough skin remained to forestall death, at least for a while. His pack, gone. It had been ripped from his back and flung somewhere inside the cave.

Still face down, he slid his hands on the ground, bringing them beside his chest. Another groan, then he pushed against the dirt. He lifted himself up a couple of inches before the pain across his back caused his body to disobey his will. He collapsed again. His face hit the ground before he could turn his head to the side.

He mumbled something.

Nadira leaned over to discern his words.

He turned his head to bring his mouth out of the dirt. He breathed out a few shallow words. "Shoot the rock."

The ground shook again.

Nadira picked up Jake's weapon from the ground beside him and shot the rock at the top of the cave entrance. Pieces shattered and flew off. She continued to shoot, walking toward the opening. The creature, still inside the cave, moved toward her. She took a position a few feet from the entrance and kept shooting. The repeated blasts combined with the thunderous steps of the monster as it moved closer shook loose the stone over the hole. A couple of large slabs broke off and dropped to form a small barrier.

Nadira stepped back and continued blasting.

The creature moved within a step of leaving the cave. It let out a howl and the hot breath and heavy smell enveloped her and Jake. The stone above the opening collapsed, piling down before the creature's path. Another roar, this time muffled behind the massive pile of rock. Thuds. Small tumbles of dirt and grit cascaded down the newly formed mound of stone. After a few moments, the beast quieted.

Nadira returned to Jake's side.

He half opened his one eye that wasn't resting on the dirt. Nadira stood over him. He noticed a glint at the corner of one of her eyes. Then his eyelid drooped. She spoke, but he couldn't make out her words.

He heard her say something again, but it didn't

sound like her voice. Then there were two voices, then more. He willed some strength into his arms and shoulders, trying to lift himself off the ground. His body ignored him.

He directed all his effort instead to open his eye once more. Three men stood before Nadira. He couldn't see her hidden behind them. They were large, strong, like himself. Well, like he was up until a minute ago.

Kharn's men, he thought.

He wanted to save her.

But he couldn't.

His eyelid gave in and shut.

Then everything faded. He felt cold. Dark.

CHAPTER SEVENTEEN

"Just be sure to keep your mouth shut."

"Come on, Rekla," Jafir said, "you know I don't even like being in the same room with him, let alone drawing more attention to myself."

The two of them stood outside the door to Crassus Kharn's audience chamber. It was as close to his inner sanctum as they had ever been.

Jafir looked himself over. He straightened his jacket, and buttoned the lapel flap. He licked his left hand before wiping it against the hair on either side of his head. He glanced down at his boots, trying to decide how they might be judged by Kharn. He reached down and wiped a spot from his left one with his thumb. None of his efforts, however, gave him the presence Rekla had.

Rekla, dark blue jack hanging open, exhibited no concern for his appearance. He was accustomed to being in charge. Sure, he stood before Kharn's domain, but he cut a deal with Kharn because it suited him. Long ago, he abandoned the fleeing Waudure that became the resistance, in favor of making his own way. This favor for Kharn was just part of him doing that, part of him doing things for himself.

He held the case Kharn asked him to deliver.

Keeping Jafir close by fed into Rekla's inflated sense of self, though he always told himself that he did it to look after Jafir.

"Are you sure you aren't trying to get noticed?" Rekla asked.

Jafir didn't have time to answer before the metal door to Kharn's audience chamber slid open, disappearing into the wall.

Rekla stepped forward without hesitation. Jafir followed less boldly.

Kharn wasn't in sight. The room, an expansive rectangular one with heavy green drapes covering most of every wall, had five oversized curved couches arranged in a broken circle in the middle of the space. The floor was jet black, some sort of stone. Several lights, noticeably dim, hung from the ceiling mostly between each of the couches, but also in each corner of the room.

A long cabinet lined the wall to the right. Rekla spotted an arrangement of bottles and glasses on it. The opposite wall displayed a series of five paintings, each graphically depicting a scene of destruction or war. He glanced at them from where he stood, but knew better than to wander over to them while he awaited Kharn's entrance. He then realized the similar style of the massive painting directly in front of him, hung from the ceiling several feet out from the wall opposite the door through which he and Jafir entered. That one, however, did not depict a scene of conflict.

The painting was of a man, a Cracian, standing on a mountain. His right arm held forth, fist clenched. Trailing the main, a mass of Cracians seemed to be climbing the summit to follow him. At the base, they were climbing out of darkness. What most disturbed Rekla was the bottom of the painting, which took a moment to make out in the dim light of the room. Scattered all around the mountain, barely visible in the heavy shadow, were countless bodies, naked and mangled. They were many assorted colors and with varied facial features, but none of them had the gray skin of the Cracians.

"Do you believe that?" Jafir said, also taking in the large painting.

Kharn walked out from behind the painting, which hid a doorway.

Rekla waited for Kharn to speak.

Kharn walked half the distance from the painting to where Rekla and Jafir stood, then he paused before looking back at the image.

"Striking, isn't it?"

Rekla waited longer than he meant to before answering. "It's an impressive work of art."

Jafir audibly swallowed.

Kharn waved his right arm toward the other paintings. "They tell a story."

"Quite a story," Rekla said. "I didn't get to take a closer look at those," he looked at the five smaller paintings Kharn gestured toward, "but I think I understand the idea."

Kharn turned his attention back to Rekla. He walked
up to him, stopping only a foot in front of him. Then he
tilted his own head from one side to the other, as if
assessing him. "Do you?"

Rekla struggled to maintain his composure. Kharn
stood several inches taller than he, but that wasn't the
issue. Something about Kharn made him unsettled. His
stomach churned and his brow grew warm. He opened
his mouth to respond, but said nothing. He became
acutely aware of the bead of sweat that was running
down his forehead.

Kharn stepped back and extended his hand, then he
raised his eyebrows and looked at the case Rekla held.

Rekla stood still.

After a moment too long, Jafir nudged him with his
shoulder. Rekla then managed to speak. "What you
asked for." He handed the case to Kharn, who
accepted it and turned away from the two men.

Kharn took a few steps. Then, his back still toward
Rekla and Jafir, he began to laugh.

Rekla didn't know if they were to leave Kharn to
relish his acquisition in private or stay there until he
decided to address them. He opted to stay. Another
bead of sweat rolled down the reddish skin of his
forehead.

Kharn turned to face them once more. He held the
package up in front of him. "You two have played a part
in something far bigger than you will ever know."

Rekla glanced at Jafir, but he didn't allow himself to
turn his head fully away from Kharn's gaze.

"I came to this world with a purpose. For too long the full potential of the Cracian people has sat dormant. We will once again draw the elements from across this world that we need to transform our people to the next stage in our development. I have led the way, but soon the rest will follow in my footsteps. We will bring a new order to the galaxy, and all will benefit from our rule."

He caressed the top of the case. "My work will continue. The disloyal activities and irritations that have delayed this heroic effort are about to end. It is for this, that I thank you."

CHAPTER EIGHTEEN

Jake felt his body cool. Then he realized the coolness was on his back. He moved slightly and felt the stone underneath him. He was lying down. He breathed in deeply. The air was damp. He smelled minerals, dirt. He couldn't quite place it.

The blackness that was in his head gave way to a less intense darkness. Through his eyelids, he saw a hint of light. He opened his eyes and glanced around. The light was from several clusters of luminescent stone embedded in the ceiling above him. Not placed there by hands, but part of the rock interior of the cave-like room in which he laid. The glow had a bluish tint. It wasn't so bright that he couldn't look directly at it. But still, it gave off enough illumination for the rectangular smallish room. He could tell from some of the rough uneven walls that it was part natural cave. But, seeing the floor and the wall to his left, which were flat and smoother, he knew it had been finished off by someone.

Aside from the three-foot high attached stone block

he was laying on, the room was empty. Across from him, at the other side, there was an opening as wide as two doors and about nine feet tall, the height of the cave room itself. The opening let out and curved. A tunnel leading to. . . Well, he wasn't quite sure.

He raised up and swung his legs off the side of the rock, sitting fully now. Then it dawned on him. The pain he had felt, as he had slipped into unconsciousness who knows how long ago, had gone. He felt healthy. He reached around to touch his back. He felt the solid garment he wore. No tears. No rips. And on his back, no sensation of pain. No sign of his wound. Only a faint ache remained.

He looked down to see the shirt wasn't his own. It was a thick cloth, made of natural fibers it seemed. Its color varied unevenly, but consisted of a mix of tans and browns. Not dyed, he thought. Just the natural coloration of the fibers.

He noticed his blaster on the floor, next to his feet, leaning against the elevated stone bed. Beside it, a flask made from the hide of some animal. It wasn't his flask. He picked it up and pulled out the stopper from the top. He smelled it. Herbs. A tea? It felt warm in his hand. He took a sip. The drink had a bitter flavor, but also a floral sweetness, as if the two wouldn't fully mix. He put the stopper back in. Then he picked up his blaster. He stood and holstered it. With the two leather straps dangling from the flask, he tied the drink to his belt.

Taking another quick glance around the room to make sure he hadn't missed anything, he noticed his leather jacket hanging on the wall. The rip across the back of it neatly repaired. He walked over and swapped the shirt for his familiar jacket. Then he stepped into the tunnel leading out.

Walking the curve, he noticed the same blue glowing stone spotting the ceiling and walls. It gave ample light. Ahead he saw another cave-like room, larger than the one he had been in. He thought to ready his blaster in case the men that had taken him and Nadira were nearby, but then realized he might have it wrong. *Why would they have left my weapon?*

He walked to the room ahead. As he got closer, he saw around the curve of the cave tunnel. On one side of the room, Nadira and three men stood around a table. They were pointing at something on it and talking. He heard the faint echo of their voices, but couldn't make out the words. As he reached the room, they stopped talking and looked up at him.

"Feeling better?" Nadira asked.

"What's going on?" Jake said. "Where are we?"

She stepped toward him. One of the other three men with her approached him as well.

"Jake, this is Yorian. He's the leader of the Waudure."

The man tipped his head toward Jake. He stood a few inches shorter than Jake, but had a definite presence about him. Small wrinkles and a slight discoloring of the skin on his forehead suggested to Jake that the man was older. He hadn't seen those details on the other Waudure.

Jake returned the gesture. "Jake Mudd," he said.

"So, maybe you can tell me what's going on."

"You have landed on a planet," Yorian said, "that has been home to a long and tragic conflict between two peoples — the vile, cruel, and oppressive Cracians, and their would-be slaves, we peace-loving Waudure." He gestured to himself. "Nadira told me she has given you some of our history, and how the Cracians brought us here to enslave us. But we Waudure are not easily conquered. There are many of us who resisted and escaped. Though our numbers are great, we could not match the forces and the weapons of the Cracians, a war-like people. Those that could, made their way here, to the Untamed Lands, beyond the reach of the Cracians. We learned the ways of the wild lands of this world. We found refuge underground, in parts unexplored and unknown to the Cracians. It is here that we have continued to live for many years, doing what we can to free our brethren still under the yoke of the Cracians. But now, because of what you brought to this world, I fear we will no longer have sanctuary here."

"Look, Yorian, I've seen this before," Jake said. "My hands aren't exactly clean, but no people deserve slavery. I don't know how many Waudure they still have. I know her father's one of them." He glanced at Nadira.

Yorian looked at her and opened his mouth, as if to say something. Then he closed it without comment.

"But I can't solve your problem," Jake said. "And thanks to her, screwing up my delivery, I've already been way more involved on this planet than I intended. But I'm having a hard time believing that whatever is in that package is gonna make much of a difference one way or the other."

Nadira looked at Yorian, as if waiting for an answer.

"That is where you are wrong," Yorian said. "You have handed Crassus Kharn the instrument of the annihilation of the Waudure people on Daedalon."

"Seriously?" Jake shifted his stance and rested his hands on his belt. "I'll be straight with you. I don't know what I delivered. Someone paid for discretion. But the damn thing couldn't have been a world-destroying weapon. It's only about this big." He held his hands as if cradling the small case. "Besides, shipping regulations don't allow dangerous cargo to go unmarked, if they allow them at all."

"Kharn must've paid handsomely to bypass those regulations," Yorian said.

"If Kharn ordered it," Jake looked at Nadira, "why did you show up for the delivery?"

"I was captured over a year ago. It took months to earn their trust," Nadira said, "but, because of my father's work for Kharn, I gained a position within the Cracian base. They came to believe I was on their side. My father, hoping I could use the opportunity to escape, convinced them to send me with the man you saw at Halcion Station."

"The guy I shot," Jake said. "You didn't look like you were trying to run away."

"My father meant well," she said, "but I knew securing the case was too important to ignore."

"So, you want the package for yourselves." Jake said.

Yorian pressed his hands together and nodded. "You assume too much, Mister Mudd."

"It's not that hard," Jake said. "The Waudure and the Cracians hate each other. You're stuck on this planet and you've been killing each other for years. Now somebody's figured out a way to finish the job."

"We only want to keep the weapon from Kharn," Nadira said, "to protect the Waudure."

"Until he uses his connections to get another contraband package down here," Jake said. "No. A delay wouldn't do."

"We've never been able to penetrate their base to any significant degree. Nadira gave us a window into what they were planning. Our best chance was to intercept the package before it reached them. Now that we've failed, it is only a matter of time."

"Doesn't make sense," Jake said. "You've been fighting for years. If you have all these subterranean hideouts, can't you keep the fight going? Or at least go deeper into hiding?"

"What you brought there is no hiding from," Nadira said.

"So, you do know what's in the package," Jake said. "And I thought I have problems."

Nadira glanced at Yorian. He nodded back to her.

"It's biological," she said. "That's why they're forcing my father to help them. They need his expertise in genetics."

"A tailor-made virus," Jake said.

They looked at him with surprise.

"Yes, I know. I don't look that smart, do I?" he said.

"The galaxy isn't all rainbows and snowflakes. I should know."

"He didn't know what they were after at first," Nadira said. "Then he refused, but they threatened to kill me. I told him I wasn't worth it. But, he thought he could keep them waiting, fool them into thinking he was going along with their plan. He muddied the research as much as he could, but their scientists spotted what he was doing. They didn't have his level of understanding of the processes involved to do what they wanted, but they began to make sense of it in time."

"So, we went after the package," Yorian said.

"And now you need to get her father out to finish the weapon." Jake shook his head.

"To code it to attack the Cracians," Yorian said, "so we can be sure they'll never use it."

Jake glanced at Nadira, then Yorian. "Why me?"

"Nadira said you saved her life," Yorian said. "We Waudure are loyal to those who stand with us. We can do what is still to come without you, but Nadira tells me you've been helpful. It's your choice. Stay here until you feel well enough to return to your ship, and we will do what we can to get you back there. Or, go with our team to recover the bioweapon and we will reward you for your help. But I warn you, don't interfere with the mission."

"How much time do we have?" Jake asked. "Either way, I need to contact my ship."

Yorian shook his head. "You can't contact your ship. We can't risk the communication signal going out from here. They don't know the location of our base."

"How much time?" Jake asked again.

"We may already be too late," Nadira said.

Yorian placed his hand on her shoulder. "There's still time. Our scientists believe it will take Kharn nearly three days to complete the process, to ready the weapon for delivery."

Jake tapped the holster strap over his blaster with his thumb. "I'll let you know if I'm in by tomorrow."

"In the meantime," Yorian said, "you may move freely among our people. You will see how important it is that our mission succeeds. Nadira."

"Yes."

"You will escort Mister Mudd. Show him the Waudure and our ways."

"I will." She glanced at Jake.

He gave her a wink and subtle grin.

She turned to leave before her flush face gave herself away. "This way."

He nodded to Yorian, then followed Nadira out of the room.

CHAPTER NINETEEN

"I trust your wounds have healed?" Nadira asked, as she and Jake walked beside each other through one of the subterranean passageways.

They were ten minutes out from the room where he met the Waudure leader. He came across several oddities in the Waudure stronghold. The rock tunnels they walked through were roughly dug out, but blue light from the patches of glowing crystal in the ceiling and walls revealed smooth metallic panels inset against the stone walls. Jake guessed they were compartments of some kind. Nadira walked with purpose. So, he didn't have the chance to look closer at them. He heard a humming noise coming through the rock at points in their walk. The air felt warmer each time he moved through a section where he heard the noise.

She said she wanted to show him something, and it seemed as if she was in a hurry to do so.

"Almost entirely," he said, reaching around to touch his back. "Though I'm not sure how. That drink given to me couldn't have done all that."

"No." She stopped and turned to him. "You almost died from the slash that creature gave you."

He noticed her eyes glistened, but the corridor was dimly lit. He couldn't decide if the glimmer was a trick of the light or not.

"The men I saw approaching before I passed out," he said, "they were Waudure from here obviously. How did they know to find us there?"

"They didn't. Just fate, I suppose." She cast him a glance.

"I don't believe in fate."

Her face turned sour. She continued walking. "Come on."

He watched her step away. *Are we talking about the same thing?*

He caught up with her. "The Waudure are much more advanced than these cave dwellings would —"

"We didn't choose to live here," she said sharply. Her words echoed against the stone.

"I know," he said. "The injury on my back. Your people's healing abilities are impressive. I mean, I have systems aboard my ship that could handle something like that, but I haven't seen any planets in this region of the galaxy with that kind of tech." He tried to stay upbeat, to sound complimentary.

"When the Cracians drove us here, to the Untamed Lands, we fought for months just to survive. In time, we came to understand the dangers — the beasts, the elements — and we learned the secrets within the planet." Still walking, she pointed to the crystals as they passed underneath another glowing cluster of them.

They walked on for a while longer. Jake wondered about the crystals he continued to see through the passageways.

"I'm taking you to meet some friends," Nadira said. She turned to look at him, up and down.

He got the impression she was conflicted about his rugged body and dominant countenance.

Not the first time I've seen that look.

"What?" he asked.

"Try not to scare them. OK?"

He held his hands up to imply he didn't know what she was talking about.

They came through a curve in the tunnel.

Jake noted the clean smooth metal of the door ahead. Nothing natural about it. And above the door, shining down from the stone roof of the tunnel, a scattered array of green beams of light, not from the usual blue crystals, a refracted laser perhaps. Sure, the Waudure had been living here underground for years, but how'd they manage to fashion such elements, he wondered. He expected the rest of the base to be mostly stone, maybe wood.

Nadira stood in the beams of green light and, for a second, looked up at their source, with her eyes closed. The door slid open. Jake watched it disappear into a slit cut into the wall of rock.

Before entering, she turned to him. "Don't kill anybody."

Now she's toying with you.

He followed her through the doorway, squinting as

he passed through the green lights.

He stood just inside the room. Stunned. He was unprepared for what he faced.

"Nadi!" The pack of children screamed in chorus, running toward Nadira with their hands extended in front of them.

She knelt and held her arms wide, receiving four of the children as they impacted her. When the other three fell against the huddle from behind the first ones, she and the entire mass of them toppled toward Jake, landing sprawled before his feet.

The children laughed and several threw questions at Nadira faster than she could respond.

"Where were you?"

"Did you see any monsters?"

"Did you kill any?"

"Who's your friend?"

Nadira chuckled as she squeezed a couple of the kids in a hug. Then she got to her feet.

"You didn't tell me it was an ambush," Jake said. Knowing he couldn't use his blaster or his fists to deal with the situation, he stepped quickly past the pile and found refuge at the other side of the room. He stood next to a long stone bench topped with a thick pad wrapped in blue cloth.

With one of the children, clinging to her leg, Nadira patted the boy on the head as she answered Jake. "I thought you were a tough guy?"

"I have my limits."

One of the girls pushed herself up from the floor and ran over to him. He looked down at her. Her curly chestnut brown hair on her head added two inches to her height, bringing her even with the top of Jakes holstered blaster on his belt.

"You look funny," she said.

The left corner of Jake's mouth drew back, pushing his cheek out slightly as he fixed his gaze at the girl.

"I've heard worse," he said.

The girl bobbed her head, as if satisfied with his answer. Then she went back to Nadira.

"This man's name is Jake Mudd," Nadira said. "He is our guest."

Jake stared at the children. He said nothing.

They stared at him.

"Well?" Nadira said to the children. Then they all ran over to Jake and jumped at him without warning, hugging him simultaneously.

He regretted that this was a situation his blaster couldn't solve. All he could do was wait it out.

"Alright," Nadira said. "I think he feels welcome now. Go tell Hodin that I'm here to see him. Then you should get back to your training."

After what seemed like a long time, the children released their death grips and waved as they left the room out a door, but not the one Jake and Nadira had entered through.

"Never figured you as the motherly type," Jake said.

"They're orphans. All but the one that spotted your good looks."

"I thought I wasn't your type," he said, wearing a wry smile.

She ignored his comment. "Her mother is still with

us, for now."

Jake felt like an ass for joking when she was talking about orphans. "For now?"

"I was told this morning that she was spotted by a Cracian patrol when she was on a scouting mission." Nadira stepped over to Jake. "I doubt she'll be with us by tomorrow."

"Can't you help her?" he asked. "Like your people healed me?"

"Her wounds were too severe."

He turned from her and began walking back and forth.

She stood still while he paced the room before speaking again.

"I need to contact my ship," he said, "to let her know I'm alright. She's expecting me back by now."

"You can't."

He stopped pacing and looked at her. "What do you mean? There must be a communications system here."

"It's too risky. Remember? The Cracians would intercept the signal. This base has stayed hidden for years. That's how we've survived for so long."

"She's not going to like it," he said.

"Like it? It's a ship, Jake."

He saw how she looked at him, head to toe. Lingering.

"I'm here… and alive," she said.

He said nothing.

She looked away. "Come on. There's someone else you should meet."

She led him out of the room and down another

corridor. She walked ahead of him the entire way without looking back, neither of them saying anything until they reached a room guarded by two men posted at either side of the door.

The guards nodded to her.

"He's with me," she said.

One of them nodded again. She glanced upward and waited for the scattered green lights to read her face. The door slid open and she entered. Jake followed.

CHAPTER TWENTY

"I'd heard you'd returned to us."

Nadira approached the man and the two extended an arm, grasping each other's forearm, as Jake had seen her do with Tay.

"I'm sorry I failed to retrieve it," she said.

"No one else could have done it then. I'm sure," Hodin said, placing his hands on his hips, hanging his thumbs off the thick leather belt he wore.

Jake took the man for a soldier. He noted Hodin's tactical boots, the right one with a formidable blade sheathed on the side, and the gear strapped to his belt — a couple of tools tucked into leather cases looped onto it, on the other side a blaster, about the same size as Jake's. It bore marks and scratches. Far from a ceremonial show piece. It had seen action, and dished out a fair bit, he would wager on it. Jake's assessment solidified as he spotted several scars on the man's arms and one on his neck. He knew knife wounds. They had that in common. Mostly it was the man's gaze. Eyes revealed a lot about someone. Those that had seen death too many times had a peculiar look. Pain. Anger. Resolve. Pain and anger belonged to everyone. But, in war, those eyes that didn't harbor resolve belonged to dead men.

Hodin stepped toward Jake. "This must be the one they found you with near the caves." He paused, taking measure of Jake. "Not sure why they brought him back here."

Jake took a step toward Hodin and offered his hand. "Jake."

Hodin looked at Jake's hand, but didn't shake it. "You aren't one of us."

Nadira spoke up to break the tension. "I brought him into this mess. And, he saved my life. He may help us infiltrate Kharn's base to get the weapon."

"Nadira." Hodin glared at her.

"Relax, Hodin. He knows. He's the one that brought it to Daedalon."

"In my defense," Jake said, "I didn't know what the package contained."

"We don't need his help," Hodin said, looking Jake over as if unimpressed. "And I don't need the distraction of looking after someone."

"Don't get worked up," Jake said to him. "I haven't agreed to help."

Hodin looked more at ease.

"Though," Jake said, looking at him, "you probably need me to get the job done."

Hodin grimaced.

Jake grinned.

Hodin clenched his fist.

"Take it easy," Nadira said.

"You heard her," Jake said. He grinned wider. Call it a test or a dance. Wolves maneuvering for dominance.

Hodin lunged at Jake, swinging his fist.

Nadira moved farther back, though she was already out of the line of fire.

Jake bobbed left and leaned, avoiding the blow. Then he sidestepped, countering with a punch to Hodin's lower ribs. He stayed his follow up, waiting to see what Hodin would do.

Hodin exhaled and sounded a heavy oomph, but otherwise seemed unfazed by the punch.

The two stood poised, a few feet apart, each sizing up his opponent. Jake grinned, and so did Hodin, giving a nod.

"Cut it out, you two!" Nadira stepped in front of them, her arms thrust out to keep them apart.

Jake and Hodin dropped their fists and stood up straight.

Nadira glared at each of them, back and forth. "Why do I get the sense that you two enjoy this sort of thing?"

"Guilty," Jake said, dipping his head slightly toward her.

"Apologies, Nadira," Hodin said. "We'll see if he's up to the task. We can run him through some of the tests the other men had to undergo." Hodin looked at Jake. "Unless you aren't up for it."

Jake rubbed his side, pretending he had been hit in the ribs instead of Hodin. "I still haven't agreed to go along, but I'm curious to see what passes for a challenge here, and I have some time to kill."

"Hodin," Nadira said, "will the team be able to get into the base? They'll be expecting us now."

"We've got a doozy of a distraction planned." Hodin moved to a table at the back of the room. "Take a look." He leaned over the table, placing his hands on a large paper that covered the entire surface.

Jake and Nadira joined him to see what he had.

Jake recognized topographical lines on the map. Two groupings of what he assumed were buildings were indicated on the paper, on opposite sides of the layout.

"They'll be plenty busy," Hodin said.

He began to explain for the next ten minutes how the Waudure forces would launch a multi-pronged full-scale assault on the Cracian base.

Their primary forces would move straight toward the base, overtaking and subduing any Cracian scouts as the Waudure advanced. It would be critical to cover as much ground as possible before the Cracians learned of the attack. With only one front to defend, they would move many of their forces toward the advancing Waudure. The hope was that the overconfident Cracians, trying to crush the Waudure, would advance beyond the natural rocky defenses surrounding the outskirts of their base. This would make them vulnerable.

As they did this, the Waudure would have a second force, which would flank the Cracian forces from the north. This would be an unconventional one, comprised of crag beast riders and a number of creatures native to the Untamed Lands that the Waudure have enlisted for aid. The creatures, whose description Jake could hardly believe, were still wild, but they could be guided sufficiently by the Waudure, who had long dealt with them. And, though the beasts lacked higher intelligence, they had enough of a mind to know the Cracians were their enemies.

Hodin, Nadira, and the rest of their small team, would move east with the primary assault. When the Cracians engaged, Hodin's infiltration team would break off from the main force and move southward before circling back up to make their way into the Cracian base.

While explaining everything, Hodin filled Jake in as to the types of weapons systems the Waudure and the Cracians had. He also discussed the pace different units could move and the distance they would cover before the Cracians discovered the attack. Jake asked quite a few questions, to which Hodin gave extensive answers. By the end of the presentation, the two had bonded over their mutual understanding of military strategy and tactics. Jake's knowledge impressed Hodin, and their posture toward one another shifted to one of mutual respect.

"There's one critical point to remember," Hodin said. "If our team fails, we won't get another chance. We are going to lose a considerable number of our forces in the main assault. In fact, there's a chance the Cracians will use the opportunity to counterattack our base, if they can determine the origin of our forces."

"And," Nadira said, "if we fail, they'll finalize the weapon."

"Then it will all be over anyway," Hodin said.

"Your plan's mostly solid," Jake said. "There are a few details you may want to reconsider."

"So, you've done this sort of thing before?" Hodin said.

"Too many times. Years ago, but it's the sort of thing that never leaves you. No matter how many of the memories you try to forget."

Hodin nodded.

Jake offered a few suggestions, such as the division of forces in the main assault into multiple groupings instead of one, to make them more difficult to target. Hodin agreed with most of the ideas, and marked up the map accordingly.

"You should come with us," Hodin said.

Nadira touched the back of Jake's hand that was nearest her on the table. "We could use you. I've seen how you handle yourself."

"Let me think about it," he said. "It's not that I don't care what happens, but I came here with other plans. I need to get back to my ship."

"Our assault happens in two days," Hodin said. "We need that much time to get everything in place. If you're in, meet me at the training arena outside the barracks in the morning. Nadira can give you directions."

"You'll have my answer in the morning," Jake said.

"Let's get something to eat," Nadira clasped Jake's hand, "and I can show you around a bit. Then I'll take you to your room for the night."

He nodded to Hodin before turning his attention to Nadira. "Lead the way."

CHAPTER TWENTY-ONE

Jake watched Nadira open the pod transport door and step out into the massive underground cavern. He turned back to the large pod dash window in front of him and took in the view of the dome. It rose high into the air and looked like a sky. The rock of the cavern ceiling only faintly showed through the glow of blue light, the same sort as that from the crystals in the tunnels. Here the glow covered the entirety of the cavern's ceiling.

He heard and watched Nadira inhale the fresh air. Then she stepped away from the pod door. He sat looking through the glass. The cavern extended several thousand feet across, he guessed, and as wide. Vegetation covered the whole of it, at least on the ground.

Nadira jutted her head back into the transport pod. "Are you going to get out?"

He undid the safety harness and tossed it over his shoulder before standing up.

Bracing himself with one arm on the chair for a

moment, he held his other hand over his stomach. He slowly turned his head toward her. "I really hate these things."

"Come on, tough guy," Nadira said, moving away from the door.

He stepped outside. The ground felt noticeably less rocky and looked less red in color than the other parts of the Waudure base. He drew his gaze from his feet upward, out over the vista. The cavern struck him as unfathomably large.

"Amazing." He stared into the distance.

Nadira watched him and smiled, giving him time to take it in.

He scanned the valley before him, darting his attention here and there.

They stood on an elevation outside the tunnel they'd traveled. To his left and right a few more such tunnels opened into the cavern. The whole of it rested underground, but the light and heavy plant growth throughout the entire space made the place appear to be topside at dusk.

A hundred feet below them, and at least a few thousand feet in every direction, lay forests and gardens. In the distance, a shimmer caught his eye. He took it to be a pond or reservoir, a sizable one.

Dozens of Waudure were in the gardens, working the soil, and tending to the plants.

"It took a long time to get to this," Nadira said. "When the first of us fled the Cracians, we nearly died in the Untamed Lands. But as we found the subterranean passageways and took to them to avoid the hunts, we made our way through the tunnels looking for refuge. Then we found this."

"It's astonishing."

"It wasn't what you see now, but there was enough plant life, fed by the water, for a start. There's a spring beneath the pool. We cultivated the cavern, bringing in more seeds from excursions deeper into the Untamed Lands. With this resource and the safety of the caves, it was decided we would remain below."

"Can we get closer?"

"Follow me. I'll take you down."

They took a trail that descended steps carved into the side of the cavern. Several minutes later they set foot on the valley below. He felt the warmth and moisture in the air. She led him through orchards and clusters of plants the likes of which he'd never seen. Each bore fruit or fulfilled other edible or medicinal needs, which she described to him. He sampled a variety of the crops as they strolled among them.

He realized the Waudure had built a new way of life here. They'd gone from fleeing captivity and persecution to creating a new home, a burgeoning society.

She introduced him to many of the people who tended the food forest. Men, women, and children who all, he learned, dedicated their days to looking after the bounty that sustained the entire base.

One of them offered him a sample from the collected harvest, picking a strange-looking fruit from a basket and handing it to him.

"Thank you," he said to the woman, before tasting it.

As he bit into it, the juices of the brown lumpy fruit tingled the inside of his mouth.

He felt dizzy for a moment.

Nadira said something to him. He watched her mouth move, but he heard no words coming from her.

Her face appeared blurry.

Poison. That b...

CHAPTER TWENTY-TWO

Jake woke to the smell. Dank. Earthy. A bitter taste coated his tongue. Slowly, feeling came to his limbs. The air around him and the floor beneath him radiated warmth. Then he remembered the fruit the Waudure woman had given him. He opened his eyes and willed some energy into his body, so he could get off the ground. His own skin still felt distant somehow, but the blurriness had left his eyes.

Whispers of smoke lingered in the room. The same blue light shown down from the rock ceiling, but more dimly than elsewhere in the caves. Three figures sat on the ground before him, a few feet away. Between them and him, a small pile of smoldering plants — the source of the smoke, and the smell.

The three were Waudure, he could tell. Much older than any he'd seen thus far. Two men and one woman, she was the most distinct, with her long neck and her slightly large eyes. Wrinkles. Tired skin. Frail-looking bodies. If he had to guess, he'd say they were ancient. But two things didn't settle with his take on them. Each of the three wore a wry smile and had eyes dazzling with life and energy. Hard to get a handle on it, but he felt their piercing gaze. It was unsettling.

He pushed himself halfway to a sitting position. "You've maybe a few seconds until strength returns to my limbs to tell me what's going on. Otherwise, I'm out of here and I don't mind putting any of you down on the way out."

"You are mistaken, Jake Mudd," the man seated in the middle of the other two said.

"Look," Jake said, "I realize I'm the outsider here, but one of yours brought me here. And then — What the hell was in that fruit?"

"We couldn't know the calip fruit would have that effect on you. We meant you no harm. We've never seen that effect on a human. You aren't the first to pass through here, though it has been a long time."

"So, I wasn't poisoned?"

"You were poisoned," the man said, "but not purposely."

Jake sat up the rest of the way. "Alright. Who are you? Where's Nadira? Why I am I here? And what's with all the smoke?"

"The smoke has cleansed your body of the calip fruit's effect. Nadira is tending to other matters. We are the Waudure Elders. And, as for why you are here, that is the question you must answer for yourself."

"I don't have time for this," Jake said, moving to stand up. He only made it half way to his feet before toppling over. He hit the stone floor with his shoulder, not bracing himself as he went down. The pain came through numbed slightly, but not completely. "Son of a bitch."

The woman seated with the others spoke. "The smoke you're breathing is serving another purpose. We should have warned you not to try to get up just yet."

Jake looked down for his blaster. "Where's my weapon?"

She continued, "You don't need it here. It will be returned to you soon enough."

Jake settled back into a seated position on the floor. He had bluffed about killing any of them, but he hadn't ruled out knocking somebody upside the head. That would have to wait. He was in no condition to do much of anything except sit and try to keep from falling over.

"We know you are not of this world," she said. "And you do not know our ways."

"I'm beginning to get the idea that I do," Jake said.

"You care for Nadira." The woman said it matter-of-factly. It wasn't a question.

"She's had a pass on me shooting her," Jake said, waving the smoke away from his face, "so far."

The woman looked at the two men beside her and smiled.

"I haven't decided about you three," Jake said.

"We know that is not our fate," the woman said. "The question remains. Why are you here?"

"Because your neighbor Kharn decided to order an illegal weapon to wipe all of you off the face of the planet. Not a nice guy, from what I hear, but maybe he has a point."

The man to her left spoke to her. "Shall I do it now?"

"Yes," she replied.

The Waudure Elder took something from the opening in his robe and dropped the substance onto the pile of smoking plants and embers.

"What's that?" Jake asked, still too weak to get up.

"The answer to your question," the woman replied.

As she spoke, the warm smoke rising from the pile changed in color to a deep red.

"Don't be afraid," she said. Then she wafted the smoke toward Jake with her arm.

The warmth of it wrapped around his cheeks. He opened his mouth to speak, but his words vanished from his mind. He looked at the red smoke as it danced in front of his face.

Not again.

Jake watched through the smoke as the three Waudure sitting before him sunk downward at the same time the ceiling of the cave swung into view. The thud pounded through the back of his head. Then the light faded.

* * *

Darkness.

Jake heard a wind. The sound grew into a howling storm. Bits of grit and sand pelted his skin. Drawing the muscles of his brow and squinting his eyes, he peered into the storm. The blackness turned to brown and gray and dust. The sand blew everywhere. A chill went up his spine. His lips quickly dried and cracked.

He stood on a precipice, his feet planted, his legs braced wide. Through the massive dust storm, he caught sight of Nadira. She stood a few feet in front of him, closer to the drop off the cliff. Below her, behind her, darkness. And still the roar of the wind. He heard her cry, drowned mostly by the storm, but he could tell, it was his name she called out.

She reached for him as her footing slipped. He extended his hand to grab hers. He would save her.

Their hands touched. He heard her voice. "Jake."

The torrents of sand crashed into his arm. Shards of ice. He struggled to hold her, to keep her from falling into the abyss.

Her lips curved at the edges. She needed him to rescue her, he thought. Warmth swelled inside him. The sound of the storm faded.

But then it turned on him. The roaring wind fought back. A terrible cold struck him. And he watched as his hand, still holding hers, turned to dust.

Her grasp slipped through the particles that were once his fingers.

He stood frozen in the storm, unable to stop her fall into the blackness.

The storm of sand and grit swelled until it filled every space around him. He could see nothing else.

He fell to his knees, grasping the wrist of his handless arm. "No!"

He trembled, but the icy wind could only lay partial claim to it.

   * * *

Darkness.

Hot burning smoke. Jake felt it. Smelled it. A roaring passing before him, not too distant. It reverberated through his muscles and rattled his bones. The darkness broke with fire. Explosions. Everywhere war-ready craft flew about, bursting through columns of sooty gray and lingering clouds of death's vapors. Blasts and crashes. Cries cut short with death's silence, while other lamentations went on. The battle raged in the air and below. Mighty beasts suffered the pulses from the advanced fighters, but the creatures did not falter. Mounted on the towering monsters of the Untamed Lands, Waudure fighters rode courageously against the forces of the Cracians, who attacked in waves and with precision. No place of respite was visible. No crag of rock nor distant valley offered refuge. War enveloped all.

Across the scene, fixed over the heavy blanket of smoke and fire, a figure came into view. Too distant to see clearly, the outline and hazy visage revealed a man of strong stature and commanding presence. Jake watched him as the man seemed to survey the battlefield. Occasionally, the figure pointed his arm at a position across the ravaged landscape, and a new group of fighter ships flew past him, following his direction, raining down energy weapons and ballistic and explosive shells on the Waudure forces below.

Jake strained to pull a clearer vision of the man through the smoke, but the fog of war swelled up to counter him. Just before it entirely obscured the man on the perch of rock across the battlefield, Jake noticed a second person step up behind the one directing the aerial forces. The other figure leaned in to the first, as if to whisper to him, and gestured with his hands. Jake heard a faint breath of the whisper, but the sounds of the battle drowned out any meaning from the words. The first man nodded, but another explosion erupted between Jake and the two men. He saw no more of them.

"Jake!" He heard the call and turned toward it as a Cracian ship came down nearby, exploding into a fireball, the hot blast of which struck him. His eyes and ears failed him as he tumbled backward.

   * * *

Darkness.

Clank. The metal cuffs dropped from his wrists and ankles, falling onto the piled chains beneath him. A cacophony of boos and jeers and cheers echoed through the massive arena. Jake rose from his knees and elbows to stand and face the man before him. The sting as his eye is invaded by the drop of blood falling from the gash on his head reminded him he was in all too familiar territory. He curled the end of the chain and shackle once around his hand. He smiled at the man across from him.

About damn time.

   * * *

A sharp pain swelled up inside his forehead. A bitter taste washed across his tongue as he swallowed. Then the pain faded and his eyes drowned the images from his mind, replacing them once again with the room, the ceiling. He turned his head and caught sight of the three Waudure Elders still seated across from him.

They didn't speak. Not until he had righted himself, returning to a seated posture in front of the now dampened pile of smoldering vegetation.

"What you saw," one of the elder men said, "was for you alone."

Jake rubbed his eyes and gently shook his head to clear his thoughts.

The woman spoke. "We have broken with tradition for you."

"Explain." Jake waved his hand toward the burnt pile before him, making sure no more smoke made it to his face.

"The stories of the future," she said, "are meant only for the Elders. But these are dangerous times." She glanced at the other two, who then nodded. "The fate of our people is at stake."

"I know you're at war with the Cracians," Jake said, "but it's not my war."

"Our visions told us you were coming. They told us you would bring death, yet also perhaps life."

"I had no idea about that delivery. Rules were broken," Jake said. "I never would've—"

"We understand," she said. "Nonetheless, the means to our end came by your hands. What we have given you is a glimpse into your future, so that you might save ours. You and the weapon are of the same tale. How it ends is up to you."

"You're asking a lot from a guy who just got swindled into doing something."

The three Elders rose to their feet. The two men left the room first.

The female Elder gazed upon Jake for a moment, as if assessing how he might act when the time came. "You must tell no one what you have seen." She turned and left him alone in the room.

He stood and stared at the pile of now ashen plants.

"What a mind screw."

Don't blame Sarah, you bum. She took the delivery, but you put the pressure on her for the big payoffs.

Contraband cargo. Hijacked. Personally responsible for impending genocide.

And I haven't even gotten paid.

Not my best day on the job.

"And this is what you do to get away from the bastard you were?"

He noticed his blaster on the floor behind where the Elders had been seated.

"Ah, hell. Guess you'll go after it."

He stepped over to his weapon and picked it up.

"Save the day, or die trying. And you know you're still not going to get paid."

CHAPTER TWENTY-THREE

Jake moved down the winding tunnel until he reached the training arena. One of the Waudure assigned to accommodate him during his stay had given him directions. She'd brought him food and drink early in the morning and, before leaving him to partake of it, told him how her husband had died, killed by the Cracians while out on his patrol.

I get it, he thought, but he simply replied, "I'm sorry for your loss. We'll do what we can."

As he made his way to the training grounds, he admitted to himself that he had adopted the Waudure, at least while he was on Daedalon. He felt responsible for their situation, even though it had been a mess long before he came there with his deadly cargo.

He stopped at the entrance to the arena, looking across the well-lit cavern to the group of men and women gathered near the other side, a hundred feet or so away.

Who knows. If you'd ended up in the Cracian base instead, maybe you'd see them as the good guys in all this.

But he hadn't, and he knew in war no side was all good. Not to argue moral equivalence, but everybody wants to live as much as the next guy. But then he thought about it some more.

No chance. Slavery. That's enough reason to take 'em down in my book.

He walked through the threshold into the arena.

One of the men in the group waved him over, and Jake made his way, scanning his surroundings as he did.

Loose gritty sand covered the expansive cavern floor. Appropriate, he thought. Who wants to fight and get knocked on their ass on a bed of rock?

A few other tunnels opened into the arena from points equally staggered around the perimeter. Aside from those, the walls were solid stone, blackish with a sheen. The familiar crystals blanketed the ceiling high above, casting their glow into the space below such that all was well lit.

The group he approached consisted of twenty Waudure, a third of them women, all of them dressed much the same as he'd seen Hodin— the warrior outfit, he thought. They stood watching Jake, awaiting his arrival.

To either side of the team rested a large crate of wood and metal. Each such box stood twice as high as any of the Waudure.

Jake heard chatter from the group as he neared, but he heard something else. Upon further approach, he realized the other noises were coming from the giant crates. Dust kicked up repeatedly from the base of the boxes, forming a low-hanging cloud a couple of feet off the ground. The Waudure seemed to take no notice of the crates or their rumblings.

There was nothing else in the entire space.

Jake stepped up to the group, spotting Nadira among them, and Hodin in front, beside another Waudure man, who wore an insignia on his left shoulder. No one else had the ornamentation, so Jake took him to be the team leader.

Jake looked at Hodin and the man next to him. "I'm here to join the idiots going into the belly of the beast."

A few of the Waudure in the rear of the group chuckled. The man with the insignia turned his head a few degrees in their direction, and the chuckling stopped.

"This is Jake Mudd," Hodin said to his superior.

The squad leader looked at Jake for a long moment before speaking. "Killed before?"

"I've been in my share of situations," Jake said. "I'm still here."

The man's expression hinted he appreciated the response. A man that felt the need to give details was either green or psychotic. Neither would serve well.

The squad leader tipped his brow slightly. "I'm Captain Drayin."

"Jake."

"Nadira vouched for you," Drayin said. "Hodin says you're probably not entirely useless."

Jake caught Hodin grinning and turned back to Drayin to await pronouncement of his judgement.

"The stakes are the highest," he said. "We need to be sure you're an asset and not a liability."

"Fair," Jake said.

Drayin nodded, then he stepped back. The group moved out of his way as he did. "Form up!"

The Waudure, including Hodin and Nadira, quickly shuffled to form a long line next to the back wall of the cavern. They each drew their weapons and held them at the ready. Drayin walked behind the oversized crate on his left. He lifted his hand to a lever on the back edge of it and paused there.

Looking at Jake, he asked, "Ready?"

Jake watched the crate shake and heard the rumbling from inside. "What the hell."

Drayin pulled down the lever, dropping the front wall of the crate to the ground. A cloud of dust and sand kicked up from the impact. Before it cleared, Jake, and everyone else, heard the snorting and growling of what he figured would be an annoyingly nasty beast.

Had to join the club, didn't you?

The creature's discharges, saliva and, no doubt, nasal projections, shot through the dust cloud. Jake watched them fly past him, spraying to the ground five feet behind him.

Drayin stepped out from behind the crate to get a better view of the scene.

Jake drew his blaster and backed up, waiting for his surprise.

The crate shook violently and out came a beast that resembled a wild boar, but with four tusks and ears that hung down to the ground like rough leather blankets, dragging through the sand.

Jake shot the creature, but the blast didn't slow the beast. The hide scorched at the impact, but wasn't penetrated. He did manage to piss it off, however.

He glanced at the Waudure, who had stayed in formation, weapons drawn and ready. "You guys are great."

The giant mutant bore, as Jake thought of it, wildly shook its head, gouging the ground before it with its tusks.

Hodin shouted from the formation, "That means she likes you!"

The monster charged Jake. He dove out of the way, but one of the large tusks caught his leg and spun him sideways in mid-dive.

Without moving from formation, the team of onlookers groaned and otherwise voiced sympathy for the blow Jake received. None of them did anything to help him, though.

His thigh would bruise heavily, but fortunately the rounded side of the tusk hit him. If it had been the point, the creature might have hooked and dragged him the twenty feet it ran before it stopped and turned to face him again.

Jake pushed himself up and spun around to a kneeling position, aiming his weapon once again at the boar monster. The creature broke into another sprint toward him. He held his fire while he tracked the creature's swaying head. He aimed for one of its eyes, large with drooped lids, caked with dried goop in the corners.

With the beast halfway to him, Jake squeezed the trigger. The blast shot dead on, piercing the creature's eye like the center spot on a target. The giant boar's head dropped at an angle, but it kept charging. Jake avoided the hit easily this time, since the monster's run skewed off course, due, no doubt, to the lost eye.

Jake backed closer to the open crate, calling with random grunts to signal the creature to his location. The beast squealed and snorted as it drew closer.

Jake stood directly in front of the fallen side panel to the crate, with the opening behind him. He shot the creature on its impenetrable hide, just above its tusks. Then he screamed at it.

His gambit worked. The four-tusked elephant-eared mutant boar charged him once more, this time more wildly than before. Animal rage drove its heavy legs, pounding the ground with a thunderous rhythm.

Jake holstered his blaster and stood in the beast's path, yelling at it. A moment before the creature was to slam into him, he pulled a small metal cylinder from a pouch on the back of his belt and tossed the device behind him, into the crate. Then, as the monster's tusks came within a foot of goring him, he jumped up. Stepping his right foot on top of one of the tusks, he pushed off, arching his head backward and extending his arms overhead. As he somersaulted, he grabbed the top edge of the open side of the crate and flipped himself onto the top.

The landing wasn't graceful. In fact, he tumbled onto his back. But he was clear of the beast's charge. The creature, with nothing in front of him to hit, continued past where Jake had been and slammed into the inside back wall of the crate. Then the device Jake tossed in detonated.

The explosion simultaneously knocked him off the top of the giant box and hurled it back against the rock wall of the cavern.

When the dust cleared and the coughing of the Waudure team stopped, they saw Jake on the ground near the back of the crate. His face bore a large scrape and a cut on his forehead. His left leg at the ankle rested wedged between the crate and the rock wall of the cavern.

Jake grinned.

"So, am I in?"

Drayin gestured with a tilt of his head to a few of his men, then he glanced at Jake on the ground next to the crate, which was still and silent now.

His men responded by hurrying over to Jake. The three of them leaned into the side of the crate. After a moment, it moved out from the cavern wall a few inches. Jake pulled his leg out from behind the giant box and got up.

He stood, looking to Drayin for a response. Out of the corner of his eye, he noticed Nadira tilting her head for a view past the men in front of her.

Drayin stepped over to Jake.

"If you're willing to die with us," he said, extending his arm to Jake, "we're willing to die for you."

Jake remembered how Nadira and Tay had embraced arms. *Bond, not birth.* He glanced at her and saw her nod to him. He took the man's arm as she had embraced Tay's.

"Dying's at the bottom of my list of priorities," he said, "but I get the sentiment. Thanks."

With mutual respect in their eyes, both men unclasped their arms.

Drayin reached under the front fold of his shirt and pulled out a sort of whistle that hung on a chain around his neck. "I would've called the beast off, if you were really in danger."

Jake shot him a raised eyebrow. "*If* I was in danger?"

Drayin smiled and tucked the whistle back under his shirt. "We'll skip the other tests." He glanced at the other crate. "That one gets a little wild. And it doesn't listen to me."

Jake looked at the second crate, wondering what precious creature waited inside. Then he turned back to Drayin.

"I figured I'd let it kill you if I decided you were a liability," Drayin said.

"Go team." Jake held his fist loosely in front of his chest, in a sarcastic gesture of enthusiasm.

Drayin walked closely past him, leaning in as he did. "Don't be a distraction to my team and we're good."

Jake looked at him as he passed, but then noticed Nadira nudging her way in front of the other Waudure to better see Jake. Her face, her eyes, made no attempt at concealing her attraction.

Where's that whistle? I think I'm in danger after all.

CHAPTER TWENTY-FOUR

Kharn stood off to the side, watching Lorian carefully remove the components from the case. Kharn paced, only a few steps in either direction. He shifted his posture, as he waited for his science administrator to do his work.

"How soon until we can encode?"

Lorian, holding a small glass vial with a pair of metal tongs, didn't respond for a moment. After he sat the vial down delicately onto the table, he answered. "Soon. Once I mix the components, there is a settling process that must take place before we can proceed."

"Yes, yes," Kharn said, "I know." He paced more.

Lorian continued, "The process can't be accelerated. The solutions are too volatile. If we force it," he withdrew another vial from within the form-fitting pad inside the case, "we risk destabilizing the solution and losing any chance of encoding the weapon."

"You are right, Lorian." Kharn turned away from him. He stepped over to the large computer display on the wall behind him. After pressing a few buttons on the controls beneath it, he brought up a map of Daedalon.

Lorian glanced over his shoulder at what Kharn was doing. "Running the simulation again?"

"I need to factor in the latest weather projections," Kharn said, continuing to type on the controls below the wall-size screen.

"It'll work," Lorian said, returning to his work. "Once the solution is ready, we can program it. The storms will do the rest."

The screen above Kharn displayed a series of numbers overlaying the map. A few moments later, contours and vector arrows plotted the predicted weather patterns onto the azimuthal equidistant projection of the planet. Kharn watched as a single point of deep red grew and then morphed as it expanded, following the vectors that were the calculated winds. Within two minutes the simulation ran its course, and the red, representing the spread of the bioweapon, covered the map of the planet.

Kharn studied the entirety of the screen.

"What are you doing?" Lorian asked. "You've run that simulation a hundred times."

"Looking for any holes. I must be sure it's complete." Kharn pressed a button on the panel. The display went black. He turned to face Lorian. "When we continue our operations, all the resistance must be wiped out. We've lost enough laborers and time over the last several years. I want no more interference."

"Perhaps if they had come to understand what we're doing." Lorian said.

Kharn walked over to him to watch him work. "You've

been loyal to the cause from the beginning."

"Your vision has allowed me to pursue levels of science I could never dream of before."

Kharn nodded. "We'll clear away these obstacles before we bring in more suitable test subjects."

"It is unfortunate that we Waudure are not pliable to the augmentation procedures," Lorian said.

Kharn turned his hand in front of himself, looking at it. "It nearly killed even me."

"I did warn against it."

Kharn scowled at Lorian. "Once we have perfected the process, we can raise my fellow Cracians."

"We loyal Waudure will stand with the Cracian as you take your rightful place in the galaxy."

"This man," Kharn said, disdain in his voice, "the one that brought us the weapon, any chance he dies from it too?"

"We can only encode it for a single species. I'm afraid it won't work on him."

"That's too bad. He's becoming a nuisance." Kharn walked back to the table on which Lorian continued to prepare the bioweapon. He smiled as he looked over the vials. "Still, he is human. They're easy enough to kill. With luck, he's rotting in the caves by now. If not, then we'll have a surprise for him along with the others who think they can overrun our defenses." Kharn picked up one of the vials from the table. "And then, for the rest of them, this."

CHAPTER TWENTY-FIVE

Jake woke early the next morning. The large assault on the Cracian base was only one more day ahead. He retrieved the food that had been left for him outside the door to his room and ate quickly, for sustenance, not pleasure. Familiar with the path, he made his way to the training area once again. His instructions were to join his unit there for a briefing.

The expansive room didn't have the large crates from the day before. Jake wondered again what sort of creature the unopened one had held, but he decided to be thankful it remained a mystery.

Nadira, Hodin, and three others had already gathered where the crates had been. Jake noticed them strapping on gear and talking as he walked over to them.

A heavy stone slab protruded out five feet from the cavern wall, with one end still embedded inside. From there Nadira and the others took canisters, blasters, and a few other pieces of equipment Jake didn't recognize.

Hodin nodded to Jake when he joined them.

"Did you sleep well?" Nadira asked, as she scanned him from head to toe with her eyes. Again.

Jake noted her interest, but offered her nothing back along those lines. He deflected with humor. "Would've been here sooner, but somebody forgot my wakeup call."

The early rise and the tactical briefing triggered something latent but familiar in him. These were the people he'd stand shoulder to shoulder with tomorrow. He took in the group as she introduced each of them by name. As she did, he decided who was likely to fall. Then he wondered who, if any, would remain standing when it was over.

Jake figured Hodin, physically close to his own stature and with the seasoning of many battles it seemed, stood the best chance.

Shortest among the group, Brun, thick with muscle, stood next to the stone table. He was opening and examining several small metal boxes and cylinders, clipping each onto his belt or the strap across his shoulder after inspection. His left cheek, with reddish skin like all the others, bore a scar that covered it, half his forehead, and part of his left ear. Jake recognized it as the remnants of a bad burn, the kind that comes with a nasty tale. Not a run-of-the-mill accident, this one left a grizzly patch of rough discolored flesh. Bet it still hurts, Jake thought. He couldn't decide the man's odds.

The character next to Brun couldn't have been a starker contrast. Taller even than Jake, thin, but with a wiry frame that looked strong and tested, Hanlan was the only one among them that said nothing, gave away no expression. His eyes spoke only focus, with an intensity that Jake recognized from his own darker days. Holding a long slender rifle, the man, at a disturbingly careful pace, turned the weapon and moved it, closely taking in every inch of it. Jake couldn't decide if he was checking the rifle's condition or merely admiring it. He knew why the man had been chosen. Even if Hanlan didn't make it back, you can bet there'd quite a few Cracian bodies scattered across the battlefield to show he'd been there.

Jake felt slightly guilty when Nadira introduced Alara, though he couldn't settle on why. He had no relationship with Nadira. In fact, she'd tried to kill him.

Still, seeing Alara caused him to become distinctly aware of his breathing, and whether he was looking at her as neutrally as he did at the others in the group. He wasn't. And if she noticed the difference.

Alara greeted him by name and then cast her gaze down, offering herself to his eyes with a long pause, while she pretended to consider a piece of gear in front of her on the table.

Nadira stepped closer to Jake. "Take whatever *gear* you require."

He turned to her, but the delicate form and exquisite features of Alara, with her rose-colored skin, still filled his mind's eye.

"Well?" Nadira spoke noticeably louder.

He raised his eyebrows, releasing Alara from his head. "Right." He looked at Nadira and then scanned the table.

Hodin pointed to the items on the stone slab. "Explosives, laser cutter, distance goggles…"

Brun had taken most of the explosive charges from the table, Jake realized. *Explains the scar.*

Taking a pair of the shoulder straps, Jake equipped himself with one of everything on the table, except the blasters. Nothing wrong with them, he thought, but he decided his would suffice. He pulled it out and pressed the button on the side. Confirming it had a sufficient charge, he holstered it again.

Hodin picked up one of the guns from the table and held it before Jake. "You sure you don't want to try one of these?" He glanced at Jake's holstered weapon. "It packs a punch. How's that one?"

"Thanks," Jake said, "but I'm used to mine. Been with me a while and never let me down."

"Suit yourself." Hodin strapped the one he held onto his right leg.

Jake, seeing all the weapons and gear Hodin had affixed to his person, barely held back a chuckle. "You sure you don't need a couple more pieces of gear?"

"You never know," Hodin said. Then he looked down at everything he'd collected and laughed.

Jake laughed with him, knowing they might not have reason to laugh much tomorrow, if at all.

Hodin put his hand on Jake's shoulder. "Let me tell you who we have here." He tipped his chin upward toward Brun. "Brun's a load of fun. He holds his own in the toughest of times, but he's particularly useful when things need livening up."

Brun patted both hands against the array of explosives clipped to the straps crossed and hung over either shoulder. "Don't won't things getting too boring."

"I see that," Jake said, eyebrows raised.

"If you take a bad hit tomorrow," Hodin said, "Alara's there to fix you up."

She pushed a knife into the sheath on her thigh, then turned to give Jake a loose two-finger salute. "Only so much a field medic can do, but I'll do my best to keep you from dying."

"Much appreciated," Jake said.

Then he heard Hanlan speak for the first time. "Course, the mission comes first."

Jake turned his gaze to Hanlan, his face now shadowed with a hood he'd donned, his head tipped downward. With his long sniper rifle slung over his left shoulder, Hanlan continued to lean against the wall at the back of the group.

"Always is," Jake said.

"Typical Hanlan," Hodin said. "You don't hear him or see him much, but he's there. He'll take a target down through the chaos of the battlefield, with nothing more than a glimpse of the man's shadow and the sound of the wind. A force multiplier. Even if he's not the best talker."

Jake didn't like a crack shot lurking behind him if he couldn't trust the guy. But, this wasn't his unit. It was Hodin's call, and he picked Hanlan. That would have to do. "Sniper can be a man's worst enemy." He made it sound like a compliment.

Jake turned his attention to Nadira, who was resting

her rear against the stone slab table. Her arms were crossed. She had been studying him, he realized. She smiled when his eyes met hers.

"You two have already been introduced, of course," Hodin said. "Nadira's been our eyes and ears inside the Cracian base. Don't let her sweet demeanor fool you. Those gears of hers are always turning. It's a good thing she's on our side."

Jake waited for her to flinch, to look away. But she didn't.

Sweet deadly demeanor.

"You've all received the briefing on the assault and our infiltration plan," Hodin said. "As you know, we head out before dawn. We'll move under cover of the main advance for the better part of our journey. Once the Cracians engage, we'll follow our route, skirting the front line. The fog of war should give us enough cover to move undetected past their defenses."

"Sounds easy," Brun said, pulling a piece of something from a pocket on his pants. He popped whatever it was into his mouth and chewed on it, rolling it around.

Alara sauntered up to Brun. "Don't worry, Bear. I'm sure there'll be something you can blow up." She leaned in a gave him a kiss on his cheek.

Brun let out a muffled grunt. He shuffled one of his feet and gestured with his hand, as if to stop her. But he moved too late to interrupt her show of affection. He glanced around at the rest of the team. No one took any notice of what Alara had done, except Jake.

Bear.

He didn't make it obvious, but he couldn't help but see the kiss. Even as he was listening to Hodin recount the plan for the next day, he found his attention drawn back to Alara. Sentiment didn't drive his gaze. How was that even possible? He'd only met the woman a few moments ago. Still, Alara, he thought, must be a prime specimen of Waudure beauty.

"If we manage to make it inside the Cracian base," Hodin said, pushing the unclaimed gear to one side of the stone slab, so he could roll out a parchment on the other half, "we must stay focused on the primary objective." He set a piece of gear on the edge of the paper to hold it in place.

"It isn't right," Brun said.

Alara placed her hand on Brun's wrist. Jake noted the contrast in size between the two of them, his arm the trunk of an oak, hers a delicate vine.

"Brun," Nadira said, "I know it's tough to swallow."

Brun pulled his arm out from under Alara's, then he raised it with a clinched fist as he looked squarely at Hodin. "We've never abandoned our people."

"My father's there," Nadira said. "I understand what's at stake, for him and the others, even those Waudure who have sided with the Cracians."

Hodin stepped into the midst of the group. "We want to save our people held by the Cracians," he glanced at Nadira, "including your father. As for the others, they have made their choice. Perhaps, in time, they will return to the fold."

Jake interrupted. "I get it. It's messy. I wouldn't want to leave anyone behind either. But you can save some of them tomorrow and watch everyone die the next day, or we can get the package, the bioweapon." Jake paused and shook his head. He still couldn't get his mind around the fact that he brought a genocidal bioweapon, or at least the precursors, to this planet. They weren't innocent, probably neither side, but come on.

"Of course, I had no idea. . ." Jake pressed his lips tightly and huffed out his nose before continuing. "I'll get the package."

He turned to see Nadira standing close beside him. Looking up at him, she smiled. "We will."

Hodin, looking frustrated by the displays of sentiment, stepped back to the table, and pointed to the elements on the plan he'd rolled out for review. "We've got perimeter defenses, here and here. Even with the distraction of the large frontal assault, those will likely still be in place."

The others drew closer and followed his overview.

He traced a line toward the base. "If we get past those—"

"When," Jake said.

Hodin shot a glance at Jake and then continued. "We'll need to make our way through a series of corridors and chambers, and eventually to one of two lifts by which we can access the lower level of the base."

"And we know the layout of these corridors?" Jake asked.

"I do," Nadira said. She looked over the drawing on the table. "This is very accurate."

"And we can trust your memory?" Hanlan asked.

"It's not the corridors we need to worry about," she said, frustrated by Hanlan's implied lack of trust in her.

"I was getting to that," Hodin said, raising his hand slightly in Hanlan's direction. "Each of the lifts and the paths to the central facility on the lower level will be guarded by a squad of the Cracian High Guard. These elite units will not be deployed in the on-going battle. Kharn maintains this ring of security at all times. We know this thanks to the risk Nadira took acting as our agent and gaining the trust of the Cracians."

"How many are we talking about," Jake asked.

Nadira answered, "There are four guards in each of these squads, but they will fight as if they are ten. Altogether, we're talking about twenty-eight guards.

"Getting past any one squad will be difficult enough," Hodin said. "We'll need to defeat two squads, one at the lift entrance and one defending whichever passageway we choose to get to the central facility."

"I've faced worse odds," Jake said.

Hodin continued, "If we succeed, we will need to make our way as swiftly as possible to the central facility on the lower level. Time is critical. If we delay, the other units will gather at the bioweapon lab before we arrive, and they'll lock it down. We can't hope to breach their defense of the lab at that point."

"We can assume," Nadira said, "that Kharn will work to get the weapon active as quickly as possible."

"Especially once the Waudure assault on the base begins," Alara said.

"Right," Hodin said, then he tipped his head down,

taking a moment to stare at the plan overview on the table. "Which is why I must say the following."

"Spit it out," Brun said.

"We will move in as a unit," Hodin said, "but should one of us fall in the attempt, the rest of you are to keeping moving, to head for the lab."

Alara looked at Brun, and to the others. "I can't leave any of you to die."

"You can, and you must," Hodin said. "If we don't get to the lab before Kharn activates it, then no Waudure on Daedalon will survive."

"He's right," Brun said, placing his arm around Alara.

"Let's just hope it doesn't come to that," Hodin said.

Jake traced the corridors on the drawing. "What are these rooms?" He pointed to areas just outside the central lab.

"Those house more equipment for the lab," Nadira said. "I've been there with my father. Those rooms and that corridor," she tapped her finger on one of the five corridors that lead to the central area, "are the only way into the lab. See. The other corridors feed into this one here." She drew their paths with her finger to illustrate.

"We go in here," Jake said, thumping one of the lifts on the drawing. "We bypass the first two corridors and target the third one, the one that leads straight to the lab, and the rooms around it."

"We'll draw fire from the squads stationed down the first two corridors as we pass them," Nadira said.

"This is correct?" Jake asked, indicating the area on the map from the targeted lift to the opening of the first two corridors?"

"What do you mean?" Nadira asked.

"The distance, the angles. Are these markings here obstructions?" Jake responded.

"Yes," she replied. "Line of sight from the lift to the openings, and halfway down the passageways, at least for the first two corridors. And that's the mechanism for the lift, just outside the lift door."

"Hanlan," Jake said, "here." He pointed to the spot just outside the lift, on the lower level, behind the large box that housed the lift engine. "It's what, about fifty yards to the first corridor entrance and a hundred to the second one."

"I see your point," Hanlan said.

"There'll be multiple targets. You'll be under fire. And the squads from the last two corridors farther down will probably engage shortly after the commotion starts."

"I can keep them at bay," Hanlan said.

"He'll be pinned down," Hodin said.

"All of us will," Jake said.

"What do you mean?" Nadira asked.

"Brun, once we're down the lift, you'll need to disable it," Jake said.

Brun smiled and tapped the explosives strapped across his chest.

"And if you can," Jake said, "I want you to take out the lift at the other end of the corridor. Blow the whole tunnel past the third entrance, if you have to."

Jake waited for the team's response. Brun's smile dropped.

He took in their faces one by one. No one spoke for several long seconds.

"We'll be trapped," Alara said.

"Twenty-eight highly trained guards," Jake said. "More on their way. We're going after the enemy's ultimate weapon during a full-scale war."

"Jake's right," Hodin said. "We can make it to the bioweapon, with luck," he removed the piece of equipment from the infiltration plan and let it curl back up to a roll, "but I don't see how we make it out again."

"And we'll need any time we can get to disable the weapon, to make it unusable," Nadira said.

Hodin clenched his jaw and composed himself with a stoic face. "We all have loved ones we're fighting for," Hodin said. "I'm not saying we're going to give up once we secure the bioweapon, but right now…"

Jake watched as each of the team gave a small nod.

"Sometimes you can see out of the fog easier than you can see through it," he said.

"What do you mean?" Nadira asked.

"Just that, while we go into this prepared to make the ultimate sacrifice, we shouldn't give in to despair," Jake said, pulling his blaster from its holster and turning it to look it over. "Fate has a way of offering an answer to those that refuse to die."

Hodin offered his arm in bond to Jake, who accepted the gesture, clasping his forearm. He couldn't pretend to fully understand the Waudure, but their struggles, their tragedies, and that which they held dear, were like things he had seen in his own life.

Hodin pressed a spot on the stone wall of the cavern beside where the slab protruded. The slab, with the remaining equipment, receded into the wall.

"Return to your loved ones. Say what must be said. Cherish what you have, what you're fighting to preserve... for all Waudure. We head out in the lull just before dawn."

With somber faces but clear resolve of conscience, they each departed, all except Jake and Nadira.

Hanlan left first, then Brun and Alara, walking together, her hand clasping his as they went out of the room.

Hodin nodded to Jake and Nadira as he passed them. Once he left, Nadira moved in front of Jake, standing with only a couple of inches between her chest and his. He looked down at her eyes and saw she had no one else to return to that evening. She didn't say anything, and he replied by wrapping his arms around her and pulling her body against his own.

After a long while, sharing stories from their respective pasts and enjoying the timeless haze of indeterminate hours lounging in bed, Jake and Nadira, equally disinterested in getting any sleep, decided to make their way to the Waudure's answer to the many other establishments for drinking and late night revelry Jake knew across the galaxy. There they left serious thoughts behind and enjoyed the lively crowd, many of whom were poised to take part in the large assault on the Cracian base the next day. As Jake imbibed a variety of Waudure spirits, his mind ever more reveled in the alien music and raucous crowd; friends and fellow warriors, that spent the better part of the night trying to forget what the dawn waited to bring.

CHAPTER TWENTY-SIX

Jake stood next to Nadira, looking at the expanse of dirt and rock ahead. They both, along with the other members of the infiltration team, watched the hundreds of Waudure ground troops move out before them. In clusters of ten to twenty each, the foot soldiers, some of them seasoned resistance fighters, others fresh-faced new recruits, made their way over the terrain that separated the underground Waudure stronghold from the Cracian base. Their target sat protected behind the stretch of jagged mountain peaks at the edge of the Untamed Lands.

"It's a long march," Hodin said. "Hours, but we'll get there, and with luck, we'll do it before they know we're coming."

They had already traversed several miles through underground tunnels to get to the open land they now faced.

"Any reason why we're standing around, then?" Jake asked.

"Oh," Nadira said, a mischievous look in her eyes,

"didn't I tell you?"

Jake looked at her, waiting for what he figured from her tone would be an annoying bit of information.

"They're bringing a pack of crag beasts for us to ride." She looked pleased with herself at getting a rise out of him.

He didn't hide his dislike for the creatures.

"You must be kidding," he said, glancing around to see if the beasts were yet in sight.

"You have something against the things?" Brun asked. He had his thumbs tucked underneath the straps on his chest. He was flicking his forefingers against the sides of two of the explosives hooked to the straps.

"Anyone but Tay ought to have a problem with them," Alara said.

Jake noted from Alara's expression that she also disliked the idea of riding the deadly oversized hounds as much as he did.

Once again lulled into a momentary stupor by Alara's flawless beauty, he caught sight of something he hadn't noticed before. Her eyes were casting daggers toward him. Then he realized they weren't directed at him. She was targeting Nadira.

Jake, without moving his head too overtly, glanced at Nadira. She hadn't noticed Alara's assault.

What's the story there?

Jake felt a nudge on his shoulder opposite Nadira. He turned to Brun who was slowly shaking his head. Jake read his eyes to say, 'leave it alone.'

"They've been conditioned well," Hodin said. "We'll

move with the mass of ground forces for the better part of the advance, but when the time comes, the crag beasts will provide us the speed and maneuverability needed to make our run for the base."

Hanlan, who as always stood off to the side, spoke while wrapping his rifle with a long band of cloth, protecting it from the swirling sand in the warm air. "Beasts acting like beasts shouldn't be blamed."

Several more Waudure came out of the tunnel openings in the mounds behind them. They'd made the long journey from the underground base.

"What are they carrying?" Jake asked.

The men and women he saw, about fifteen of them, wore large packs on their backs. Affixed to the outside of the brown bulky packs, metal tripods, the legs of which were as long as the Waudure were tall.

"Those are the anti-ship defense units," Hodin said.

"Right," Jake said. "I thought they'd be bigger."

"Don't underestimate them," Nadira said. "Besides, we may cross the mountains before the Cracians launch the ships. If we do, we won't have to worry about them."

"One thing I've learned over the years," Jake said, watching another group of anti-ship forces move past him and the team, "war rarely goes according to plan."

The wind picked up, a building rush of sound and reddish haze moved across the staging area where Jake and the others waited. He, like Nadira, pulled the cloth that dangled around his neck and secured it over his nose and mouth. Hanlan pulled his hood lower to shield his eyes from the sand. Brun grabbed the goggles on his forehead and lowered them into place.

"They're here." Alara stepped in front of Jake, then walked past Nadira, glaring at her again as she did.

Jake heard the growls and smacking jowls of the crag beasts before he saw them. Alara walked around a large formation of rock that jutted out from the mounds leading to the underground tunnels. He watched her extend her hand to meet the head of a massive crag beast, as it came into view. Following the first creature were five others, all equally intimidating and questionable, in Jake's mind.

Alara wasted no time in mounting the first one, who knelt before her as she touched her hand to its head.

"Well," Jake said, an inflection of surprise in his voice, "she seems to know what she's doing."

He was caught off guard by the bump in the back of his shoulder. Nadira stepped past him without a word. She moved toward the second animal. He watched her steps. Quick. But he saw the anxiety in her body as she approached the creature.

She raised her arm to place her hand on the its head, much as Alara had done. The crag beast snarled. Her hand shook slightly, but she otherwise didn't move.

"Excuse me," Brun said to Jake. Then he walked over to Alara, ignoring her mount. "What do you think you're doing?" He glanced at her hands, which were clenching the neck of the creature she sat upon.

"I figured Tay taught her how to approach," she said.

Brun tipped his head slightly. "Alara."

"Fine." She released her grip on the animal. Once

she did, the lead crag beast, hers, sounded a faint snort.

The one standing before Nadira ceased to snarl. Then it lowered its head.

Careful not to face Alara as she walked around to the side of her mount, she climbed onto its back.

"Maybe we should walk," Jake said, rolling his eyes for Hodin to see.

"Come on," Hodin said, as he headed to the group of beasts and took one for his mount.

Hanlan, without a word, did the same, followed by Brun.

Jake shook his head. *I can't believe I'm doing this again.* He walked up to the unclaimed crag beast and stood before it, eye to eye.

"You gonna behave?"

Without waiting for a response he knew wouldn't come, he stepped to its side and climbed on.

"Alara." Hodin called out, louder than before to overcome the sound of the growing wind.

She let out a guttural noise that triggered her crag beast to move. The others fell in behind and beside hers, and they made their way out into the vast land before them.

Jake surveyed the Waudure forces, many well ahead of them. Hundreds moved onward, grouped in clusters of a dozen or so each.

He wondered how all of them would fare when the Cracians brought their might to bear.

The sky enveloped the land below with a banded blanket of ever-darkening clouds. Though it was dawn, the light of the day hadn't made a full appearance. Instead, the whole of the scene was cast with an eerie glow, the reticent daylight muted by the approaching storm.

Jake felt the air as he rode. The still air warmed him, only to give way to currents of cold that brought a chill to his spine. Even the sky knew the day would be wrought with conflict, he thought.

"The weather serves us," Hodin said, riding up beside him.

Jake continued to look skyward. "From what I've seen, the weather cares little for those beneath it."

Alara and Brun rode a short distance in front of the others, beyond the reach of Hodin's words. "Tay was her brother," Hodin said, and he nodded toward Alara.

Jake glanced at Alara. "I had no idea."

"She honors him in her own way. She's always been hard to read."

Jake nodded. After an appropriate pause, out of respect for the subject of Tay's passing, he spoke. "It wasn't hard to read her feelings about Nadira."

"Hmm, well."

Echoes drifted around him from the battle-ready forces all around. The drum beat of war.

Jake thought Nadira, who rode behind him next to Hanlan, couldn't hear his conversation with Hodin. He was wrong.

"She wants you to notice," Nadira said, her mount catching up with his.

Caught off guard, he turned to face her. "What do I know?"

He could tell she wasn't buying his feign of ignorance.

"You're not the first man to fall for it," she said.

He decided he wanted no part of the contrived guilt she was offering. He prodded his crag beast with his heels, and it responded by picking up the pace.

"What the?" Jake heard her say, as he rode to the front of the group.

After several minutes riding as they were, the terrain became more challenging. The beasts covered ground at the same rate, but they were jumping over large rocks and uneven sections where the slabs of dirt-covered stone had shifted long ago, leaving ridges. There were sudden drops of several feet quite regularly.

Jake forgot about the conversation he had been avoiding and instead focused on staying upright on the constantly shifting mass of bone and muscle beneath him. It didn't help that the wind, which seemed to be calming before, suddenly picked up, gusting against his body.

He could no longer discern the Waudure forces he had been watching walk ahead of him in the distance, spread out across the landscape. The brewing storm had lifted enough sand and grit from the ground that the land looked like a hazy red lake.

They rode for a long while.

Maybe it was his growing sense of unease that drove his attention elsewhere. Whatever it was, he became acutely aware of the stench coming from the creature beneath him.

Hodin rode up beside him. "It's their sweat."

"What?" Jake said.

"The smell. You'd think the bastards sweat out their bowels."

"And I said I didn't like these things."

He chuckled, and so did Hodin.

Jake heard a rumbling somewhere behind him, in the distance. He repositioned his hand gripping the crag beast, then turned to discover the cause of the noise.

Hodin tossed him a pair of viewing lenses. Jake drew them to his eyes.

Twenty or more vehicles advanced, pushing a thick red cloud of dirt as they did. They moved over the ground with an occasional bump, almost a bounce, as they cleared the larger clusters of rock. Square at their base and domed on the top, the vehicles measured about ten feet high and the same in width. Large, deeply grooved wheels, six of them, carried each mass of rust-colored metal forward.

"The troop carriers?" Jake asked Hodin.

"We have fifty of them," he said proudly.

Jake, thinking of all the ground troops, and of the mountains ahead, and of the Cracian forces and weapons he heard about in the briefing, said, "Will it be enough?"

Just then, Nadira and Hanlan rode quickly past Jake. He heard Nadira yell as she closed in on Alara and Brun. "Take us left!"

Alara, hearing her, reached down to the right side of her crag beast's neck and slapped it repeatedly. The creature responded by swiftly turning leftward and breaking into a run. The other beasts, with their riders holding fast, did the same.

Jake looked back to see half of the troop carriers moving off to one side and the other half moving the opposite direction.

"Here they come!" Hodin guided his mount onto a large rock that protruded like a ramp above the ground to form a higher vantage point from which to watch.

Bursting through the opening between the divided line of troop carriers far behind Jake and the rest of the team, a transport pod came into view. Jake recognized it as the same sort that had nauseated him days before when he rode with Nadira away from Halcion Station.

He watched the large sphere race toward him. It was moving at what he guessed was top speed.

"Ride!" Hodin roused his mount by kicking his heels into it. It leapt from the large rock and took off at a full run.

Jake, not remembering this part from the briefing, looked around to see what the others were doing. Hanlan rode past him. Nadira moved her crag beast beside Jake's and reached over to his, slapping it on the backside. Jake felt the jerking pull against his arms as his mount took off. He held on and leaned forward against the creature.

All six members of the infiltration team rode at breakneck speed. Jake grunted with each landing as his mount lunged and jumped over every obstacle, never slowing its run. Soon, they moved among the first waves of Waudure that advanced on foot. He saw all of them, hundreds, now running.

The first transport pod shot past him. He felt the strong push from the displaced air as it passed him. The pod was a blur, but it looked to him that no one was inside piloting the sphere.

Seconds apart, nine more transport pods rolled past him, every one of them moving at the same phenomenal rate of speed.

After the last one, Hodin rode next to Jake. "Get ready. That's our way through the mountains. There's a passage between them. Not much rock to the other side. No large mountains. The pods will clear it for us."

"They'll die on impact," Jake said, his beast still running fast with the others.

Nadira slowed her mount for a moment to settle in beside his.

"There's no one inside them, of course," she said.

"Explosives!" Brun yelled to Jake.

They rode forward. With his peripheral vision, Jake saw scores more Waudure running for the mountains, for the path set by the spheres rushing to crash into the rock defenses of the Cracians. He heard a rolling rumble. Their numbers were great.

At the horizon, rising slowly into view, the tips of the mountains. The ride across the border of the Untamed Lands was near an end. War was in sight.

The sky darkened, as if on cue. The sound of his crag beast's legs striking the ground became drowned out by a sudden ear-numbing crack and a thunderous boom that swelled though his body. For a second, he thought it must be the transport pods, now far ahead and out of sight. But he realized the sound came from the sky, from every direction. The storm was upon him. It was upon them all.

He looked skyward and remembered the storm by the cave, and Tay.

He leaned toward his mount's neck and drove the beast faster.

CHAPTER TWENTY-SEVEN

Fire and explosive might formed from shooting debris, black torrents of pulverized rock from the mountains, took over the horizon. The flashes lit the barren plains, revealing all the Waudure forces for the brief time it took for the transport pods to do their work. The crashing sounds of explosives cracked the air across the battlefield, declaring the Waudure people's freedom from their Cracian oppressors. Jake felt the noise reverberate in his bones, and his ears rang.

When his hearing returned, he heard the roar of cheers from the forces rushing toward the blasts. Hodin, Brun, and the others in his team joined the many hundreds in celebration. Jake noticed that Nadira stayed silent. No cheer. No smile.

Me neither. But why just her?

He rode his beast near hers. "This is it."

His words broke her away from her thoughts. She hadn't seen him until he spoke, though he was beside her for a moment before he did.

"I don't know what's going to happen," she said,

turning to him, even as they rode on.

He knew her to be strong, but her face spoke fear. *She's not a fool.* People were about to die, he thought. But he sensed it was more, something else.

He thought about the time they'd shared in the cave before he'd been knocked out by the monster they'd encountered, and the hours they spent talking after meeting the team.

"Stay close to me," he said. It was the only thing he could offer her. No promises. War took without permission. He promised himself that he would have something to say about that if it came down to it.

She swallowed whatever thoughts had called her mind away, then she nodded to him and smiled.

With the others, they rode toward the pass that the pods had blasted through the mountains.

Ash floated slowly downward upon them, drifting and meandering in the sky as it did. The closer they rode to the impact site the warmer and thicker the air grew. Smoke and dust hung in the sky and draped to the ground, as did the tease of death.

Darkness settled in ahead. Jake and the rest of the infiltration team rode the fearless crag beasts toward the foot of the Cracian mountains. As they approached, he heard the blasts of weapons, a few at first, then a rush of firings, some accompanied by explosions. Flickers of the fighting lit up the now swirling gray canopy into which they rode.

The sounds of battle filled in all around as Jake pushed into the chaos.

An earthy metallic smell overwhelmed his nose. And

a charring.

Not good.

Then he saw the first of many. His mount nearly struck the body, but managed to leap over it.

Jake instinctively pulled back on the neck of his crag beast. The creature slowed. He wanted to look back at the man, to see that the soldier wasn't dead. He didn't look back. He knew there was no point. The wounds were too grave. Soon he passed dozens more Waudure. All lifeless.

"Jake!" Nadira called out to him from somewhere nearby, but he couldn't see her.

Blasts of high-powered lasers rained down onto the battlefield, pitting the ground, as even the rock succumbed to their power.

"Here!"

He looked around, struggling to see her through the explosions.

She rode toward his voice, and he saw her.

"They knew we were coming," she said.

"We don't stand a chance out here. Their ships are picking us off."

Hodin appeared between the two of them on his beast. "The mountains!"

Jake nodded to Nadira, and the two of them took off, following Hodin. They rode blind for the better part of a minute, only avoiding the fire from the Cracian ships by a hair's breadth on several occasions.

Screams of agony rang out around them.

Poor bastards.

They moved into a clearing in the smoke-filled air,

still riding hard for the cover of the rocks ahead. Jake saw scores of fallen Waudure that cleared the plain before him only to meet the waiting Cracian ships above them. He kicked his beast into a gallop and, Nadira at his side and Hodin just ahead, watched the enemy aircraft soar past. The fighters flew toward the remaining Waudure troops still approaching.

"We're nearly there," he said, surmounting a large hill.

When he moved past the crest of the hill, he yanked on the neck of his crag beast, forcing it to a stop.

From his mount, Hodin was firing at dozens of Cracian ground troops, who were rushing toward him from fifty yards or so away. Jake grabbed his blaster and added his fire to the fight. A moment later, Nadira and Alara rode down the hill and joined in.

The uneven terrain between them and the Cracians proved decent cover against the advancing troops. But the already overwhelming odds took a turn for the worse.

"We have to move now!" Hodin shouted.

Another ship flew down, hovering just ahead of the advancing Cracian ground troops. The bottom of the craft opened and black cables dropped down to within a few feet of the ground. Down the dozen cords, which hung from inside the ship's lower opening, as many Cracian soldiers slid down.

Jake took a few more shots while Nadira and Alara rode with Hodin off toward the rocks to the right, making for better cover behind the debris piled there by the transport pod explosions.

He glanced around. The Cracian troops shooting at them blocked the only path through the mountains. Hiding in the rocks without something to change the tide would amount to suicide, he realized.

Screw that.

Taking another shot just to let the enemy know he was still fighting, he looked around for another way. Then he saw it. Halfway to where Hodin and the others had ridden, a jagged path rose across the side of the mountain. It wasn't man-made — *or whatever race* — but it would work, he thought.

He eyed the cliff's edge at the top of the rocky path, fifty or sixty feet up. He glanced at the ship again. It was hovering at almost the same height, slightly lower, and maybe twenty feet from that side of the mountain. He could see the pilot through an open portal on the side.

The Cracian reinforcements sliding down the ship's cables were halfway to the ground.

"What the hell," Jake said to himself. He kicked into the side of his crag beast, and the two of them sped up the rocky path on the side of the mountain.

"Jake!" Nadira's voice floated toward him from the distance.

No time to explain. Either they all died or maybe he died, maybe he didn't. With any luck, it would be the Cracians' turn.

The crag beast, accustomed to rocks and unsure footing, leapt up the path, carrying Jake, who felt a little uneasy in his gut once they reached the top. As he and the creature turned the last cut of the path and climbed over the loose stones piled up around the edge where the rest of the mountain had been blown off, a blast struck his mount's hind leg. Jake saw that the shot hadn't come from the ship itself, but from a soldier who was making his way down one of the dangling cables.

His mount stumbled. Jake slipped to one side, though he didn't mean to do so. The side of his head hit one of the larger rocks on the precipice. He sat stunned on the beast for a split second before the creature fell on its side, badly wounded from the blast to its leg and Jake tumbled off its back and onto his own.

Another shot from the man on the cable flew overhead. Jake scrambled to check the damage to the crag beast.

"That won't do."

The creature flexed its muscles, trying to stand, but it couldn't. Jake placed his hand on the animal's back and felt it breathe.

He peered over the creature's drooping head to see if the Cracian ship had moved. It had, but now it looked even closer to the cliff than before. He could hear one of troops below yelling commands to his comrades. No doubt, they're going after Nadira and the others, Jake thought.

"Now or never."

He rose to his feet and looked past the edge of the cliff, guessing the distance to the ship. He put a mental bullseye on the pilot. Then he hurried several steps away from the edge of the cliff. He took a deep breath, as if it might be his last, before sprinting past the wounded crag beast and leaping off the mountain.

When his feet left the solid ground, he had second thoughts.

He'd achieved a fully horizontal pose, with his blaster hand leading him slightly. It must've taken no more than a second to travel the distance from the cliff to the hovering ship. Nonetheless, as is usually the case with imminent death, time slowed. Or so it seemed to Jake.

He counted the troops on the ground, fifty feet below him. There were twenty-five. A few must've gone out of view, he decided, chasing Nadira and Alara and Hodin.

The Cracian that had shot at him, that struck his mount, looked up at Jake as he flew across the gap. Jake, tucking his blaster hand downward and below his chest, smiled and squeezed the trigger on his weapon. The man's eyes bulged at the sight. Jake watched the soldier's hand slip from the cable as the shot hit the man.

His aerial marksmanship took his focus off the opening on the side of the ship at precisely the wrong time. His shoulder clipped the hard metal edge of the portal, but he still somehow managed to land inside, crashing into one very surprised pilot.

He and the pilot tumbled onto the controls of the craft. Jake's face smacked against the glass of the cockpit and the other man's knee hit Jake's back. The ship spilled forward, and Jake could once again see the soldiers beneath, many of whom had fallen from the cables. They were sprawled out on the rock below. A few still clung to the cords, but they were swinging toward the side of the mountain.

He watched them slam into the mountainside. The ship began to fall. He shoved the pilot off him, knocking the man against the back wall of the cockpit. Without checking to see if the pilot remained a threat, Jake took the controls. He pulled them back. The nose of the ship lifted a little.

The pilot punched Jake in his right kidney. Jake exhaled and crunched to that side. His hands still on the ship's controls, the craft darted to the right. The left wing of the craft plowed into the side of the mountain. The impact sounded with a fury of crunching metal. A small explosion went off on the left side of the craft. Jake and the pilot tumbled about the cockpit. The ship wasn't flying now. It was a burning wreck, spinning and plummeting to the ground.

Jake watched the border between the ground and the sky flash past him three times, then he jumped. The fact that the ship fell in the opposite direction is the only reason he made it to the ground alive. He was bruised, and had what felt like a broken toe, several scrapes, a gash above his left eye, and a headache for the record books.

The rocks near the base of the mountain opposite his landing shielded him from the shockwave and fire as the ship exploded. Jake took a two-second timeout. Then he pushed himself up and stood. Only three of the Cracian soldiers were still alive and they were running away from the ball of fire and flying debris, the only remains of the ship.

Satisfied all his parts still worked, Jake didn't bother to chase down the last three soldiers. Instead, he made his way in the direction he'd seen Nadira and the others go for cover. Ignoring his body's pleas for sympathy, he corrected a stumble and then set out at a jog.

After a minute of negotiating the rocks on the ground, he spotted Nadira. She stood beside a boulder. She hadn't yet seen him. He watched her head dart here and there. He knew she was looking for him, for signs he'd made it. When she saw him, her face lit up without restraint.

He wished it was his ship Sarah looking for him, but at least she was safe in orbit, for now.

He heard her rejoice. It was a gasp that tightened to a short chirp. He liked that.

Hodin and Alara stepped out from behind the boulder. Hodin waved to Jake. Moments later they all stood together.

Hodin shook his head. "You're one…"

"Crazy bastard," Jake said. "Remind me not to listen to myself." He rubbed the side of his head, wincing when he inadvertently touched the cut on his cheek.

Nadira hugged him.

He stood there, not sure what to do. But he didn't stop her.

"You two are sweet," Alara said.

Nadira, still holding him, turned her head toward Alara. "Shut up." Jake noticed she said it without malice.

She let go of him and took a step back, glancing at Hodin. He was looking across the battlefield. The mass of Waudure forces, those that hadn't been killed by the

Cracian ships, were gathering before the passage blown through the mountains.

"Do you want me to tend to those?" Alara pointed to the more obvious of Jake's many wounds.

"Maybe later," he said, adrenaline still rushing through his body.

"They're advancing," Hodin said. "The anti-ship units are getting into place. They'll be able to hold the Cracians back, and with any luck, push through the pass."

"Where's Brun," Jake asked, "and Hanlan?"

"You didn't think you were the only one with a hare-brained plan, did you?" Nadira tipped her head to the side as she stepped toward Hodin and Alara. "Come on. We're not going that way."

Before he took the last few steps over the ridge of the mountain, Jake turned to survey the battlefield behind him. The wind blew strong against his face. He shielded his eyes with his hands. A whistling passed over his ears. A few more ships flew toward the mass of Waudure and Cracian ground troops. He pulled out the viewing goggles Hodin had given him and peered through them.

He spotted an anti-ship unit setting up their gear amidst smoke and laser blasts. He watched them perform with a precision that comes from rigorous training. One of the men knelt beside the tripod structure they'd erected. He turned a large gear on the side of the equipment, adjusting the angle of the central cylinder that sat affixed to the mid-point where the legs joined.

The man raised his hand from the gear and held his arm up, signaling one of the other men of the team with a clenched fist. The other man responded by dropping what appeared to be a ball of mud into the cylinder. Whatever he actually fed into the pipe launched right back out of it with an explosive force.

Jake could barely follow the projectile as it flew skyward toward one of the Cracian ships. The mud, lit with a tinge of glowing embers, or maybe a crackling of fire or sparks of some kind, spread out as it rose. When it struck the hull of the ship a second later, the substance splattered across the bottom of the craft and clung to it.

He watched the glowing mud burn through the metal. A moment later, a ten-foot diameter circular section of the underneath of the ship fell to the ground. The crew of the ship plummeted down behind the pieces of metal. Then the empty craft rolled to one side and veered downward, before crashing into the ground in a fiery heap of destruction.

Jake swept the battlefield with his goggles, taking in the scene. Hundreds of Waudure survived the initial strikes by the Cracian ships. Now, across the land, as far as he could see, skirmishes raged between the two sides. A large contingent of Waudure troops, joined by transport vehicles for cover, were making their way into the newly formed pass through the mountain defenses. There was resistance, but they looked to be pushing Kharn's forces back.

He clipped the binoculars onto his belt and headed over the ridge to join Nadira and the others.

They sat on a grouping of rocks twenty feet below. Nadira drank from a flask, then wiped her brow. Alara applied a salve to a cut on Hodin's arm.

Jake maneuvered down the slope of the mountain, managing not to fall from the gravel, though he had to run the last few steps to stay upright.

"I see why Nadira insisted on you joining our unit," Hodin said.

Jake walked over to the group. "How far to the other side?"

"If Hanlan's right," Hodin tapped a small piece of equipment strung from his ear, "we can make it through within the hour. He and Brun have been clearing a path."

"Through mountains?" Jake spoke with incredulity.

Nadira hopped from her seat on a large rock. "Brun and his toys."

"Right," Jake said. "He did take a lot of those explosives."

Alara put her first-aid supplies away. "Hanlan has been scouting this area for weeks — he and the others."

"Others?" Jake asked.

"Snipers." Hodin said. "They stick together even though they do their thing solo." Hodin rose to his feet and repositioned his gear, straightening his belt and checking to be sure all was secured in its place. "They're the only ones that can elude the Cracian patrols."

Hodin helped Alara get her pack onto her back. "The location targeted by the transport pods was chosen based on the proximity to this weakness in the mountain defenses. We're heading toward the narrowest point of the range."

She shrugged her pack higher onto her back and drew the cinching strap tighter across her chest. "Brun should be in position by now to take out the last section of rock blocking us from Cracian land. That part of mountain is too high and treacherous to scale, but there's a cave that cuts into it far enough that we think it's possible to blast through to the other side."

"You must be kidding," Jake said. "So, we're heading into a cave, beneath hundreds of tons of rock, and we're going to set off a bunch of explosives in there."

"Sorry I didn't tell you before," Hodin said. "I had to be sure about you. Too much at stake."

Jake nodded.

Nadira walked past Jake, slapping him on his stomach as she did. "Exactly."

He looked at Alara and Hodin. "You two think this is a good idea?"

"You just jumped off a cliff into an enemy ship and crashed it," Hodin said.

Alara moved her hands apart, extending her fingers as she did. "Boom."

Jake raised his brow and sighed. "Just checking."

Hodin shuffled past the others and into the lead, heading down the path. "Come on. We still have a job to do."

Nadira and Alara fell in behind him.

Jake brought up the tail of the group. "I need a vacation."

CHAPTER TWENTY-EIGHT

Kharn, with his back to his administrator, stood before a shelf of glass figures of Cracians, Waudure, and several other races. The man had just informed Kharn of the initial results of the Waudure assault on the mountain defenses, and of the losses the Cracian side suffered.

Kharn stayed silent. He stared at the foot-high figures in front of him, his record of the failed attempts at the augmentation process. Each figure represented hundreds of attempts. Only he, so far, had survived it.

The administrator raised his hand, extending a shaky finger to make his next comment. "We've held them off, my lord."

Kharn, his back still to the man, quietly replied, "Have we?"

"Yes. We've lost a few ships, but the Waudure have been unable to penetrate the mountains."

"Oh," Kharn said, "this is good news."

"Y-yes." The administrator's stutter was more pronounced in front of Kharn.

The man waited for a response. For several seconds, there was no reply.

Kharn lashed out with his arm, striking the figures on the shelf before him, smashing them as he flung them across the room in one move.

"Good news?" he screamed.

He turned to face the administrator, who shook and cowered.

Kharn yelled at the man. "The resistance forces pound at our gate, our ships have been destroyed, and this is good news?"

"They have been unable—"

"They should never have tried!"

Kharn stormed over to the man, whose body quivered. Then, lowering his voice, said, "The threat is not from the weapons they fire at us."

He leaned in close to the man and shook his head, coaxing the man to shake his own to signify understanding. The administrator did so, though his face looked bewildered.

"The threat," Kharn said, "is that they dared to attack in the first place."

"Yes, Lord Kharn," the man said, his words weak and muttering.

"I want every Cracian soldier moved into the pass. No Waudure in sight is to be left standing. If the bodies pile too high, tell them to climb over them and continue attacking."

"Yes, Lord Kharn."

"Tell your security counterpart that if he doesn't crush the assault by nightfall, I'll tie his body to the head of his ship and send it crashing into the Waudure's front line. Maybe that will do the job."

The administrator, as if his neck could barely comply with his will, nodded slowly as he spoke. "Yes, Lord Kharn. I will give him the message."

Kharn raised the back of his hand to strike the man's face, but then lowered it without doing so. He turned away. "Leave me now."

The administrator lowered his head and gave a short bow. Then took a few steps backward toward the door, before turning and leaving, picking up speed with each foot closer to the door.

Kharn stood for a moment after the door shut, then he crossed the room to his personal elevator and rode it down to the lab where the work on the bioweapon was still in progress.

The door of the lift opened and he stepped out into the lab.

Hearing the sliding door and Kharn's footsteps, Lorian looked up from his work. "Everything is progressing nicely."

"When?" Kharn asked.

"The timetable is the same. I've told you before. It's a process."

"Speed up the process!"

Lorian, visibly shaken by Kharn's tone, replied, "Yes. Of course. I'll do everything I can."

"Good."

"I still think we can do it with just a tissue sample, if you're willing to wait longer. Perhaps a few more days."

"I will have no further delays, Lorian. You will do the

encoding as we discussed."

"But why take another life to do it, when I can achieve the encoding with tissue samples? I'm sure of it."

"You have pledged your loyalty to our cause," Kharn said. "You will continue as planned. I have selected one of your own for the encoding."

Lorian's face was awash with conflicting emotions. "Who?"

"I have selected someone whose loss will not diminish our efforts. Finish the preparations. I will return for the encoding procedure."

With that, Kharn turned and walked back into the lift, and its door closed.

CHAPTER TWENTY-NINE

Hanlan sat near the peak of the mountain high above the cave to which Jake and the others traveled. From where he perched, he took in both sides of the battlefield. Behind him, the overwhelming numbers of Waudure and Cracian troops tried to kill each other, but to Hanlan on his lofty seat, they appeared as little more than insects facing off over territory.

He preferred where he sat, above the fray. His loyalty lay with his people, the Waudure, no question. But he cared little for the chaos of battle. Why wallow in the mud when his work could be carried out much more efficiently from afar? He'd trained as a scout and a sniper since he was a child. If Kharn had known his skill set, or that of the others in his guild, he and his fellow snipers would have been culled from the enslaved Waudure that were brought here. But fading into the shadows, becoming uninteresting, came to him as easy as breathing.

Ahead of him, far below, in Cracian territory, the land to the south remained still and empty. He could only partially see the tail of the Cracian forces to the north. They continued to feed into the pass the Waudure had blown through the mountains. But his focus remained below, in the empty plateau. He scoured the ground for any sign of movement.

Soon Hodin and the others would set off the explosive charges in the caves, blowing out the rock that sat between them and Kharn's land. Hanlan looked for Cracian patrols.

He listened to the muffled sounds that drifted up. Explosions. The blasts of weapons. Fury and lamentations. They were faint, but he heard them nonetheless.

The wind shifted rapidly at the top of the mountain where he kept watch. He took notice each time, effortlessly calculating the adjustment he'd need to make for the shot, should a patrol appear. Such things were second nature. The layers he wore, knowing his mission, protected his body from the frigid air. And the cold he breathed in gave his mind calm.

The land from the foot of the mountain range to the Cracian base were cleared long ago of any vegetation, and anything else that would hide approaching threats to the base. Thus, the survey for Hanlan was easy.

Satisfied the route where the other members of the infiltration team would exit the mountain and cross the plateau was free of any immediate threats, he turned once more to view the panorama of war in the distance.

He pulled his viewing goggles from the pouch on his side. He lifted them under his hood and adjusted the range on them to bring the details of carnage and sorrow into view. He watched without relish, but to remember. For he knew tomorrow, if he carried on with the living, there would be many Waudure who would not. For them he chronicled the battle with his eyes.

Any semblance of formations had disappeared from the battlefield. The well-laid plans either side had made, it looked to him, were long abandoned. Small bands of Waudure men and women that stood together against the now rising tide of Kharn's forces only proved to be easier targets for their enemies.

High-voltage channels, bands of Cracian lightning, crawled across the ground in lines and angles, a supercharged fence, emanating from several charge vehicles, the power supplies for the system. The lightning fences posed an impassable barrier to the Waudure. And for those standing in its path when a new section of fence deployed, a quick electrocution of a magnitude that left nothing but dust and cinders awaited.

Dozens of sections had been deployed, leaving some Cracian troops on the Waudure side to continue fighting, while the ships stayed their advance. Instead, they struck targets from the relative safety in the air behind the surging electric channels that ran from the charge vehicles to a series of coiled relay posts.

Hanlan followed a Cracian team with his viewing goggles as they ran farther into Waudure territory and deployed another post. Once it was fixed into the ground, they stood to one side of the equipment. As a member of their team was struck down by a blast from a Waudure soldier, another of them smacked a panel on top of the post. The lightning shot to it from an identical post already charged a hundred feet away.

Hanlan turned to the Cracian side of the mountains for a moment. He scanned the landscape far below. With no activity there on the ground, he unslung his sniper rifle from his back and repositioned himself to face the ongoing battle once more.

Now using the scope on his weapon to inspect the battlefield, he witnessed three more extensions of the lightning fence system. The Cracians were using it to surround the Waudure, rounding them together for an easier kill.

He removed the portion of his glove that covered his trigger finger, pulling the leather back at the cut in the glove just below the middle knuckle point. Then he reached up with his other arm and pushed his hood from his head, letting it drop to the back of his neck. The wind caressed his cheek, and he set his aim.

The pad on his fingertip touched the curved metal of the trigger. The rifle recoiled, but he kept it firmly against him, so the movement was slight.

At one second intervals, he performed the ritual seven more times.

When he had done so, he leaned back and lowered his rifle. All but one of the lightning charge fields disappeared. He had targeted the posts nearest the charge vehicles, rendering the other posts in each chain useless.

He sat and watched the Waudure forces, galvanized by what he'd done, regroup and surge into the Cracian front line.

CHAPTER THIRTY

"Jake, through here." Nadira reached for him as she walked in front of him, deeper into the cave, but he didn't notice her hand.

He listened to the faint echo of her words.

The two of them, along with Hodin and Alara, made their way over rough ground, squeezing through narrow passages in the cave. The air felt cool and damp. Their footsteps and the shuffling dirt and rocks they walked over sounded throughout the cave.

Hodin, in the lead, held a device inset with a clump of the same blue glowing crystals Jake marveled at when he first awoke in the underground Waudure stronghold. Far from the entrance to the cave now, the light did its job, but Jake, who walked behind Nadira, could only see a few feet past his feet. The walls of the cave to his sides were dark, as was behind him.

Stopping while Nadira scaled a three-foot rise in the rocky path, Jake felt Alara press against him from behind.

"Sorry," she said softly. "I couldn't see."

"It's fine." He didn't turn around. The passage at this point was too narrow to do so.

He still felt her chest pressed against his back. Then he felt her weight against him increase, as she leaned into him more.

"Still standing here," he said.

Nadira made it up the rock onto the elevated path ahead. She walked on, catching up with Hodin, who had turned a curve in the path. The light before Jake dimmed.

He took a step forward, preparing to scale the rock Nadira had climbed.

Alara kept pace with him and once again pressed herself against his back.

"Hey," he said.

She reached around his waist with her left arm and rested her hand on his pelvis.

Jake's mind wrestled with the circumstances, and he stood there while it did.

He felt her right arm slide against his waist on the other side.

"It's really dark in here," she said in a whisper.

In the blackness, she moved her left hand down and reached with her other hand for his blaster. He couldn't see what she was doing with her right hand. It was too dark, and his attention stayed elsewhere.

He made a deep grunt, clearing his throat. Then, before she grasped either of her objectives, he stepped forward, leaving her arms to drop away from him. He didn't look back at her, but instead scaled the rock before him and walked after Nadira and Hodin.

He took the turn in the cave and spotted them up ahead, and with them, standing at the back of the cave, Brun.

"So, this is it," Jake said, walking up to the three.

Brun, who was kneeling beside the rock wall dead end and facing it, twisted a pair of wires together. Then he rose and stepped back and to the side, giving the others a clear view of his work.

"That ought to do it," he said. "I had to take a good look at the rock first, the walls, and overhead. Want to make sure it goes right."

Brun had fitted explosive charges to the wall, stuck into the rock with small spikes, driven into cracks. Jake counted nineteen charges on the back of the cave and four more on the walls to either side.

"Those are supposed to give a little counter force for the main blast," Brun said. "If I put them in the right places, they'll keep the mountain from falling down on top of us."

Jake looked uneasy about the prospect of being buried alive under a mountain, especially after escaping death at least a few times since he arrived on Daedalon.

Nadira put her hand on his arm and gave it a playful shove. "Don't worry. He knows what he's doing."

"She's right," Hodin said.

Jake tipped the palms of his hands upward halfway and shrugged. "We've made it this far."

Alara rounded the curve and came into the wider part of the cave where they stood.

Jake glanced at her, but made sure he didn't look too

long.

"Alara," Brun said, his eyes lightning up at her, "your bear did it."

"Brun," she said in a reprimanding tone, evidently because he openly used her pet name for him.

"Take it easy," Hodin said. "No one here has a problem with you two."

Jake tapped his foot, but only once before he realized it and stopped.

Awkward.

Hodin looked over Brun's work. "How far back did you say for the blast?"

"Back around that turn and down the drop in the path should do it," Brun said.

"Good." Hodin looked satisfied. "Let's do it."

He headed back down the path. Nadira followed.

Brun knelt to pick up a few pieces of gear he'd left on the ground. He opened the small pack next to him and put them inside.

Alara, while Brun put away his things, walked over to Jake and looked up at him. She puckered her lips. Then she smiled and continued around the turn in the cave, toward the designated safe spot.

Jake gave her a good head start before leaving Brun to join the others.

Half a minute later, all five of them huddled down against the wall of the cave.

Brun pulled out the triggering device for the explosives. He grabbed the switch on top after flipping open the safety guard. Then he looked at everyone.

"You may want to cover your ears," he said.

They all did so with their hands.

He took a deep breath and exhaled. "Hope this works."

He moved the toggle switch, and the lot of them fell to the ground as the explosive force of the blast far on the other side of several tons of rock shook every bit of stone around them.

A torrent of dust, heavy and gray, shot out into the path to the exploded wall. It quickly filled the entire space around them. They waved their arms about to displace the cloud, as they coughed. Covering their mouths and noses with their hands, they stood and cautiously moved to see if the explosives had done their job.

Jake's ears rang, as did everyone else's from the looks on their faces. Brun's face was the exception. He looked unfazed. He pulled a set of plugs from his ears and shoved them into a pocket on his shirt.

The large opening leading out of the cave allowed part of the cloud of powdered stone to drift outside. The room cleared, and they could once again breath without filtering the air with their hands, which hadn't helped much anyway.

"Nice work," Hodin said, glancing at the ceiling above them. "I'm not sure how you managed it without a cave in, but you did."

Brun, hands on his hips, beamed with pride. "What can I say. I'm an artist."

"Yes, you are," Jake said, slapping him on the back.

Hodin touched the communication device in his ear. "Hanlan, how's it look?"

Jake pulled his blaster from its holster and checked the charge reading. Satisfied, he put it back and stepped to the edge of the newly created portal into Kharn's territory.

"Ok," Hodin said before tapping the device in his ear once more.

"Well?" Nadira asked.

Hodin moved next to Jake and looked outside. "So far our plan is working."

"The Cracian forces are engaging?" Alara asked.

"They've moved through the pass we cleared with the transport pods," Hodin said, staring out at the hundreds of acres that surrounded Kharn's base, the top of which was just barely visible in the distance.

"How does it look for our people?" Nadira asked.

Hodin turned to her. "It's war."

They stood silent for moment. Everyone knew what he meant.

"That's why we're going to get in there," Jake said, changing his posture to that of a man ready to get on with it. "They're counting on us to stop Kharn, to get that weapon from him."

"He's right," Brun said.

"We need to do more than just get the bioweapon," Nadira said.

"Your father," Hodin said. "We'll do everything we can to get him out too."

"Kharn," she said. Her eyes swam in a distant pool, one of malice and darkness.

Jake and the others said nothing.

A calm came over her face, as if from the comfort of

an epiphany. "I'm going to kill him."

Alara stepped up to her. "Our mission is the bioweapon."

Nadira tensed. Her shoulders drew up slightly, and a fiery countenance washed over her face as she glared at Alara.

"That's not going to get your father back," Alara said.

"Of course it will," Nadira replied.

Jake noticed that Nadira looked as if she was about to explode, maybe even louder than Brun's handiwork. He reached his arm between the two women, laying his hand on her shoulder to persuade her to walk with away from Alara. It took her a couple of seconds, but she did.

They're going to kill each other before this is over.

Once they moved closer to Hodin and the portal blasted through the rock, Jake spoke to all of them. "The faster we do this, the more Waudure lives we can save. For those that still fight, our actions may turn the tide. For those already fallen, we need to make their sacrifice worthwhile."

Brun assented with a bellowing grunt.

Hodin nodded. "Well said."

They stepped through the opening, one by one. The terrain set before them posed little challenge by way of topography. Mostly a barren flat plain, a few small hills and ridges broke the continuity, but posed no significant hurdle. Most of the hills lined the perimeter of the grounds. The same such rock and dirt as in the Waudure land covered the surface, but with sparsely scattered vegetation, nothing larger than a fistful of weeds.

Jake noted how little dust was in the air compared to the other side of the mountains. The cloud from the blast through the mountain had dissipated, except for a thin wisp of it, which rose high above them now.

Hodin touched his ear device again. "We're moving."

Nadira walked over to Jake and pulled her weapon from its holster.

"Finally decide to shoot me?" he asked.

"Still thinking about it."

"Give me a heads up. OK?"

She laughed, not too boisterously. The situation demanded she didn't.

"You may want to be ready," she said, glancing down at his blaster.

"Yes," he said. Then he called out to Hodin, who stood ten feet away, surveying the land from them toward the base, "Hanlan's got eyes on us?"

Hodin called back, "For a few more minutes. He's making his way down the mountain. He'll join us when he can."

"Let's do this." Jake walked past the others and took the lead, heading toward the Kharn's stronghold.

Hodin joined him. "Keep your eyes open. Hanlan said there's nothing out there, but that could change."

Brun, Alara, and Nadira followed. Once they'd caught up with the others, everyone fanned out.

They moved at a brisk pace, short of a jog.

"We should reach the base in twenty minutes," Hodin said.

"Brun," Nadira said, "the entrance may be

unguarded, but they'll have it monitored from inside. You'll need to be quick."

"Watch my back," he said, "and I'll have us inside in ten seconds."

Another few minutes of travel took them over one of the ridges, easy enough to scale. They paused at Hodin's signal. He gestured with his fingers first to his eyes and then out, pointing at the land ahead.

Jake pulled out the viewing goggles Hodin had given him. He scanned the horizon. Nothing in sight but more empty land, and the base, now half visible. A stark contrast from the natural surroundings of rock and dirt and mountains in the distance to the west, the Cracian facility, with huge curved structures and smaller rectangular buildings below them, was larger than Jake had expected. He saw a series of stacked and overlapping long rectangles, all made from metal, but weathered in appearance. No doubt the harsh elements of Daedalon had taken what must've once been polished surfaces and turned them into a patchwork of rust and pitted steel, or whatever material made up the series of fused buildings. No guards in sight. He couldn't see the bottom of the structure. He saw no windows. No doors. No openings of any kind.

As he dropped his goggles, out of the corner of his eye he caught Nadira and Brun doing the same.

"It's clear," Nadira called out.

Hodin waved his arm forward. "Let's move."

They traveled another minute or so, the air cooling noticeably. The sky grew darker, as thick clouds of heavy gray and muted amber moved in across the mountains. The wind picked up, filling the air with a constant rushing noise, soon to be too loud to hear one another.

A loud crashing sound struck from the west and echoed through them. All of them halted. Jake looked to the mountains behind them, thinking they'd been struck again or collapsed where they'd blown through the cave. They'd traveled far from the cave, but from what he could see, it still looked as they left it.

Alara, seeing him look back, yelled through the wind, "It's the storm, Daedalon's anger. It's coming for—."

Did she say 'you' or 'us'?

"You're right," Nadira looked skyward toward the mountains, "the storms are cresting the mountains. But if the sky is angry, its wrath is for Kharn."

Jake watched the dark mass roll over the peaks. "Where's the flash?"

"What?" Nadira said.

"Lightning, it comes with light."

"He's right," Hodin said. "I fear it is the thunder of war, but we Waudure have nothing that would shake the earth as that."

Hanlan, who had run as only his kind could, caught up with them as Hodin spoke. "Our task is all the direr."

"Hanlan!" Brun turned to greet him as everyone stopped at hearing the sniper's words. Brun embraced his brother-in-arms with the Waudure bond, arms clasped. The two were glad to see the life still well in the other.

"Good to see you," Nadira said.

Hodin went up to Hanlan and greeted him as Brun

had done. "Yes, it is."

"How'd you get down here so fast?" Jake asked.

Hanlan didn't respond.

Nadira approached Jake, and leaned in to him to whisper. "He won't admit it, but I've seen the apparatus he uses to fall from the sky. Must've used it to get down the mountain."

"Hmm. I see."

"The storms," Hanlan said, looking even more serious than usual, "they're unlike anything we've ever seen."

"That bad?" Hodin asked. "We saw the clouds. Didn't think they ever made it over the mountains, at least not the high ones surrounding this land."

"If not for the weapon fire," Hanlan said, "and the light from the explosions, they'd be fighting in utter darkness. Just before I headed down here— the storms —I couldn't see what was happening on the battlefield."

"It's a sign," Alara said. She spoke, peering into the distance, toward the Cracian base.

Jake thought he saw her lips form a faint smile, but he wasn't sure.

"We can't help them by standing here," Hodin said.

"He's right." Nadira looked toward the mountains as she spoke. "And I'd rather not be standing out here when those storms reach us."

Most of them nodded their assent. They resumed their path across the plateau. Soon, crossing another ridge, Kharn's base came into full view. Only a few hundred feet to go, Jake thought.

To their left, far away, through the pass in the mountain range, the tail end of the Cracian forces were visible. The ground troops and several transport vehicles, along with a few ships overhead, looked to be driving back the Waudure advance. Kharn's forces were moving deeper into the mountain pass, attacking relentlessly. Little return fire pierced the gloom. Garbled, muted echoes of the battle reverberated off the mountains.

The storm's creeping mass of blackness spread across the sky, enveloping the tops of the mountains, and casting a single shadow over all below.

Then a flash blinded Jake. His vision returned slowly as the boom of thunder sounded a second later. He, along with the others, shifted footing to avoid falling to the ground from the quake caused by the shockwave.

Once he recovered, he grabbed his viewing goggles. He saw rain pouring down into the pass between the mountains. The fight of the Cracian forces he could see collapsed under the deluge. The flood turned the ground in the pass into a slurry. Few could stand, let alone continue their attack. The Cracian ground transport vehicles lost all traction and became immobile.

The rain had not yet made it to where Jake and the others stood. It continued to spill into the mountain pass, and slowly overflowing beyond the mountain range. The mighty storm was moving toward the base. It would be upon Jake and his companions soon.

"I've never seen such a thing," Brun said. Then he slowly lowered his viewing goggles.

Jake saw the stunned look on his face.

"We need to keep moving," Hodin said.

They set off again, this time at a near run.

Jake watched the scene unfolding at the mountain pass. The storm did not respite. Only flickers of weapon fire were visible, coming from farther inside the pass. A bolt of lightning struck one of the Cracian ships. It exploded in the air. Jake saw one of the larger pieces of the craft, aflame and spinning, fly into the side of a mountain. The other two ships turned away from the battle and flew toward the Cracian base, headed toward Jake and his team.

Jake waved his arm to Nadira and the others, as he took off toward the cluster of buildings beneath the curved metal superstructure. "We need to get inside before they see us!"

Nadira saw the two craft approaching and cried out, "Net ships! Hurry!"

She and the rest of them ran with Jake toward the base.

The two ships flew in close to the base, then one of them turned toward the infiltration team.

Nadira, seeing it targeting them, screamed to the others. "Don't let it get over you!"

They ran as fast as they could to take cover under the half-domed construction that loomed high above the base's many connected buildings, but there was too much distance to clear.

The storm pushed beyond the confines of the mountains and rolled toward them, crossing the plateau rapidly.

The ship swooped in and took a position above Hodin, tracking his movements as he ran.

Jake turned and fired at the ship with his blaster, but it wasn't enough to penetrate the ship's armor. Nadira and the others joined their weapons with his, firing relentlessly at the net ship. They couldn't stop it. Their handheld weapons weren't enough. The net ships, built to operate at low altitudes in the midst of enemy fire, were constructed to withstand more than Jake and the others had available to them.

A panel on the bottom of the craft slid open and a heavy net of thick metal cable shot out toward Hodin. Fixed on the edges with weighted balls of iron, the net spread wider as it flew down toward Hodin. The central point of the mesh web tethered to the ship by a single cable, the same metal as the net itself. The device fell onto Hodin and enveloped him, knocking him to the ground with its weight. Then, the thing electrified.

Jake watched as the charge lit up the cables with a white glow, and sparks arced across several points. He aimed at the line connecting the net to the ship that fed it the charge. He fired. His blaster shot couldn't get through the energy field built up around the cable. He couldn't cut the connection.

Hodin screamed as Jake and the others ran to him. It took only a few seconds for them to reach him, but when they made it to the edge of the netting, Hodin fell silent.

"No!" Nadira cried out before turning her weapon on the ship once again.

Jake peered through the cabled web and saw Hodin

no longer needed saving.

"He's gone," Jake said. "The other ship is coming. We need to get inside."

Brun pulled Nadira by the arm and forced her to run toward one of the buildings. Alara, Hanlan, and Jake headed for it as well.

The leading edge of the storm reached them. The rush of wind, cold with a heavy mist, bowled into them from their left as they ran. Shielding their faces from the weather, they struggled to keep going. Gusts almost pushed them off their feet. The rain crashed against them, pelting them in sheets, obscuring their view of the Cracian base ahead. But they knew they were close, so they kept going.

The other ship circled in on them. They pushed their legs to move faster, trying to escape the second net ship. Jake reached back as he ran, shooting against the cockpit to obscure the pilot's view. Then he veered away from the rest of the group, continuing to fire at the craft. The net ship took the bait, maneuvering to chase him down. Jake continued to shoot at it.

Jake led the ship away from the others, giving them time to reach the base and find one of the entrances. Brun slid into the wet ground, slamming against a steel door. He pulled his pack off his back and dug into it, taking out several explosive charges and their triggers.

Alara, Hanlan, and Nadira settled in beside him, surrounding him and aiming their weapons back toward the net ship, which still flew after Jake.

Jake managed to out maneuver the ship by running erratically, changing directions and pace multiple times.

He continued to shoot into the ship's cockpit viewing window as much as possible.

Nadira reached past Brun, who furiously put together his explosive array, and tried the handle on the door. It didn't move. Brun looked up at her.

"Had to try it," she said.

Brun shook his head and then raised the now connected explosive charges to the door and attached them to it with an adhesive putty.

"He'll never make it," Nadira said, looking at Jake as he ran from the ship, leaping over rocks and mounds. "Can't we do something?"

"I am doing something," Brun said. "Now everyone needs to get back." He gestured for them to move away from the door.

They repositioned themselves farther down the wall, to what seemed like a safe distance.

"That's good," Brun said. Then he made a last adjustment to the charge and joined them.

"Jake!" Nadira holstered her weapon and waved him down with both arms.

Brun flipped the trigger on the device in his hand. The explosives attached to the door blew a hole through it. Not only did the door fly off its hinges, breaking into numerous pieces, but the wall around where the door had been also collapsed. The blast splayed the metal and curled it inwards, creating a bigger opening than they needed to get through. They rushed over to see it was done.

Alara peered inside, her weapon drawn. "It's clear. Get in." She stepped in through the space where the door had been.

Brun followed. "Be careful."

Nadira watched Jake run toward them. The ship stayed with him.

Jake caught his pack on a large rock as he planted his hands midway onto it and leapt over it. The strap tore, and his pack fell to the ground, but he kept moving.

"He's not going to make it," she said, then she looked at Hanlan, pleading with him with her eyes.

"I'll put him out of his misery." Hanlan unslung his rifle from his back and slipped off the wrap that protected it. He held the rifle up to his cheek, tucked his shoulder in against it, and took aim.

"What are you doing?" Nadira said, reaching for his rifle.

Before she struck it with her hand, he let loose a shot. As she knocked the barrel down, she looked at Jake.

He continued running toward them. The ship flying in low after him stuttered and veered off course, slowing slightly. Jake, kept going, putting more distance between him and the pursuing Cracian.

"He's going to make it," Nadira said.

"You're welcome." Hanlan wrapped his rifle again and swung it around onto his back.

"I thought you were going to—"

"Why would I do that?" Hanlan asked.

After a few more seconds of the ship tipping this way and that, the pilot seemed to recover from the shot Hanlan placed directly in front of his face. The flash that close to him must have startled the pilot, but now the net ship corrected its course and renewed its pursuit of Jake, who still had a couple hundred feet to make it to the door.

"Oh no!" Nadira grabbed Hanlan's arm and pointed to Jake and the ship.

"He'll make it," Hanlan said.

"Wait. Look. The storm."

As Jake ran toward them, the ship flew above him.

Keeping pace with Jake, the pilot opened the panel on the underside of his ship to launch the net. As he reached for the lever to send it out, a mass of thick dark clouds dropped onto the ship like a weight. The Cracian craft disappeared into the storm momentarily.

Jake heard the event but didn't look back. He ran, reaching Nadira and Hanlan seconds later.

Standing next to the opening into the Cracian base, he looked back only to see the net ship ejected from bottom of the black clouds. It flew out at an odd angle, hurtling toward the ground. Just before impact, Jake saw the nose of the ship pull up slightly. Then the whole of it crashed against the dense dirt and hard rock, exploding in a fireball whose black smoke rose and fed into the darkened sky above.

"Unbelievable," he said.

Nadira took his hand. "Daedalon bestows her fortune on the Waudure when our cause is just."

He gazed upon the flaming wreckage for a moment before turning his attention to her. A tear clung to the corner of her eye. He felt her hand tremble in his own.

"I'm sorry we couldn't save, Hodin," Jake said,

glancing at Hanlan for a split second, but focusing his words more toward Nadira.

Hanlan moved to step through the opening in the wall. Then he paused. "He'd say he died well, but I'd say he lived well." He passed through the opening into the base.

Jake reached a hand to Nadira's face, extending his index finger.

She didn't move, but continued to look at him.

He wiped the tear from her eye. He spoke softly. "Come on. We've got a job to do."

CHAPTER THIRTY-ONE

The lone guard stood in the cave, many levels above the heart of the Waudure stronghold hidden underground. Accustomed to the wind and dust, to the shifting elements of Daedalon, he stood in his well-worn uniform, tan like the rocks around him, only his face and hands showing the Waudure red. He could no longer see the hundreds of his fellow people that had earlier set out across the vast rocky plain toward the Cracian mountains. He would have served with them in battle, but his place was here, keeping watch over those that remained.

One of only a handful of trained soldiers not facing off against Kharn's forces, he, like the other guards stationed in similar caves around the great perimeter of their home, took pride in his position. To guard the stronghold meant honor and trust. No stranger to fighting, he'd risen to his current station by choice of the Elders. They recognized his steadfastness and bravery. No Waudure would think of turning down a decision of the Elders, whose mystic ways were unfathomable to all but those of royal blood. He wasn't royal, like the three Elders; he was a Waudure man, humbly doing his part for his people.

For hours after his people's forces were no longer in sight, he scoured the horizon for any signs of Cracian scouts or spies. As it was most weeks on watch, whether with his naked eyes or with his viewing goggles, he saw nothing but the occasional pack of wild crag beasts or a few scurrying drasils making their way from the cracks and shade of one cluster of rocks to the protection of another. The ever-changing sky loomed overhead, often confusing day for night and night for day.

He saw nothing unusual. Yet, in the distance, beyond even the scope of his goggles, he knew his people would face the might of the Kharn's army. He'd heard rumors as to why his people, who had spent years avoiding detection deep in the Untamed Lands, now set out to attack the Cracian land. He remembered the times when the daily huntings took many of his neighbors and friends, never to reappear.

Rumors. Rumors that the de facto peace they who resisted enslavement enjoyed for so long was near an end. Rumors that Crassus Kharn, the diabolical leader of the Cracians, had found a way to root them out, even in the safety of their deep hidden home. He will turn the sky against us, many whispered.

As a guard of the stronghold, he had his place. The council of the Waudure military leaders and of the Elders was not his to be heard. Rumors. But, as he stood, watching across the vast plain for signs of the enemy, he could think of no other reason sufficient to send their forces in a direct assault against the Cracian land.

And then, his reverie broke.

It was to the north, so faint at first, he questioned his eyes. Grabbing his viewing goggles, he homed in on the spot where he'd seen a glimmer far in the distance. Something approached, but he couldn't yet make out what it was.

Every so often, light would dance off the back of a crag beast or some other wild creature, only to later reveal the beast for what it truly was. He adjusted his goggles and focused on the object of interest. It was moving fast.

The light spread to five times its width, then it faded. In its place, four Cracian assault vehicles drove toward him. They were miles away, but from the dust cloud they were kicking up, he could tell they weren't wasting any time making their way to the Waudure stronghold. Before he lowered his goggles to head downstairs to alert those in the base and the few guards and soldiers still there, he caught sight of several more vehicles.

"They must've known," he said. "We've no chance."

He raced to the back of the cave and down a set of stairs carved into the rock.

"Cracians! It's a large assault force coming in from the north. At least nine vehicles, heavily equipped, probably two hundred men."

The men in the room, five of them, clambered to their feet. They ran down the five corridors that fed out of the room toward different sections of the stronghold.

Each racing to alert their counterparts in the base, setting off a chain reaction of communication. Within minutes, the entire base knew of the approaching threat.

Teams, each led by the most seasoned of the fighters that hadn't left to take part in the assault on the Kharn's base, took positions at every point along the northern end of the stronghold, armed with the meager supply of weapons not taken to the Cracian mountains.

The guard who'd first seen the approaching vehicles was stopped as he was running back to his post to do what he could from there.

"Wait." A Waudure woman grabbed him by his shoulder as he passed her. "The Elders want to speak to you."

The guard looked at her and at his rifle he'd planned to use from his post.

"Come with me," the woman said.

"Of course."

He followed her through a series of corridors, some of which sloped downward. He knew the Elders met deep down in the caves, where they were secure and undisturbed. He'd never been as close to them as he was getting. Soon, the woman brought him to a door.

"Here. Leave your weapon and enter," she said.

He did as she instructed.

"You have seen them?" The Elder spoke as he entered. He saw the woman standing near the middle of the room. Behind her, seated on the ground, were the other two Elders.

He stopped short of coming up to her. "Yes. At least

nine vehicles. Assault vehicles. Coming fast from the north."

He noticed the lack of alarm on her face. A condition quite different from his own.

"When will they arrive?" she asked.

"They'll have to pass the crags that lie in the north. The beasts might slow them slightly, but I'd say an hour. They were moving fast."

"I see."

"They must've known our forces would be away," he said.

"I feared such a thing," the Elder said. "She denies her path."

"Who? What?"

"Never mind," she said. "Go and join the others. Do what you can to slow the Cracians' approach."

"We don't have the numbers to stop them," the guard said.

"Do what I have told you. The Cracians do not belong here. You will not fight them alone. Now, leave us."

The guard nodded and left the room.

As he closed the door, he paused, thinking of what the Elder had said. "We won't fight alone?" He placed his ear against the door. He heard the female Elder speak to the other two.

"We will enjoin them to come to our aid."

He spoke to himself again, "Who?"

Then the guard ran back to take his station to do what he could to slow the Cracian advance.

CHAPTER THIRTY-TWO

The storm whipped about just outside. In the corridor where they stood, Jake and the other four of them girded themselves for what came next, though none of them knew for certain what that would be. The hall stretched long in either direction. It was clean and barren, aside from the dust and debris blowing in through the open wound in the outside wall. Lights ran every ten feet along the ceiling. Jake recognized them as closer to the sort he was used to seeing elsewhere, not the glowing blue crystals the Waudure had.

He peered down the hall to each end. "Which way to the lifts?"

Nadira looked at both options before answering. "I think they're this way." She headed down the path to the right of where they'd entered.

"You heard the lady," Jake said, pulling his blaster out again and following her.

Brun went next. The width of the hall spanned only a few feet, so they moved single file.

Alara held up her pistol, checking the side of it and

wiping a spot with the thumb of her other hand. "You go ahead." She gestured, waving the barrel of her weapon at Hanlan then down the hall toward Brun.

"It's alright," Hanlan said, flipping open the bottom portion of his jacket and retrieving a distinctly unusual blaster. The barrel came to twice the length of that carried by Alara, Nadira, or any of them. He reached under his jacket on the opposite side, pulling a small metal cylinder from a pouch affixed to his belt. "From back here," he said, pushing the cylinder into an opening in the back of his gun, "I'll be better able to handle any surprises that come our way."

Alara stared at him, but he only returned the stare. She waited. He didn't move.

Finally, she said, "Suit yourself." Then she went down the hall after Brun.

Hanlan followed her.

Without incident, they traveled down several corridors, following Nadira as she decided each path to take. Then Jake held his arm up, signaling the others behind him to stop, and they did so.

He watched Nadira slowly back up. He could see her effort to step as quietly as possible as she took three steps behind her, moving away from the corner she'd passed.

She turned to him and held up four fingers, then jutted her hand toward the corner. He took that to mean they'd come upon four guards. Since no one was shooting at him or anyone else, he assumed the guards hadn't seen Nadira.

He looked behind him. Brun, Alara, and Hanlan had

seen Nadira's pantomime. He brandished his blaster, cuing the others to be ready.

With weapons drawn and trigger fingers primed, they rushed around the corner. The four Cracian High Guards embarrassed themselves at how slowly they reacted to the ambush. Only four shots were fired. The sounds of the blasts echoed down the hall, resonating off the hollow walls.

All the guards lay on the floor, blast burns on their uniforms. Three of them had managed to draw their weapons, but none fired, though Jake saw they would have, given enough time. He wasn't interested in being so generous, nor was anyone else on his team.

Nadira turned to the group. "The next ones will be ready."

"So will we," Jake said. "Let's get to one of those lifts before they have time to call everybody in."

They rushed down two more corridors before coming to one of the elevators that lead down to the central facility level.

Nadira pulled a card from her pocket and passed it over the reader on the wall to open the lift door. It didn't open.

"I don't understand," she said. Then she tried it again, but still nothing happened.

"They must've locked your access out of the system," Brun said.

"No," Nadira said, giving the card one more try. "They wouldn't have known about this one. It isn't mine. I got it long before I left. It should still work."

"They must've shut down the lifts," Jake said.

"Maybe because of the Waudure attack. Maybe they heard our shots and locked it down."

Nadira slammed her fist against the wall above the card reader. "We have to get down there!"

"The other lift," Alara said. "You said there were two. We should try the other one."

"She's right," Jake said. "Where is it?"

Nadira, who had been shaking her head and looking at the ground after hitting the wall, looked up. She seemed to collect herself mentally, then she answered. "Farther down this corridor. We take several turns, but the other lift lines up with this one. It's quite a way. We'll pass by several rooms. It's not going to be easy. We're sure to run into more guards."

"It's still our best option," Jake said. "We can't just sit here waiting for them to come after us."

"He's right," Brun said. Then he looked at Alara and Hanlan.

"I'm with you," Alara said, leaning against him, hugging him with one arm.

Jake watched her. She was so convincing, he thought.

You poor bastard.

Hanlan merely gave a nod to the others.

With all on board, they set out. Weapons ready.

It took a while, but no one stopped them. They made it to the other lift. It was easy. No alarms. No Guards. They reached it without incident.

"We got worked up for nothing, I guess," Brun said.

Nadira took out the access card once more.

"Hold on," Jake said. "That was too damn easy.

"What do you propose?" Alara asked.

"Brun," Jake said, "can you shape a charge to blast in only one direction?"

Brun raised one eyebrow. "Can you hit the side of a mountain with your blaster?"

"Ok then." Jake turned to Nadira. "Can we keep the lift from going down long enough for Brun to set something up inside?"

She looked at Brun.

"Thirty seconds," Brun said.

She turned back to Jake. "Yes. I can hold it, but if they realize we've activated it they'll be waiting for us."

"That's what I'm counting on," Jake said. "Hold on."

He ran a short distance back down the way they'd come and stopped at the first door he came across. Standing off to the side of it, he blasted the hinges. They were metal, like the door, but not nearly as thick as it was. The door fell from the frame, hitting the floor with a loud thud. He picked it up and hustled back to the others.

"What the hell do you have planned?" Nadira asked.

"Trust me," Jake said. "Swipe the card and hold the lift while Brun does his thing."

She did as he asked. Brun got to work, pulling equipment from his pack and one of the two explosive charges left on the strap across his chest.

Everyone stood by watching Brun set up the blast. He was positioning it so that it would go off in the direction of the lift door.

"It'll go off when the door opens again," he said. "I've attached a sensor to it."

The elevator was large enough for ten people, as it was used to transport squads of guards, as well as the other officers and staff of the Cracian base.

After a few seconds of silence, Nadira asked the question. "Why are you holding a door, Jake?"

Brun, not looking up from his work, said, "So we don't die when this thing goes off. It's steel. Should block much of the blowback from the blast."

"Oh, no," Nadira said. "We're not riding down with the bomb, are we?"

"We can't be sure the lift will still be working once that thing goes off," Jake said. "We have to risk it."

"It's ready," Brun said, standing up and tucking away the rest of his gear.

"Right then," Alara said, extending her arm toward the door.

Everyone piled in, Nadira, Hanlan, then Alara. Jake got in last, since he had trouble getting the steel door through the lift opening. He bumped somebody with it, but wasn't sure whom. "Sorry about that. Almost there."

There was some repositioning. All of them settled in behind the door, which Jake braced in front of him. The explosive charge sat on the ground on the other side of the makeshift shield.

"If we're ready then," Nadira said, drawing her blaster. She reached for the button on the inside of the lift, next to the door, just past where Alara stood. She had to stretch. Brun scooted forward to give her room. Then she pressed the button to close the door.

As it began to slide closed, Alara quickly stepped out of the elevator.

"Alara." Brun reached for her, but couldn't get to her in time.

The door shut. The lift started moving.

"What the hell!" Nadira turned toward the door, bumping into Brun with her arm and shoulder.

"That's what I thought," Hanlan said.

"What's she doing?" Jake asked.

Brun stepped out from behind the metal door Jake held.

"Brun!" Nadira swiped her hand to catch his coat as he moved. She couldn't reach him. She, along with Hanlan, were pinned behind Jake and the door.

Brun smacked the button on the wall with his fist. "Come on!"

They felt the elevator settle onto the floor below.

"Get back here," Jake said, still holding the door to shield himself and the others from the impending blast.

The elevator opened, and Jake, his head tilting to the edge of the door he held, caught a glimpse of the Cracian High Guards positioned outside the lift, about ten feet away. He counted twelve of them, but he couldn't be sure. All of them targeting the elevator with their weapons.

The blast went off as the elevator was still opening. Almost all the force escaped the enclosed space, hitting the guards as intended. Powerful, the detonation shredded most of the guards. The delayed smaller explosions of several of the guards' weapons, each fitted with high-energy capacitors, took out the few guards that didn't die from the primary blast.

Jake's hands, holding the sides of the metal door

shield, burned. He let go of it, though the metal barrier stayed upright. Then it smacked him in the face and pushed him back against Hanlan and Nadira.

Unfortunately, some of the blast hadn't made it out of the lift door, which wasn't yet fully open when the bomb went off. Aside from the burns on his hands and his busted now bleeding nose, Jake fared as well as could be expected. Nadira and Hanlan only suffered bruises from being pressed between Jake and the back wall of the lift.

Brun, however, wasn't as fortunate. When the door opened and the blast went off, he was standing next to the button he'd been hitting. He didn't have the protection of the metal barrier Jake held. Enough of the blast pushed back as it hit the still opening lift door to do Brun severe damage. His head struck the wall. His arms, legs, and face were badly burned. He fell to the ground unconscious.

Seeing the guards were no longer a threat and Brun badly injured, Jake pushed away the door he'd been holding, and it flew out of the elevator, landing on top of the pile of dead Cracian guards. He stepped forward, allowing Nadira and Hanlan free from behind him.

Then the three gathered around Brun to look him over and see how badly he was hurt.

The lift started to close again, but the bottom edges of the sliding door, mangled from the blast, dragged against the floor, keeping it from shutting.

"It looks bad," Nadira said, kneeling beside Brun. She felt for a pulse. "He's alive."

"We can't stay here," Jake said, stepping into the

open lift doorway. He leaned into it, pushing it all the way open. He held his blaster up and looked around, past the pile of guards. He noted a single long hallway at the back left of the room.

"Hold the door open," he said to Nadira. "Hanlan and I will get him out of there."

She switched places with Jake. He and Hanlan lifted Brun, one at his legs, the other from his shoulders. They carried him out of the elevator and to a couch at the far side of the room.

Hanlan looked more closely at Brun. "He'll make it, but he's going to be recovering for months. He's strong, strongest I know."

Jake kept an eye on the hallway. He still had his blaster at the ready.

Nadira joined them. She pulled a few bandages from her pack, and a small canister. "This is a salve. It may ease the pain slightly." She opened it and applied it generously to the burns. "If Alara was here, we could do more. She has most of the medic gear. That bitch."

"I hate to be the insensitive one," Jake said, "but we still have a mission, and I'm sure it's becoming more impossible by the second."

"He's right," Hanlan said. "You need to make it to the bioweapon lab. From what I saw of the battle before I joined you, Kharn will want to make that weapon deployable as soon as possible."

Nadira looked at Brun, and then to Jake, as if needing his answer.

"I'll stop Kharn from activating the weapon," he said, looking at her, "but I need you to get me there."

Hanlan looked across the room at the metal door they'd used as a shield, and at the bodies of the guards underneath it. "I'll stay with Brun. I can build a barrier and hold off any Cracians as long as it takes."

Jake nodded to Nadira.

"Ok," she said. "You'll watch over him?"

Hanlan unslung his rifle. "We'll be here waiting for you."

Jake held out his hand to Nadira. "Let's go."

CHAPTER THIRTY-THREE

The two male Elders braced the woman Elder under her arms, helping her to stand. The chamber was empty aside from the three of them. What they had done, was for only those of royal blood to witness. She stood, but only with their aid. Passing her mind into the creatures' realm took a heavy toll on her.

"It is done," she said. "I must go now to the top to await their arrival. They will listen to me."

The man bracing her by her left elbow spoke. "You'll be in danger there, exposed to the Cracian attack."

"Yes," she said. "It's the only way. We've summoned the creatures. If I'm not there to meet them, they will destroy everything in their path, including this place."

The other two Elders nodded. Then they helped her on the long walk to the topside of the stronghold.

As they made their way up the series of corridors and rock stairways, they felt the attacks of Kharn's forces. While the Elders had contacted the strange elusive creatures from deeper within the Untamed Lands, the Cracian assault vehicles made their way across the barren northern plain. Now, the enemy, with heavy barreled energy cannons on their vehicles and dozens of ground troops equipped with laser assault rifles, pummeled the hills and rocks that served as the protective barrier around and over the subterranean Waudure base.

The three Elders stumbled as the blasts overhead shook the rock pathways under their feet. The closer they got to the upper levels of the base the louder the cries of the terror-filled civilians grew. They heard thunderous crashes, rock ceilings caving in. Many tunnels filled with dust too thick to move through. They pushed past throngs of people who were fleeing the upper levels of the stronghold to escape the destruction wrought by the attack.

The Elder woman called out to a nearby guard as he crossed in front of the Elders, no doubt hurrying to another position from which to counterattack the Cracians. The guard, seeing the three of them and the determined look upon the woman's face, came to their side.

"Lead us to the highest point outside," she said. "And quickly."

The man looked at her, and the other two, but didn't question her, as it was not his place to do so.

She and the other two Elders followed the man until they reached a set of stairs that lead to an opening in the rock ceiling. They climbed the stairs, coming out on top of the highest point of the natural formation that capped the underground Waudure stronghold.

"Thank you," she said to the guard.

He nodded to her. "Of course." Then he ran back down the stairs.

She stood up straighter and glanced to each of her companions. They removed their hands from under her elbows, and she stood unassisted.

Shielding her eyes from the wind with her hand, she looked out over the land to the west, farther into the Untamed Lands than any Waudure had ever ventured.

The ground shook as the attack continued. Sounds of their weapons, the charging cannons of their vehicles and the rapid firing of the ground troops' rifles, combined with the rushing sounds of the wind, which blew strong. Sporadic flurries of Waudure weapon fire blew in, but paled against the overwhelming power of the Cracian assault.

"There!" She raised her arm and pointed to a brewing lightning storm on the western horizon.

One of the other Elders nodded. "They are coming."

They watched the storm as it approached, even as the fight continued at the distant edge of the rock formation, far below where they stood.

"You two must leave me here," she said.

One of the men took a deep breath and exhaled before speaking. "Yes. I know, but if something happened to you…"

"What will happen, will happen," she said. "They will listen to me. They know the Waudure are no threat to their land."

"You speak truth," the other man said, "and still, it is unsafe here." He looked to the edge of the rock, in the direction of the Cracian forces.

"We must protect the Elders," she said. "We must always protect the Elders, and that is why you two must go. We risk only one of us, and this is my task."

One and then the other of the two men extended his arm and embraced hers before parting.

The woman looked at her two friends. "She will return one day to take my place."

The two men nodded, then they left her to wait for the creatures which she had summoned.

She watched the storm grow in both size and wrath as it drew near. The rock beneath her feet continued to tremble. She knew the base would fall soon, and with that her people would have no protection from the Cracian forces amassed outside.

And then she saw them. Born of the Untamed Lands, the creatures for which the storms sounded. Cracking and crushing the ground before them as they moved, gargantuan things, thick-bodied legless tube-like monsters. There were four of them. With heads pushed down into the earth, their undulating bodies drove them half buried, scarring the landscape as they traversed toward the mass of hills and rocks that protected the Waudure base. The storm traveled with them, obeying their direction.

She felt their presence, and their connection with the elements around them. Reaching back into the depths of her mind, to the channel she'd formed in the mystic trance before coming to the surface, she gave her thoughts to the creatures. Joined in consciousness with them, she stood, no longer aware of her other senses or her surroundings.

The giant beings cut a path toward Kharn's forces outside the northern part of the Waudure base.

Seeing the monsters approach, the Cracians redirected their fire at them, but their weapons did little to deter the creatures.

Within moments the ground before the Cracians burst up and toppled over upon them. The gigantic bodies of the creatures pushed through the amassed equipment and troops. The explosions of their vehicles as they were crushed became smothered under the weight and breadth of the monsters. As they obliterated the Cracian forces, one of the four giants sloughed through the edge of the rock formation on which the Elder stood, still folded into their mind. The quake from the impact cast her down against the rocky ground, and, as the creature continued through the crumbling stone of the hill, caused her body to tumble. Without breaking her connection with the creatures, she fell over the edge of the cliff, dropping fifty feet below to her death.

The storms gathered overhead, raining down onto the rock that covered the Waudure base, which stood far below, still partially intact, and with scores of her people alive. The creatures withdrew and made their way back to the depths of the Untamed Lands.

CHAPTER THIRTY-FOUR

"I want him dead!" Kharn thrust one hand into the chest of the uniformed Cracian, shoving him. The man, captain of the High Guards, flew back from the push, his feet coming off the ground. He struck the wall five feet behind him.

Kharn looked at his hand, turning it over and then clenching and opening it. He seemed to relish what the augmentation process had done for him.

The captain, who had fallen to the floor after hitting the wall, picked himself up. He straightened the coat of his gray uniform. "I will see to it myself."

Kharn, wrapped in his own thoughts and not looking at him, merely tipped his head down slightly in response.

The captain took his leave from the room.

Kharn squeezed his hand into a fist and held it until it shook. "Jake Mudd, how many times must I kill you?"

Lorian, who witnessed the exchange with the captain from his seat in one of two oversized upholstered chairs nearby, spoke up. "He's only one man.

Insignificant to our plans."

Kharn directed his attention to Lorian. "One man? My High Guards have been attacked. My base, which sits behind impenetrable mountains, has been infiltrated. As we speak, filthy Waudure rebels run through our corridors."

"A foolish and lucky few. By the day's end, their forces will abandon the mountain assault and return to their stronghold in the Untamed Lands where they belong."

"And do you know who is leading this foolish few, as you call them?"

Lorian shook his head.

"Your precious daughter."

"Nadira? No. She's returned?"

"I had Rekla place a tracker in her. Our sensors picked it up when she got close enough to the base. I was right not to trust her. Your feelings for her blinded you to her true allegiance. She's brought a team here to sabotage the weapon."

"I'll speak with her. I'm sure I can get her to see reason."

"No! You will finish the work. My guards will deal with her and her friends."

"You must let me see her."

"I must? How dare you. I am Crassus Kharn! You live at my pleasure. You will complete the weapon as planned. Then your daughter, along with every one of the Waudure traitors will be wiped from the face of Daedalon." He walked to the window and looked upon the raging battle among the mountains in the distance.

"I will have my world. The true Cracians will rise!"

Lorian rose from his seat and watched Kharn take in the flickers of fires and explosions and death on the horizon. *Nadira, forgive me.*

CHAPTER THIRTY-FIVE

"The lab will be heavily guarded," Nadira said to Jake as they hurried down the hall. They were several passages from where they'd left Hanlan and Brun.

"We'll deal with that when we get there." He held out his arm in front of her, halting her progress. Then he stepped forward, raising his blaster. He fired across the room from the corridor, but with a shaky grip on his blaster. His hands still felt tender from the burns; he missed.

The Cracian guard standing beside a door sixty feet ahead, returned fire, but also missed. Jake and Nadira slid down behind a long row of waist-high cabinets that divided the room in half.

She glanced at his hands. "Those look bad."

"I'll make it," he said. "How's your aim?"

"Right now, better than yours." She popped up from behind the metal storage units and shot the guard.

Jake stood and saw the guard on the floor. "Nice work."

Nadira moved around the end of the row of cabinets

and toward the door where the guard had been standing. "Come on. The lab's this way."

Jake followed. Before she opened the door, he holstered his blaster and tore a long strip of fabric from the bottom of his shirt. Then he ripped it in two and began wrapping each of his hands, around his palms and knuckles.

"What are you doing?" she asked.

"Changing weapons."

"Right."

After a few seconds, he'd finished. Then he nodded to her.

She quickly opened the door. He went through first.

He ducked as the guard on his left swung the barrel of his arm's-length weapon at Jake's head. Landing a solid punch into the man's midsection, Jake dipped one knee to the ground and spun around with his elbow, striking the second guard in the groin.

Nadira stepped in to hit the first guard, who now leaned forward from Jake's blow. She raised her pistol arm and brought the butt of her weapon's grip down against the back of the man's head. The guard hit the floor hard.

Jake, from a kneeling position, shot up to his feet, striking the second guard in the face with his forearm. He followed through on the move, which lifted the man a few inches off the ground and knocked him against the wall behind him. Then the guard collapsed like a loose sack of rocks.

Nadira looked at the two unconscious guards. "Changing weapons."

Jake looked at one of his hands. The cloth he'd wrapped around it had dark spots now. The burned skin underneath had torn from the punch.

"How do you do it?" Nadira asked.

"What?"

"The pain. First you jump off a cliff and crash a ship with your bare hands. Now those hands are burned and bleeding and you're hitting people in the face."

"I've built up a tolerance, you could say. And for the record, I didn't hit them in the face."

Nadira shook her head and walked off down the hall.

"How much farther?" Jake said, catching up with her.

"Just a bit more."

CHAPTER THIRTY-SIX

"Down!" Jake threw his arm around Nadira's shoulders and pulled her toward himself.

A bolt of energy narrowly missed her head. The sound of the blast striking the wall behind her echoed down the corridor.

She dropped to a crouch and braced her firing arm with her opposite hand before taking the shot at the Cracian standing thirty feet away in an open doorway at the end of the hall, half his body behind the wall.

She hit the edge of doorway and the blast reflected at a wide angle, grazing the attacker's arm. He dropped his weapon as the shot burned his sleeve and the flesh underneath it.

Jake saw a faint shadow on the floor as he was keeping Nadira's head protected. In the same second, the shadow grew and loomed over him. He saw the shaded outline of an arm swinging toward him, a weapon in its hand. Acting even before he looked to see his assailant, Jake rose as he stepped in to give an uppercut. His fist, still bandaged, but as powerful as ever, connected with the guard's chin. The force of the blow knocked the man unconscious, his blaster flinging from his hand. Jake saw a second attacker behind the one he'd struck. He drove forward into the first man before the guard hit the floor and pushed the unconscious guard backward onto the other.

Nadira rolled to the opposite side of the corridor, landing with her back against the wall. She took another shot. The Cracian, still reeling from the wound on his arm, didn't see her second attempt. She hit him in his chest this time. He spun around to his right, slamming against the wall. The thud was noticeable. Then he dropped to the floor, his leg sliding out across the opening.

The two men Jake knocked down landed a few feet from him. The conscious one, still half underneath the other man, looked at Jake and stretched his arm to grab his weapon that lay on floor a few inches from his fingertips. Jake leapt forward towards the man's blaster with arms outstretched. The guard grabbed his weapon at the same time both Jake's hands landed on it. In an instant of struggle, Jake forced the man's hand into an unnatural position, breaking the Cracian's wrist and a few fingers. A blast shot low down the hall from the weapon. The man screamed in anguish at the damage done to his hand. Jake wrested the blaster away and stood up. Then he gave the man a kick to his chin, knocking him out.

Two more men appeared in the portal at the end of the hall. They hadn't drawn their weapons yet. They stood for a moment, until Nadira saw them.

"You!" She blasted her weapon down the hall at them, but missed. "How could you?"

Rekla and Jafir stepped back behind the wall to the right of the opening.

Nadira continued firing down the hall, though her former comrades were out of sight.

Jake quickly moved over to her and pulled her up by her arm. She let off another shot, still with no target in sight. He moved her several feet back until the two of them also had cover, taking a position around the nearest corner.

Rekla's voice sounded from the end of the hall. "We should've finished you two off the last time."

"Oooh!" Nadira started to come out from behind the corner, but Jake held her back. She shouted at them, "Step into the open and try it!"

"They're blocking the entrance to the lab, right?" Jake asked her.

"Yes, it's through that room, in the one beyond it. They knew we'd head there. I can't believe those bastards." She peered around the corner and took another shot.

"No other way in?"

"No."

Jake pushed his hand against the wall beside him.

"What are you doing?" Nadira asked.

"I'm thinking of doing something stupid."

He took a step back. Then he swung his fist into the wall. His hand, still wrapped in cloth, and half his arm plunged through the wall. He winced. "Man, that hurt."

"Are you crazy?" Nadira said, looking at his muscled

arm and shoulder.

"Probably. The blasts reflect off this material, but it's not that strong." He pulled his arm out of the hole, which went clear through to the room on the other side. The structure inside the walls looked flimsy.

Nadira looked through the opening. "The lab walls are armored. You can't punch your way in."

Jake glanced at her blaster. "You ready to use that?"

"What do you have in mind?"

He looked to the corner opposite them. "Move over there. Keep them occupied. Don't let them out into the open doorway."

"And?"

"And don't shoot me."

"What?"

"Trust me. Just keep shooting near the edge. Keep them ducking against the wall for cover."

She looked at him in disbelief. Then she quickly moved to the corner across from him.

"Ready?" he asked.

She nodded. She took a stance at the edge of the wall and laid down a stream of fire next to the wall Rekla and Jafir hid behind.

"You're not a very good shot, are you?" Rekla yelled from behind the wall of the room at the end of the hall.

"What are you going to do now?" Jafir asked.

"You're too late," Rekla said. "We've won."

Jake shook his right hand, letting his fingers move loosely. He felt the warmth in his knuckles from the burns they'd taken. The throbbing sensation, he noted, was from driving his fist through the wall.

Seems I'm inflicting more damage to myself than the Cracians.

He ran down the right side of the hall, staying close to the wall and clear of the blasts from Nadira's weapon.

She called out to him, but continued shooting. "Jake!"

"Don't stop," he said as he ran. A couple of seconds later he reached the end of the hall, sliding on his feet toward the wall to the right of the doorway.

Nadira's shots whizzed by his left side.

With a heavy audible exhale, using the momentum from his run, Jake plowed his right fist through the wall and followed through with his arm, his elbow, his shoulder, and, much to his regret, his face. The wall caved inward, hitting Rekla and Jafir, who leaned against it on the other side.

All three of them fell into a pile, along with the rubble from the wall.

Nadira raced down the hall.

When she stepped through the doorway, which was much larger now, and quite oddly shaped, she found Jake on his back grinning. Rekla and Jafir were still and quiet, half-buried under debris.

"Give me a second, if you don't mind," Jake said, "then we can head into the lab."

CHAPTER THIRTY-SEVEN

Nadira helped Jake up from the pile of debris, some of which clung to his clothes and skin.

"Thanks," he said, dusting himself off. "Good as new." The scrapes on his arms and face, along with an actively bleeding cut on his cheek, said otherwise.

"You." Nadira shook her head.

"Hell of a delivery, huh?"

She chuckled, but then her face recomposed at the seriousness of the situation.

He nodded toward the door that led into the lab.

She readied her weapon, and they entered.

Jake stepped inside first, ready to take on the next Cracian he saw, but only one person stood in the room.

"Father!" Nadira moved quickly in front of Jake, but then halted.

The room was large, three times the size of any they'd seen in the base. White floors and walls, well lit, it was a sterile working environment, as was to be expected. A sharp antiseptic smell filled the chilled air.

The Waudure man Nadira spoke to stood beside a

massive steel rectangular vat, filled with a murky brown-colored liquid. The sides of the vat extended, forming work surfaces, cluttered with laboratory equipment — a rack of vials, metal tongs, and other assorted items. A large robotic arm hung from the ceiling above the vat. The man, her father, and the functional part of the laboratory were behind a thick glass wall that extended the width of the greater room and divided it evenly in half.

To the right of the door Jake and Nadira came through was a couch and a single end table. To the left, the wall on their side of the glass divide stood behind cabinets, shelves of books above them.

Her father, Lorian, looked up when she called to him. Jake watched him mouth a response. "My child."

Lorian half turned away from the vat before him and reached out to a panel on the wall behind him, pressing a button.

Jake heard a click, followed by a faint hum of static.

"I'm so glad to see you," Lorian said, his voice coming from above Jake and Nadira.

Jake glanced up, spotting the speakers in the ceiling.

"Why?" Nadira asked. "How can you do this?"

Jake scanned the glass divide for a door, which he saw at the far end to the right. Also glass, it had two wide steel bands connecting from the wall inside the enclosure where Nadira's father was to the inside of the door itself.

"Our work is a worthwhile cause," Lorian said. He moved around to the opposite side of the vat, approaching the glass between himself and Nadira.

"You've known the importance of what we're doing."

Jake headed over to the glass door and tried to open it. The door wouldn't budge.

Lorian looked at him. "I'm sorry. I'm afraid I can't let you in. I know the two of you are here to stop us, but I can't allow that to happen."

Jake worked some more to open the door, but still he couldn't do so. He heaved his shoulder into it, but neither the door, nor the glass wall around it moved in the slightest.

"It's a material I developed," Lorian said. "Completely impervious."

Jake walked back over to Nadira. "So, he's is in on it? You've been lying to me."

She looked at him, but then turned her attention back to her father. "I understood why you did what you had to all those years, why you worked for Kharn. You had no choice."

Her father held his hand up to the glass in front of her. "I protected you."

"Yes," she said, strain of swelling emotion in her voice. "You protected me and so many others. You did everything you could."

"Kharn recognized my abilities. He allowed me to continue my research, and in return I assisted him and his scientists with their work."

"But this?" Nadira placed her hands against the glass, still holding her blaster in one hand.

Her father looked at her silently for a moment, and then turned away. "Kharn is a brilliant man. I didn't understand at first what he was trying to accomplish, but now I do. Together we can do so much, for all peoples."

"By killing the Waudure?" Nadira's face flushed. Her eyes grew glossy.

Jake slammed his fist against the glass. "Ok. I hate to break up the touching reunion, but this isn't happening. You open the lab or I'll find a way to do it. And I'm not above blowing the whole place up if that's what it takes."

Lorian moved back to the instruments on the counter beside the vat. "The rebels are the treacherous ones." He picked up a large dropper and stuck it into the solution in the vat. Then he squeezed a few drops of the liquid onto a petri dish. "If it weren't for their saboteurs stalling our efforts, collapsing the mines, and hitting our supply caravans, we'd have achieved a stable augmentation process by now."

"You have been murdering them," Nadira said. "Our people!"

Jake took his blaster out and shot at the glass wall where Lorian stood on the other side. The shot reflected off the surface, zipping back between Jake and Nadira.

"Ok," he said. "Maybe not the best idea."

Nadira's father stirred the solution in the dish with the tip of the dropper. "We had to use a variety of test subjects. Studying how each race reacts to the process is critical to achieving the correct formula. Their deaths served the greater good."

Jake leaned over to Nadira. "I think he's too committed. Might as well be Kharn in there."

She cast him a glare, before turning back to face her father. "Please, father. This is not who you are." Tears streamed from the outer corners of her eyes. "You would kill your own daughter?"

Jake looked around the room for something that might help to get into the lab, a control panel, something he could use to smash the wall. "We're not getting this far to fail!"

"My dear Nadira," Lorian said, "you were right. I have protected you. The bioweapon will not affect you, just as it will not affect me, or any of the people here in this base, Cracian or Waudure." He held the petri dish up to the light and tilted it slightly, looking at the solution in it. "During your routine medical examinations while you were here, minor alterations were made to you. You are different from the Waudure rebels you insist on supporting."

"What?" Nadira helped her hands up, looking at them as if to see what he'd done.

Her father placed the petri dish back on the counter. "I am a scientist, not a monster. I would not harm the innocent. They led you astray. You, my sweet daughter, you can now return to your rightful place."

"So, your great science," Jake said, "calls for you to kill off thousands of people!"

"They chose their fate," Lorian said. "Kharn has built the foundation to a great future for all peoples. Unfortunately, some of the Waudure could not accept that."

"Screw that," Jake said. "There has to be a way in." He ran over to the clear door to the right of the enclosed lab space again. He squared his shoulders to the door and stepped forward, lunging into it with a kick. Nothing. He slammed against it twice with his body weight, hitting the door with his shoulder. The door didn't budge.

Lorian stepped over to the wall behind him, raising his hand to a button beside a perforated panel. "You two will witness as we overcome the final hurdle. With the Waudure rebels eliminated, we will be on our way to mastering the augmentation process that will usher in a new age of hope for the galaxy." He pressed the button down and turned toward the panel. "It is time."

Through the panel came a reply. "Excellent."

Nadira turned to Jake. "Explosives?"

He shook his head. "They were in my pack."

A moment later, a door slid open at the back of the enclosed side of the lab. Jake hadn't noticed the door, as it was flush to the wall and made to look like part of it, with only a seam showing.

"Kharn," Nadira said.

Jake saw him for the first time. He only had the few Cracians he'd fought for comparison, but Kharn stood notably taller. His dark gray uniform and light gray skin made him look like a villain, Jake thought. But the expression on his face sealed the deal in Jake's mind.

Kharn seemed to be relishing the thought of activating the weapon, of killing thousands of people.

Jake felt nauseated by the smile Kharn wore.

Kharn stepped out of his private elevator. "We have guests, Lorian."

"I was going to notify you," Lorian said, "but the

facility is secure."

Kharn moved past him, approaching the clear wall toward Jake and Nadira. "It's quite alright. In fact, I rather prefer it this way."

Jake took a step closer to the glass divide. "So, you're the crazy son of a bitch in charge."

"Mister Mudd," Kharn said, plying the tips of his bony fingers against one another in front of him as he spoke, "we meet at last."

"An unpleasant necessity," Jake said.

Kharn pulled a credit chip out of his pocket. "I believe this is what you came for, isn't it? You see, Mudd, I am an honorable man." He turned the credit chip over with his fingers. "A million credits. Say we have an agreement, and I'll hand it over. Then you walk away and go back to your ship."

"Go to hell," Jake said.

"Despite the trouble you've caused," Kharn said, "I must thank you for your cooperation." He tucked the credit chip back into his pocket.

Jake clenched his bandaged hands into fists. "Why don't you open the door and we can thank each other properly."

Kharn gave no notice to his comment, nor to his fists, and continued. "You see," he turned and extended his arm toward the vat behind him, "this wouldn't have been possible without your help."

Nadira looked at Jake, and he noticed her stare.

Jake turned to her. "I told you, I had no idea of the cargo!"

"Still," Kharn said, "with the help of an old friend of

yours, you came through quite nicely."

"What's he talking about?" Nadira asked Jake.

He shook his head.

Kharn spoke to Nadira. "Your father had such faith in you. He always believed you'd be loyal in the end."

"Kharn." Lorian slapped the counter in front of him, toppling over a few of the instruments.

"I must say, I had my doubts. Turns out, I was right to have my people keep a close watch on you. Your rebels continued to pose problems. Fortunately, there are avenues for finding solutions to such problems. It took a while, but I found a man who specializes in such solutions, and he was willing to help, for a price."

Nadira, her cheeks flush and her eyes red, asked, "What's he talking about?"

"No friend of mine would ever help you, Kharn." Jake's chest rose and fell visibly. He stared at Kharn with the intensity of a man ready to cross any line to do what was necessary.

Kharn raised his eyebrows, mocking surprise. "Oh? He seemed to know you. He knew all about you, Jake Mudd, about your past."

"I'm going to kill you," Jake said.

"Father!" Nadira stood at the dividing wall, her palms touching it, bracing herself as she leaned against it.

"That's more like the man he described." Kharn walked away from the clear partition, moving to the comm switch on the wall behind Lorian. Then he turned to face Jake again. "Jake is well acquainted with death, it turns out. Aren't you Mudd?"

"We're not talking about my past. That's not me

anymore," Jake said. "The Waudure are good people. I've seen them. We're talking about women and men who just want to live without fear of being hunted, to live without being a slave to your sick dream. And children."

Kharn pressed the comm button. "Bring her in."

He looked at Lorian. "It is ready?"

"Yes," Lorian said. "We only need to encode the solution. Then the system will convert it to gas and expel it into the atmosphere. Just a few hours to spread."

Nadira staggered back a few steps, watching her father as he spoke to Kharn.

"The beauty," Kharn said, again addressing Jake, "is the price I had to pay for such a black-market commodity. Do you know what it cost me?"

"Enough games, Kharn," Jake said. He hurried to the wall of cabinets nearby. Then he grabbed one and yanked it away from the wall. Lifting it overhead, the strain showing in his neck and by the vein bulging on his forehead, he hurled the cabinet against the barrier between Kharn and himself. The wall vibrated for a second at the impact, but the cabinet crashed to the ground, and the wall stayed intact.

Kharn walked up to the clear divide, staring at Jake. "You. All your friend wanted in exchange for the bioweapon precursors was to know that you would be here, so he knew where to hunt you down and kill you."

Kharn turned and took Lorian's place in front of the vat.

"Hyde," Jake said.

"Oh," Kharn said, as if recalling the detail, "he also said something about destroying your ship, Sarah. Apparently, you're quite fond of her."

Jake ran to the transparent wall guarding Kharn and pounded on it with his fists. Blood wicked through the bandages on his hands and smeared onto the unbreakable glass.

Kharn laughed as he watched Jake beat against the barrier.

CHAPTER THIRTY-EIGHT

The door through which Kharn had entered the lab again slid open. Held firmly by two guards clasping her wrists, a young Waudure girl, no older than eleven, squirmed and fought to get free. Her face was wrought with terror, tears streamed down her cheeks.

Jake heard her cries through the speakers above him and watched in disbelief. "She's a child!"

Nadira pounded the glass barrier. "No! Don't!"

Kharn gestured for the two guards to bring the girl to him. "Her sacrifice will not be in vain," he said. "Once the weapon is encoded, it is irreversible. The loyal Waudure here within the walls of the Cracian base have nothing to fear. They, unlike this daughter of a rebel, have been protected for their loyalty."

Jake stepped back a few feet, then gave the clear wall a strong sidekick, but his foot only deflected off the surface. "How about we throw you into the vat instead?"

Kharn chuckled at him. "Of course, we engineered a failsafe into the weapon from the beginning. It will have no impact on Cracians. The Daedalon storms will carry the weapon to every inch of the planet. Soon, the rebel interruptions I've tolerated for too long will cease."

Nadira slapped her hands repeatedly against the transparent barrier. "Father! Do something! You can't let him get away with this. Please!"

Lorian watched his daughter's tearful pleading. He stepped between Kharn and the guards who were holding the Waudure girl. "Couldn't we use one of the adult prisoners? She's an innocent child."

A look of rage flashed over Kharn's face as he turned to Lorian. "Innocent? The sins of her parents abide in her."

Lorian, glancing first to the crying girl, said, "I don't think we should do it this way."

Kharn raised his arm and swung it fiercely at him, striking him on his temple. Kharn's blow knocked Lorian back. He fell against a set of metal levers, hitting his head on them.

Jake noticed the large robotic arm above the vat moved when Lorian fell onto the levers behind Kharn. He could see blood pooling on the floor beside Lorian, who slid to the ground against the back wall.

"No!" Nadira screamed and wailed. "Father!" She continued with unrestrained lamentations as she slumped to the floor before the glass wall, her body convulsing with each sob.

Jake ran to the door of the inner lab again and pushed and pounded on it. "Kharn! Damn you!"

Kharn ignored him. The door held firm. He signaled the two guards to bring the girl to him. They did so.

Then they held the girl up by her wrists as Kharn moved to the controls beside Lorian's body. Kharn paused to look at Lorian on the floor, his head had a large gash, blood still running down to the growing pool on the floor. Kharn kicked him in the chest, shoving his body away from the controls to the robotic arm. Lorian's body flipped over from the thrust, resting a few feet away, under the control panel on the wall.

While Jake still pounded on the door, Kharn used the control levers to activate the robotic arm and guide it to take hold of the girl from her waist. Once he had, the two guards stepped back to watch the procedure.

Kharn, intently focused on what he was doing, didn't notice what Jake saw. The guards didn't notice either. Lorian turned his head to see Jake outside the transparent door. Lorian's left eye was swollen shut and his head was glazed with blood, but with his right eye he looked at Jake.

Nadira couldn't see her father moving behind the two guards. She continued to weep.

Kharn worked the levers to lift the girl higher off the ground.

Jake watched Lorian slide his arm up the wall toward the intercom control panel, painting a red smear on the surface as he did.

The robotic arm, still under Kharn's control, maneuvered the Waudure girl over the vat. With his attention only on the girl and the vat below her, Kharn said, "No one will ever dare to interfere with my life's work again."

The girl screamed repeatedly.

Jake watched Lorian, still laying on the floor, push his upper body up slightly with one of his legs, managing to rise a foot off the ground. He stretched his arm out. With his hand shaking, he extended a finger and pushed a button on the panel.

Jake saw Lorian collapse to the floor again as the inner lab door in front of Jake slid open.

He rushed in.

Kharn, with his hand on the lever to release the girl into the vat, turned to see him running toward him.

Jake dove through the air with his arms out in front of him.

Kharn pushed the lever, causing the robotic arm to release the girl over the vat.

She dropped as Jake flew toward her. He caught her in his outstretched arms just before her foot touched the surface of the solution in the vat. The two of them tumbled onto the floor beyond the tank, Jake rolling his body and wrapping his arms around her to brace her against the impact.

"Jake!" Nadira got up and ran toward the entrance to the lab room.

Kharn yelled, "Mudd!"

Jake opened his arms. "Are you OK?"

The girl, trembling, nodded her head.

"Go," Jake said to her, pointing toward the door as Nadira came to it.

The young girl ran across the lab to Nadira who knelt to receive her. Then she carried the girl away from the entrance, away from Kharn, taking her to the farthest corner of the room. She stayed with her. "You're safe now."

Jake got up and faced Kharn.

"You will die for that," Kharn said. "Your friend be damned. The pleasure will be mine."

Jake stood with his arms a little out to his sides, hands wrapped in tattered blood-soaked bandages. "Bring it."

Kharn stepped forward, throwing a punch at Jake's head. Jake bobbed to the side and moved diagonally into Kharn's space, landing a blow to his midsection. As he did, Kharn, barely reacting to Jake's punch, struck Jake on the side of his head with his other fist. The two men traded blows for a few seconds, and then locked into a grapple with one another.

Jake came inside, taking hold of Kharn's uniform just below his shoulders. Kharn used his longer arms to wrap his bony fingers around Jake's neck, squeezing with a strength Jake didn't think possible.

He felt his focus drift as Kharn choked the flow of air from his lungs. He leaned into Kharn, still holding him near the collar. He doubled down, heaving his body weight behind his strength, pushing Kharn backwards. He drove him off balance and charged with him toward the wall. Kharn's back hit the wall hard and Jake followed through, slamming into him. Kharn's choke hold on Jake's neck fell away.

As the two men fought, Nadira comforted the Waudure girl as best she could. The girl stopped crying, but sat curled up, holding her knees. Nadira darted her eyes around the room and toward the entrance, checking for any other threats to the girl or herself.

"Stay here," she said. "I'm going to help my friend."

The girl nodded, but said nothing.

Nadira stood and, pulling her blaster from its holster, ran back toward the entrance to the contained lab. As she reached the door, the girl screamed.

Nadira looked back to see two Cracian guards grabbing the girl and pulling her up. The girl kicked and continued to scream, but the men overpowered her, carrying her toward the lab.

Nadira, glanced at Jake, who was trading blows again with Kharn. They were turning about. She didn't have a clear shot. She swung her blaster up toward the approaching guards carrying the girl.

One of the guards had already trained his weapon on her. He fired. The blast hit her shoulder, blowing a chunk from it. She screamed and dropped her weapon as she stumbled, grabbing her injured arm with her opposite hand.

The two guards, forcing the girl along with them, stood over Nadira, training their weapons at her head. "Inside," one of them said.

Wincing, she got up and made her way into the lab. The guards, still holding the Waudure child, came in behind her.

Kharn, his back to Nadira and his guards, reached out and took hold of Jake's throat again. Jake struggled to pry Kharn's hand from his neck, but the grip was too strong. He swung for Kharn, but his blows onto his chest were grazing. Kharn's long limbs gave him greater reach.

"Jake," Nadira called out to him, "I'm sorry."

Jake, trying desperately to breathe, glanced past Kharn and saw her holding her right arm, her shoulder dripping blood from the wound caused by the blast. She looked as if she could barely stand. Then he saw the Waudure girl, sobbing and writhing to get free from the grasp of the guards on either side of her.

Drawing strength from some untapped reserve, he repeatedly struck the inside of Kharn's bicep on the arm gripping his own neck. Kharn's hold loosened, and Jake pushed forward, ramming the top of his forehead into Kharn's face. Kharn's battered nose bled. He staggered back, and Jake advanced, plying him with multiple blows to his body and head. Kharn's fight seemed to be fading. Jake paused to catch his breath.

Then, Kharn shook his head, as if throwing off the effects of the attack.

He came back at Jake with renewed energy. Jake hit him as he advanced toward him, but Kharn was unflinching. He moved in and took hold of Jake by his arm and belt, lifting him over his head.

"No!" Nadira tried to come to Jake's aid, but one of the Cracian guards grabbed her injured shoulder, and the pain caused her to drop to her knees with a whimper.

Kharn yelled loud enough to drown out Nadira and the crying girl still held by the guards. "I am Crassus Kharn!" He threw Jake to the wall at the back of the lab.

Jake crashed into the white wall at shoulder height. The impact rattled everything at the back of the lab, as well as the large robotic arm attached to the ceiling above the vat. He fell to the floor and lay motionless. A smattering of sweat and blood marked the wall where his body struck.

Kharn wiped his own blood from under his nose with the back of his hand. He looked at Jake, who neither moved nor made any sound. Then he stepped over to the vat. "Bring her!"

The two guards dragged the unwilling girl past Nadira and brought her by her arms over to Kharn. One of them kicked Nadira in the back of her head as they passed. She fell with her face to the floor, moaning from the pain, before turning to watch them go by.

Kharn looked at Jake. "Wake up, Mudd. I want you to see this."

Jake didn't move.

Kharn grabbed the girl's arm. He looked to one of the guards and nodded toward Jake. "Get him up."

The two guards stepped over to Jake and pulled him off the floor. His eyes were closed and his body hung like dead weight. One of the guards shook him to rouse him. Then the two of them lifted him to his feet, each of them moving a shoulder under one of Jake's arms to keep him standing.

Jake mumbled and barely opened his eyes.

Kharn, seeing Jake was up and watching him, turned his attention back to the vat and the girl. He pulled the girl to himself. She struggled, but against his strength she had no chance of getting free.

Jake mumbled again, dropping his right arm off the

guard's shoulder and leaning his head against him. He reached around the man and grabbed the guard's blaster from his holster. As the man noticed what he was doing, Jake tipped the weapon up and shot him in the chest at near point-blank range. The Cracian fell dead, and Jake, still weak, dropped to the ground at the same time, holding onto the man's weapon.

The other guard reached for his blaster, but Jake shot again. The man cried out in pain as he fell to the floor.

Kharn turned to Jake as the two guards fell.

Jake pointed the blaster at Kharn, but before he could pull the trigger again, Kharn kicked his arm that was wielding the weapon. The blaster flew out of his hand, landing across the room. He tipped forward, bracing himself with his forearm against the floor.

The girl struggled to get free from Kharn's hold, but he yanked her closer to him. She screamed. The scream broke down into sobbing. "Please," she said. "Please, no."

Jake heard her. Despite exhaustion and the shooting pains throughout his body, from broken bones he couldn't even begin to name, he found the will to move.

He looked up at Kharn, who was holding the girl's arm and grabbing her leg with his other hand to lift her. Jake sprung forward to stop him, but something held him back. The second of the two guards he'd shot had a grip on Jake's leg by the ankle. The guard couldn't get up, but still had the strength to keep Jake down.

Kharn lifted the girl over his head. "No more rebels standing in my way."

Jake strained against the pull on his leg, dragging the guard with him. Jake's body convulsed in protest, as internal injuries caused him to heave under the effort.

Nadira, still hazy from the blow to her head, realized what Jake was about to do. "Stop! It'll kill you!"

Taking hold of the edge of the work surface beside the vat, Jake clawed his way across the counter toward the stew of imminent genocide. He couldn't get to Kharn in time, but there was another way, he thought.

Kharn raised the girl higher, and a mania lit up his face.

"Not today," Jake said, then he thrust his arm into the vat.

The torrent of pain consumed all other sensations in his body. His head reflexively whipped back, and he screamed in agony.

The solution in the vat violently filled with froth, as it churned and sloshed. He felt the flesh dropping from his arm. He couldn't remove his hand from the vat. The current held it in as the deadly liquid worked to devour the encoding material he had offered it.

Sarah.

Kharn cast the girl down to the floor. "You fool! What have you done?"

The girl scampered away, hiding on the other side of the vat.

Jake stayed slumped over the metal table, with his arm, hooked over the top of the vat, submerged up to his bicep. The dark solution inside the massive steel container settled.

He raised his gaze to Kharn. "Set things right."

"You, Mudd," Kharn said, "will die when the weapon becomes active." He reached over to Jake and lifted him by the throat with one hand.

Jake's body had gone into shock from the pain of the vat, but he still felt the squeeze on his neck and the warmth building in his face. But he didn't feel the pain or panic typically associated with choking. He noticed his eyes growing glossy and his vision blurry.

Kharn held him aloft. "No need to wait for the weapon to do its job." Jake's feet dangled a few inches off the floor. "But I want to enjoy this." He threw Jake against the wall at the back of the lab.

Jake felt something thrust into his lower back as he landed. He nearly passed out. Then he realized what he'd just seen. The robotic arm above Kharn moved. The idea formed slowly.

Kharn, still standing next to the huge vat, scowled at Jake before peering into the pool of dark liquid, the instrument of Waudure destruction ripped from his grasp.

Jake twisted his body off the controls to the robotic arm. Then he took hold of them with his intact arm, bracing against them and the wall to keep himself upright. He nudged one of the control sticks and watched how the long jointed mechanical arm moved, as it swiveled at the base set in the ceiling. He figured out which lever did what with the arm. Kharn turned to face him again, and saw Jake's hand on the lever.

Million credits. Damn. So close.

Jake pushed it to its limit. The robotic arm plowed

down, crashing into Kharn's head and toppling him into the vat. The brackish liquid splashed as he fell in, and heavy sloshes spilled over the edge of the container.

Jake felt the lever push against his hand, but he held it down. After several seconds, the vibrations in the lever stopped. The liquid in the vat smoothed over around the large robotic arm still sunk into it, with Kharn underneath it.

CHAPTER THIRTY-NINE

She was a blur to him at first, then Jake's eyesight cleared enough to see Nadira rushing over to him. He saw the young girl clinging to the wall beside the open door to the lab.

"I'm here," Nadira said as she came to his side.

He tipped his head back to see her face. "I'm sorry I couldn't save him."

Nadira sharply inhaled and turned her attention to her father on the ground just past Jake. She moved and knelt beside Lorian. She took his lifeless arm in hers, clasping it by the forearm as was the custom. Her back faced Jake, but he heard her crying softly.

Then she stood and turned back to Jake. "Your arm."

"Yes. It hurts." He shifted between gritting his teeth and wincing from the pain.

"I think that might be a slight understatement," Nadira said. She dug through the pocket on her pant leg and pulled out a small tube.

"I think you can finally shoot me now," he said.

After removing the cap from one end, she jabbed the

exposed needle of the tube into his leg and pressed the other end with her thumb.

"Oh, that's just cruel," Jake said, as he clenched his jaw and drew his shoulders inward.

"You'll thank me."

She stood over him, waiting.

He felt the drug kick in. The pain from his arm, and throughout his body didn't go away, but the injection certainly made an improvement.

"Thanks," he said. "What was that?"

"We call it Comfort. It's usually given to soldiers with mortal wounds, to take away their suffering until they pass on."

"Maybe I'm delusional, but I think I'm gonna make it."

"I know, but you needed something that strong. Your wounds are severe, and we don't have time to deal with them here."

She gathered his weapon and stepped over to look into the vat. "It's draining. Must be converting to the gas. I don't think there's a way to stop it now."

"It won't hurt anybody now. It's encoded with my DNA."

"What about you? It'll kill you, I'm afraid, and any human that tries to come to Daedalon. Can you walk?" She held her arm out to him.

He noticed the wound on her shoulder. The blood had clotted, but it looked bad. He tipped his chin upward, glancing at her shoulder. "You?"

"I'll make it." She moved her hand still extended to him. "Come on. We need to get out of here."

He reached up and took her hand. He stood, and the

two of them leaned on each other as they hobbled toward the door.

He smiled at the girl, who was looking up at him. "Stick with us. You'll be OK. Time to go home."

The girl nodded to him and walked just behind them, staying close and grasping the bottom of Jake's shirt from behind.

Nadira walked with her arm wrapped around his waist. "Sorry you didn't get paid."

"Yes, me too." He glanced to his mangled arm. "At least I got these souvenirs."

"You're nuts," she said, as they headed out of the lab.

"I know."

They headed down the corridor, making their way back to where they'd left Hanlan and Brun. Halfway there, a guard turned a corner and saw them. The man stopped in his tracks at the sight of them.

"What?" Jake said. "You didn't think we were going to make it?"

The guard reached for his weapon.

Nadira shot him with Jake's blaster, and the two of them continued down the corridor, stepping over the body when they came to it.

As they walked down the next couple of hallways, they felt the ground tremble and heard explosions beyond the walls of the base.

"We've made it through the mountains," Nadira said.

"The Cracian forces must be falling, if the battle's come here now."

"We've done our part."

They came to the room Hanlan and Brun held up in.

From behind a pile of Cracian bodies, a voice called out. "You two missed the excitement."

"Hanlan?" Nadira asked.

Hanlan stood up from behind the barricade of corpses. "Well, maybe you didn't miss the action after all."

"It's done," Nadira said. "Brun?"

Hanlan turned and looked down behind him. "He's here. Doing better."

Brun stood up, bracing himself with one arm on the wall. "Glad you made it. I'm sorry I wasn't there with you. Looks like you two had one hell of a fight."

"Jake here took the worst of it," Nadira said.

Jake waved a hand to Brun and Hanlan. "I'll live. But, her father."

Nadira dropped her gaze to the ground. "I didn't want to accept it, but he actually shared Kharn's mad dream."

"Son of a bitch," Hanlan said.

"Oh," Brun said, "I'm sorry, Nadira. And here we were trying to save him."

"In the end," Jake said, "he did what he could to help stop Kharn."

"And Kharn?" Hanlan asked.

"Dead," Jake said.

Brun nodded his head. "You're a good man, Jake."

"Not sure about that," Jake replied. "Maybe today."

"Alara?" Brun asked.

Nadira shook her head. "Haven't seen her."

"I know," Brun said. "She must've been working for

him. There were always little signs, but I've been ignoring them. I didn't want to believe it."

"I'm sorry, Brun," Jake said. "That's hard."

"You deserve better," Nadira said. "I know she and I didn't get along, but I can't fathom how she could do that to you."

Brun gave him a quick nod, acknowledging the comment.

Jake looked at the stack of guards in front of Hanlan and Brun. The bodies were piled onto one another, staggered like large bricks in a wall. They came up to Jake's chest. "So, what's the story here?"

"They kept coming," Hanlan said. "I decided to put them to use."

Another explosion nearby rumbled the walls. Bits of the ceiling broke loose and dropped.

"We need to get out of here," Nadira said.

Hanlan and Brun stepped out from behind their Cracian barricade.

"What about the weapon?" Brun asked.

Nadira patted Jake's chest. "He took care of it."

"It's disabled?" Hanlan asked.

"Not exactly," Jake said. "But it's not a threat to the Waudure anymore."

"What do you mean?" Brun asked.

"Look at his arm," Nadira said. "The weapon's encoded for humans. He's the target for it now."

Brun stepped over to Jake and helped to brace him. "We're getting you out of here."

Hanlan took point in front of them, and they headed out of the base.

CHAPTER FORTY

After Hanlan and Nadira, Jake stepped outside to see hundreds of Waudure troops across the plain surrounding the Cracian base. The Waudure fighters cheered. Many of them raising their weapons overhead, shaking them in celebration. Plumes of dark smoke rose from fiery wreckage of Cracian ships. At scattered points in the distance, weapon fire flashed, but those seemed to be the final skirmishes. Jake took a few steps before stumbling.

Brun caught Jake's good arm. "Looks like we did it."

Jake nodded, then he continued out into the clearing. He turned to look at the base. Many of the walls had been destroyed. Waudure vehicles formed an arc around the western part of the clustered buildings. He saw large holes blown through the walls there, and Waudure troops funneling inside. Only the occasional shot from displaced Cracian fighters challenged the conquering forces, but those threats now faced overwhelming numbers. From the edge of the base to the mountains in the distance, signs of the struggle that took place were visible. Fallen soldiers, smoldering vehicles, scars of war on the land.

Nadira stepped to Jake's side. "They say after the aerial forces were taken out, many of the ground forces disbanded."

"For all his blustering," Jake said, "Kharn couldn't give his soldiers what the Waudure have."

"What's that?"

"The desire to be free."

A roaring sound came from within the Cracian compound. Jake turned to see what it was. A massive jet of brown smoke shot up into the clouds.

"That must be the weapon," Nadira said.

Looking skyward at the storms still coalescing near the mountains, Jake drew a deep breath and exhaled. "That doesn't bode well. Not for me, anyway."

He heard Brun yelling nearby. "Over there. He needs it more than I do."

A team of two medics came up to Jake. "Sir, let me help you." He held out a canister.

Jake glanced at his mangled arm. "I almost forgot." He held it up for the woman to apply the treatment. "She gave me a Comfort injection."

The second medic knelt and pulled a roll of bandages from the bag he carried. "Here, please."

Jake allowed the man to wrap his arm, while the other medic applied the foaming spray to Nadira's shoulder wound.

"Where's your commanding officer?" Nadira asked the one attending to her.

The woman pointed to a man nearby.

Nadira glanced at Jake as she addressed the medic. "Tell him we need to get him out of out here."

"His wound is bad," the woman said, "but he'll recover. The treatment—"

"It's not his arm I'm worried about," Nadira said.

Jake directed the woman's attention to the torrent of brown smoke rising to the clouds. "That's the bioweapon."

The medic looked shocked. "No. We're too late!"

"Take it easy," Jake said. "You're safe. You're all safe."

"What?" she asked.

"The weapon is harmless to the Waudure now," Jake said.

Nadira placed her hand on the medic's shoulder. "But not to him, or any humans. We'll need to send word that Daedalon is off-limits to their race, for now."

The woman looked at Jake, and then at Nadira. She didn't seem to understand what she was being told.

Nadira looked squarely at the woman. "Tell your captain Kharn's dead and the weapon can no longer target the Waudure."

The woman nodded as she listened.

Nadira continued, "And tell him the man responsible for saving all of us is about to die from that plume of smoke if we don't get him out of here. Now!"

The medic nodded again. Then she ran to her captain.

The other medic finished wrapping Jake's arm. Then he stood up and looked Jake in the eye. "Thank you, sir." He held out his arm to Jake's good one.

Jake looked at the man, who glanced down at his hand and then back to Jake. Jake embraced the man's arm, clasping his forearm as Nadira had done with Tay. "Bond, not birth," Jake said.

"Bond, not birth," the man said in reply. Then he left Jake and Nadira and headed off to tend to others.

Nadira stepped closer to Jake, taking his hand. "There's not another way, is there?" She looked deep into his eyes.

He had no doubt what she was saying. "If I stay on Daedalon, I'll die. Perhaps one day I can return."

"I know. I only wish…"

"I know."

"You're a good man, Jake Mudd."

"Just a man." He would have shrugged but it hurt too much.

She leaned against him, and he wrapped his one good arm around her.

They stood for a moment, lost to everything going on around them.

Behind them, someone spoke. "It's here, sir."

Jake and Nadira turned around. The woman was pointing to a ship landing not far away. Hundreds of Waudure gathered around it.

"Follow me," she said. "It's a Cracian ship, but I don't think they need it any more. We have a pilot ready to take you where you need to go."

Jake and Nadira walked toward the ship as it touched down. Upon their approach the large crowd of Waudure fighters erupted into cheers and applause.

"What's this?" Jake asked.

"You're their hero," Nadira said.

He looked at her.

She took his hand again. "I'll miss you, Jake."

"We weren't bad, were we?"

He stepped up to the front of the crowd. Hanlan and Brun were there to greet him.

"Not too shabby," Brun said.

Jake smiled. "Couldn't have done it without you." He looked at Hanlan. "And you."

"We made a good team," Nadira said.

"I wish you could stay," Brun said. "Keep things interesting around here."

Jake looked up at the brown cloud high above the Cracian base. "I wish I could, but if that does what Kharn claimed, there's no place for me here."

"Yes," Brun said. "Just wish it weren't so."

"Besides," Jake said, "I need to get back to my ship. There's something I need to do. Something Kharn said that I need to follow up on."

"I'm not sure I understand," Brun said, "but if you ever can come back, when it's safe, you'll always have a place with us."

The door to the ship opened. The crowd of Waudure parted to make a path for Jake.

He turned to Nadira. "This is goodbye, then."

"No," she said. "This is goodbye." She reached up and put her hand on the side of his neck, gazing up at him. He leaned in and they shared a long kiss.

"That's a proper goodbye," Brun said.

The crowd roared.

"Now save yourself, Jake Mudd," Nadira said. "I'll be

here if you ever want to come looking for trouble again."

He gave the three of them one last glance, then he made his way through the crowd and boarded the ship.

CHAPTER FORTY-ONE

Jake took a seat beside the Waudure pilot, a young man who seemed pleased with the task of ferrying the day's hero to his destination. He and Jake exchanged brief pleasantries before Jake turned his attention to the window beside him. He could see the large crowd below, and among them, his three new friends. He wondered if he'd ever see them again.

He tipped his chair back as the craft took off in a steady climb. "Did they tell you where we're going?"

"Yes, sir," the pilot answered, while staying focused on the controls and screens in front of him.

"Does this thing have a comm link?"

"One second, sir." The pilot pressed a switch on the panel in front of him. "The channel is open to your ship."

Jake swiveled in his chair. "Hey, darlin'. You there?"

"Jake?" Sarah sounded both exasperated and relieved at the same time.

"Miss me?"

"I expected to hear from you a long time ago. You're

OK?" Her voice dipped into a tender tone.

"A little worse for wear, but I'll make it. Sounds like you've been worried."

Nothing came through the comm speakers for a few seconds.

"Sarah?"

"I was just trying to decide whether to cancel the request I put out for your replacement."

"You're hilarious," Jake said.

"How did the delivery go?"

Jake turned his chair and looked at the pilot. The young man raised his eyebrows while tilting his head and shrugging.

"There were a few hiccups," Jake said, "I'm not going to lie to you."

The pilot chuckled.

"What was that?" Sarah asked.

"Never mind," Jake said. "There's something I want you to do."

"Did you get the payment?"

"That was one of the hiccups," Jake said. "But listen, I need you to fire up the drives. We're going to need to fold out of here as soon as I'm on board."

"What? Why the hurry?"

"Just do it. Open the bay door when you see us coming."

"I see you now," she said. "Jake."

"Yes."

"My sensors are picking up several ships folding into our space. They're coming in not too far from me."

Hyde.

"Get the drives ready to go!"

"What's going on?"

"I don't think we want to be there when those ships come in," Jake said. "As soon as I'm on board and my escort is clear from you, we need to go."

"You're the boss." Sarah laced her response with sarcasm.

Jake opened his mouth to respond, but then let it slide, and instead shook his head.

"Trouble?" the pilot asked.

"Just don't hang around after you drop me off. I don't think they're interested in Daedalon."

The pilot nodded then returned to his controls to guide the craft through Sarah's bay door.

CHAPTER FORTY-TWO

Jake waved to the pilot from the door leading out of the landing bay, as the commandeered Cracian ship turned and headed back out through the energized field that guarded the interior from the cold vacuum of space. With a noticeable stagger, he made his way down the hall and into the lift that rose to the captain's deck.

With the camera in the elevator, Sarah saw him — cuts, blood, and bandages. She had to comment. "Hiccups?"

He looked up at the camera. "Nice to see you too."

"You look like —"

The door opened with a swoosh.

He went to his captain's chair and dropped into it. "Can we fold space yet?"

"I'll need another minute," she said. "I didn't know you were coming until a short while ago. I had the drives shut down to conserve energy."

"As soon as we can."

"You sure you don't want to head down to the med bay?"

Jake repositioned himself in his chair, although he still remained obviously uncomfortable. "Believe me. That sounds like a great idea, but not until we're safe."

"Safe?"

Jake pressed a few buttons on the arm of his captain's chair to bring up the approaching ships on the large display in front of him.

"Jake, whose ships are those?"

"People we don't want to talk to."

"They're hailing us on the comm link," Sarah said. "Should I open the channel."

"Are the drives ready yet?"

"No."

Jake exhaled with a groan. "Put them on."

The distant view of the approaching fleet of ships flickered before being replaced by a closeup of a man seated in a chair like Jake's.

"Not the video link," Jake said under his breath.

The man on the screen wore a black and gray uniform that was ripped in a few places and anything but crisp and clean. Dark green skinned, he churned his jaw and licked his lips with a forked crimson tongue before speaking. "Mudd. All the places in the galaxy to hide, and somehow, I run into you here."

Jake leaned in slightly and to the side of his chair. "Hyde. I've been looking all over for you."

"I'll bet you have."

"And I see you brought your friends." Jake smiled.

"More the merrier, right?"

"You don't have friends, Hyde," Jake said, losing the pleasant pretense.

"Aren't you curious how I knew where to find you?" Hyde asked.

"Seems you were in on a black-market deal," Jake said. "Serious stuff, genocide, even for you, Hyde."

Hyde's face lit up. He looked proud. "Hacked the Galactic Shipping Registry. Broke the encryption on your anonymized shipping license."

"Really? That's impressive."

Hyde nodded and bobbed his head, looking pleased with himself.

"I figured I'd make some money off the contraband cargo," Hyde said, "and maybe get you killed in the process. But I'm glad you made it out alive. I think I'd prefer to kill you myself." He jostled in his chair and laughed. "And take your ship when I'm done."

"Jake," Sarah said.

"Uh huh?"

"That thing you asked about is ready."

"Good to know," Jake said. He leaned forward, staring into the two-way video transmission. "Hyde, I always hated you. You are the vilest, most dishonorable, dumbest mercenary I've ever met. I'm not sure who did the leg work on this job, but I'm willing to bet you have no idea how to hack the shipping registry, let alone the shipping license encryption. No, somebody much smarter than you had to do it. I'm guessing you're just the dumb pawn in someone's game. But, you know what Hyde?"

Hyde seemed to be boiling with rage as Jake spoke.

"The sad thing is, Hyde," Jake said, "you probably don't even realize that."

Hyde got up from his chair, raising his hand in front of him and clenching it into a fist. "Jake Mudd! I will—"

"Let's go," Jake said, as he flipped a switch on the arm of his chair to cut the comm link.

"You got it," Sarah replied.

The charged field around the ship pulsed and Sarah and Jake were gone.

CHAPTER FORTY-THREE

In the timeless place between space, Jake sat in his captain's chair watching the cosmic dance of light around his ship, Sarah.

"Where to?" she asked.

"I don't really know."

"How about somewhere off the charts for a while?"

"That sounds like a good idea. Sorry I didn't get the payment on this one."

"That's OK. We'll manage. We always do."

"We do, don't we?" Jake rubbed the edge of his chair, and Sarah felt it. "You're always there for me."

"Always will be."

THANK YOU FOR READING

You, the reader, are of the utmost importance to any author, including this one.

If you enjoyed this book, please take the time to leave a review online at the following link.

http://HalArcher.com/review1
(You can just search for Deadly Cargo on Amazon.)

Reviews help others discover great books, and they help authors, such as myself, continue writing stories for readers to enjoy.

I would be most grateful if you write one for this book.

Sign up to the Hal Archer Readers Group email list and be the first to hear of new releases and sales. No spam. I promise.

http://HalArcher.com/signup

ACKNOWLEDGMENTS

Thank you to the following people for the invaluable contributions they have made to the success of this book.

To my editor, Graham, of Fading Street, your work has immeasurably improved this story. It has been a pleasure working with you.

To the wonderful team at Deranged Doctor Design, particularly Milo, Kim, and Darja, thank you for sharing my vision for this work and for bringing it to life through your wonderful cover design. It's been great working through the whole process with your team.

To my fellow writer friends Gary, Nick, and Adam— sources of inspiration and invaluable feedback, as well as unwavering friendship. Thank you.

Lastly, but most importantly, to my three children, Lewis, Ben, and Abbie, you bring unceasing joy and purpose to my life. May you soar with your dreams and bring your particular genius to the world.

ABOUT THE AUTHOR

Hal Archer was born in Texas, where, after many travels, he again resides. He has worked as a bookseller, a research library assistant, and a military computer network expert (often in hostile enemy territory). He eventually took a position in international shipping and worked for twelve years, while pursuing the writing craft in his spare time. After several early attempts in sci-fi, action/adventure, and thriller genres, he developed a character that he found truly compelling, and the Jake Mudd Adventures series was born.

BOOKS BY HAL ARCHER

JAKE MUDD ADVENTURES:
DEADLY CARGO
FORCED VENGEANCE
HEAT SEEKER
BROKEN SOLACE
LOST HUMANITY
To be continued…

JAKE MUDD TALES:
TANGLED PERIL (a prequel novelette)

Visit http://HalArcher.com to find out about the latest available titles.

There you can sign up to the Hal Archer Readers' Group email list and be the first to hear of new releases and sales.

To say thanks, I'll send you the Jake Mudd novelette, Tangled Peril, for free when you sign up.
http://HalArcher.com/signup

A Preview of

Forced Vengeance
Jake Mudd Adventures Book Two

FORCED VENGEANCE, CHAPTER ONE

The drop out of the fold in space was smooth, as usual, but Jake awoke seconds later to his ship's frustrating sense of humor. His head rose a few inches above the padded roll on his bed shelf before coming back down with a thud. The pillow gave some protection against the hard surface beneath it, but not enough to keep him from experiencing the onset of a slight headache.

He groaned as he sat up and swung his legs over the side of his bed. Before his eyes were ready, the lights came on.

"Good morning, Jake." His ship Sarah spoke with a cheerfulness that Jake took as the perfection of sarcasm.

"Yeah, right. You too."

"You asked me to wake you when we reached Eon Station."

"How'd you manage to hit a bump in space? Did you run over something?"

"What? Oh, no. I must've made an error when

activating the impulse drive. Sorry about that."

Jake got up and stretched his arms. He rubbed some feeling into his stubbled jaw. Then he reached for his brown leather jacket that hung on the hook nearby. He donned it over his broad shoulders and slipped his feet into his boots. He left his holstered blaster and belt hanging on the other hook.

"How far out are we?"

"Far enough to allow for the fold without drawing attention to ourselves. A few minutes to the space station at this speed."

"When we get closer, slow down and notify me."

"Will do, boss. You know…"

"What is it?"

"A shower might be a good idea."

Jake looked into the camera on the wall above his holster belt. "Funny."

"You know I have sensors, right?"

Jake took his belt off the hook and put it on. "I'm heading to the bridge. I want to get a look at the station. It's been a long time."

"Of course. It's coming into view now."

Jake walked over to the door of the elevator to the bridge. He stepped in front of it and caught a glimpse of his tousled brown hair in the reflection before the door slid open. As he entered, he raised his arm, tilted his head toward it, and sniffed. "She's crazy."

Coming out of the lift he got his first look at the massive space city of Eon. It had been a couple of years since he'd visited the space station metropolis. He could see that it had grown even from the sprawling conglomeration he remembered it to be.

Eon first served as a refueling and trading outpost for those braving the uncertain frontier of this part of the galaxy. Over the years, it drew the wayward and the unseemly with its offer of unbridled opportunities for profit and mischief, and for the absence of interference by the various policing organizations that hampered much of the galaxy with law and order.

Word quickly spread through the many networks of ruffians and the unruly. In time, more of that sort came from across the vastness of space to do business at Eon, and often settled there. The remote space station grew to accommodate those that came.

Now it stood as a gargantuan city, fixed in space, alone in its galactic neighborhood. It played host to the underbelly of the universe, with kingpins and factions carving out their own sleazy pieces of the city. A dangerous place where anything could happen and all could be had for a price, it was just the place Jake needed.

"Are you sure you can get one there?" Sarah asked as Jake walked over to the large viewing window and took in the sight.

"No doubt someone has one. If it's black market, then you can get it in Eon. An anonymized shipping license will be harder to track down than some things, but I'm sure I can find one."

"I'm sorry about what happened."

"It wasn't your fault. I don't know how Hyde did it. He must've paid off the right people. Still, I've never heard of a shadow license being cracked."

"You don't think he'll come after us here, do you? I know he can't trace us on the shipping registry this time, but..."

"Doubtful. As bad a character as he is, this isn't his neck of the galaxy. He may not even know how to find Eon. It's not exactly on the official maps."

"I'm just glad you got back on board from Daedalon before his ships could attack."

"Me too. You're a tough lady, but I didn't want to test his fleet."

Jake stared at Eon. A thousand times larger than his cargo ship, the space station city crawled with activity. Vessels docked and took off at multiple hubs around the perimeter of the station. The glow of lights from the hundreds of buildings created an effect like a sky at sunset. That's how it always was, Jake remembered, perpetual dusk. The inhabitants of Eon liked it that way. Nothing was ever exposed to the light of day.

"They're hailing us now," Sarah said.

Jake stepped over to his captain's chair and sat, resting his hands on the wide arms of the seat. He swiveled the blocky unit to face the wall-sized display screen off to his right.

"Bring them up."

An Eon border official appeared on the screen. It was a humanoid creature, with soot black skin that overlapped itself in rolls across its face. Jake couldn't see the rest of the official, and he couldn't decide if it was male or female.

"Identity?" the border officer said, though its mouth moved for longer than the time it took for Jake to hear the word.

"You sure you're giving me the whole translation?" he asked.

"Yes," Sarah said, "that's all."

"Class 4 Tarian Cargo Vessel in need of supplies," Jake said. "No passengers. Just passing through. Permission to land."

Everyone was 'just passing through' at Eon, or at least that was the answer everybody gave. Jake knew the routine.

The creature turned to look at something off-screen for a moment, then it faced front again. "Denied."

"What?" Jake shifted in his chair, then leaned forward. "We're just passing through. We need to refuel and get some basic supplies. Requesting permission to land."

"Denied."

"Seriously?"

"Why do you question my seriousness?"

Jake glared at one of Sarah's cameras. Then he quickly ran through his options in his head. He remembered a name from his last visit. There was a man, using the term loosely, that helped him out of a run-in with one of the officials.

"Actually," he said, "I'm also here to see Chori Kawf."

The official once again looked off-screen. Jake saw him mouthing something.

"What's he saying?" Jake asked Sarah, deciding the alien was male.

"I don't know. He's muted the audio."

The alien officer paused, appearing to listen to

someone. Then he turned back to Jake.

"You will dock your ship in the secure holding area where it will undergo inspection. It will remain there in quarantine until you depart Eon."

"You must be kidding. Don't translate that."

"What shall I tell him?" Sarah asked.

Jake considered whether he could talk the official out of having his ship on lockdown. What if he needed to get back to Sarah in a hurry? And inspected? That was just asking for trouble. Especially since he was nearly tapped out of credits. No chance he could offer a respectable bribe if it came up. He could decline and come back in the shuttle to see if they'd let him in that way. But, he realized, coming there in a shuttle would arouse suspicion.

"We're not carrying anything too illegal, are we?" he asked Sarah.

"Not really," she said. "Nothing that would be out of place here, anyway."

"Tell him we'll dock as advised."

"You're just going to leave me there and let them snoop around in me?"

"You'll be fine. All you need to do is act… try not to piss them off."

"Fine. But you better not take too long."

Sarah relayed the edited version of Jake's response to the Eon Station border official and received the clearance code and directions to the assigned docking point.

The screen went to black.

"If you go down there and get yourself locked up, or

worse," Sarah said, "I'm not hanging around waiting for you."

"You don't mean that, darlin'."

"Well… just be careful. OK?"

"Careful's my middle name."

"Oh! Honestly! Why do I put up with you?"

Jake rose from his chair. "Because you couldn't go on without me."

"Ugh."

He went back to the viewing window and watched as they flew in for the approach and made their way around the perimeter of the station, heading toward the docking port.

FORCED VENGEANCE, CHAPTER TWO

Jake felt bad leaving Sarah in the holding area, but he realized he had no choice. At least he knew where to find her if things went sour, though under those circumstances getting through the layers of security to get back to her would be no easy task. He knew he could reach her on the comm link on his belt, but running the streets without drawing too much attention meant not having her on the line providing commentary the whole time.

As he stood holding the identification card he was assigned when he first stepped out of his ship, he nearly laughed at the extent of the security ring he'd passed through.

Somebody's really taking things seriously around here now.

The man in front of him appeared to be the last one who would need to check his ID card. Jake held it up to the man.

"Reason for your visit?"

The uniformed officer wore a small metal box fixed in

front of his throat by a band that wrapped around his neck. Jake noticed five red lights flicker out of sync as he heard the man's words. He also heard a second vocalization from the officer at the same time, but it was more of an undertone. His native language, no doubt, Jake thought.

"Do you want the same answer I gave the other six guys or something new?"

The man had obviously heard that one before. He sighed before speaking again. "Reason for your visit?"

Jake noted the color and style of the officer's uniform looked remarkably like that of Crassus Kharn, the tyrant he'd faced off against on Daedalon weeks earlier.

"You ever met a Cracian?"

"Are you a Cracian?"

"Not by a long shot. Never mind. I'm here to pick up some supplies. Just routine. Passing through."

"Right. Passing through. OK, then." The officer stepped to the side and waved Jake on.

He winked at the man, then walked past him and out the door at the end of the hall.

When he stepped out of the building, Eon looked, sounded, and smelled more like he remembered. Tall buildings blocked out a third of the celestial view, and the blanket of clouds, which he knew to be smog, obscured another third. He noted a few of the flaming spires and pipes on the tops of the buildings; they belched into the space station's artificial atmosphere. A mist, the settling pollution, drifted down in the warm air to cover everything with a dank odor.

Jake felt it coat his face and hands as he stood, deciding which way to head. He nudged a piece of trash away from his foot, and listened to the clamor of activity — conversations of passers-by, the hum of transport vehicles as they flew between the buildings, the shuffle of feet, the heated voices of confrontations, and the whispers of shady deals.

The street, lit from all around with a play of color and glow, stretched far to his left and right. In front of him, towers of metal and brownish glass formed a wall that rose into the dirty pseudo clouds. Alien signage jutted out the sides of the buildings, offering goods and services a guy would be jailed for in any civilized place. Jake could make out some of the signs. He'd picked up a few alien tongues in his travels. But many of them made their offers clear enough with pictures.

Storefront shacks huddled against the buildings and down into the alleyways between them. They were scraped together, collections of castaway materials. Merchants gestured and presented items to potential customers that stepped up to the shops.

He found himself in a busy scene of people headed down the walkways in every direction. People is an easy term. They were aliens. Every shape, size, color, and who-knows-what you could imagine. But then again, so was he.

The dim lighting and long shadows of the tall buildings all around made everyone look like they were up to no good. Or maybe, Jake thought, they were up to no good. But then again, so was he.

Where to start?

Jake appreciated that he could walk the city without drawing attention, at least until he had to punch somebody in the face. And even then, most would mind their own business. Everyone had an agenda. If he didn't cross their path, and they stayed out of his way, finding a seller for the license would be just a matter of time.

"I would never do that!" A man's voice cried out.

Jake turned to the source. A thin elderly man working the nearest shop cowered away from two creatures twice his size. Big around the waist, and with a thick matted streak of hair down their shirtless backs, each of the two appeared to be a cross between an oversized man and a herd animal, though their legs were normal aside from being large. The heavyset pair leaned in toward the shop owner. One of the two bumped the corrugated rusted tin that served as the shack's roof, knocking it back a foot and tilting one of the two posts that supported it.

Jake kept his distance, observing. He couldn't understand what the two were saying to the frightened merchant, but they obviously were unhappy with the man.

The one that bumped the roof reached in and took hold of the shopkeeper's collar, yanking him forward across the counter.

"No. Please don't," the man said as he floundered on top of his wares. Electronic devices and parts spilled off the display. The bruiser held the shopkeeper up with one hand and threatened him with the fist of his other.

Jake heard more alien gibberish from the thug. He

felt like jumping in and sorting the two goons out, but he knew he needed to move around the city with discretion, given his purpose there. Eon Station officials expected the city's inhabitants to run on the shady side, but a contraband galactic shipping license bordered on stepping over the line.

Better to let it go. They're just scaring him. Shame. No respect for the elderly these days.

Then the second one patted his partner on the shoulder. The one holding the merchant shook the trembling man. Then he glanced to his left at his interfering partner. Jake watched a heated exchange between the two bruisers. The one on the left shoved the other. The one on the right released the old man and shoved his partner back. The merchant scrambled off the counter and ducked underneath the display table.

Jake imagined what the two partners screamed at each other for the next few seconds, but it still sounded like gibberish to him. He saw the shopkeeper scurry across the floor of his shop and rush through a door at the back, slamming it shut.

"Good for him," Jake said. He peered down the street, blindly choosing a path for himself. *Might as well start walking.*

He made a point of giving the two arguing thugs a wide berth as he passed them. When he crossed in front of the shop, the two men traded punches. Then one of them rammed the other one, knocking him back several feet. Jake tried to get out of the man's path, but a crowd of people behind him watching the scuffle blocked his path. The beast man slammed into Jake. He stumbled but kept on his feet.

"Easy, big guy," Jake said.

The thug whipped around toward him. He screamed something that came out with a great deal of spit. Jake figured that little nugget of alien gibberish was a well-chosen profanity. He didn't fault the man for that, but the nasty-smelling saliva he felt splash across his face wasn't so easy to ignore.

That's the problem with cities, you can't just shoot someone and be done with it.

He wiped his cheek clean and shook his head at the guy. He threw in a pretty decent scowl too. His point must've gotten across, because the hairy-backed spitting alien took a swing at him. Jake saw the move coming and stepped in before the punch smacked him in the face. He put his left forearm up and inside to stifle the swing and clocked the man on his chin with a powerful right fist. Jake felt and heard the crack of knuckles to jawbone, and he watched the lights go out in the thug's eyes. The man fell backward. Then Jake heard the gasp from the crowd behind him.

The other thug stood across from Jake, on the other side of his partner, who lay sprawled out on the pavement. He figured the guy might thank him for settling the dispute, but that didn't happen. Instead, Jake listened to more alien screaming. He still couldn't figure what any of it meant, but he was glad the sprays of saliva were falling on the guy's partner instead of him.

Jake realized this guy was bigger than the other one.

And he looked even more pissed off. When the enraged beast man brandished his fists, and hunkered toward him, on the attack, Jake wasted no time taking the guy up on his offer. He stepped onto the chest of the fallen thug before him and, pushing off the man's gut with his second step, sprung toward the ill-tempered troublemaker. His full body weight hit the man in his chest, and the two flew backward, crashing into the front of the abandoned shop stand. Random pieces of the shop's offerings scattered across the ground, and the bulk of the displayed wares fell onto the shop floor behind the counter.

Jake pushed himself up with one arm and flexed his brow, trying to clear the blur from his vision. A second later he could see again. The thug's face loomed a foot in front of him. Jake clenched his hand and chambered his arm to strike, but then realized the man was out cold.

Jake got to his feet. He noticed the cracked support post behind the goon's head. No blood. He held little sympathy for his attacker, but he was glad he didn't have a death on his hands. That could complicate matters.

He turned around to work the city's puzzle once again.

Where to look?

He expected the crowd that had been watching the fight to have fanned out by now, but they stayed huddled. He noticed slips of paper and credit markers circulating around in the group. Half the faces in the crowd wore looks of disappointment. The other half of them seemed pleased with the outcome.

"Nice," Jake said to himself. "I risk my neck, and they get to profit from it."

He spotted a couple of city officers, wearing their distinct black hats with the black and white checkered band around the edge of the wide brim. And those shiny black boots, like midnight mirrors. Each officer had a shock stick dangling from the clip that held it to his belt.

Damn, those things sting.

They started across the street, coming toward the scene from behind the crowd of street gamblers.

Since when is a good old fashioned fist fight illegal in Eon? Maybe it's the street gambling. But that'd be a new law.

The crowd of onlookers settled their bets and peeled off a few at a time. Jake got a better view of the patrol officers. They had eyes on him through the crowd of the remaining gamblers.

Not good.

Jake walked, not too fast, and kept watch with his peripheral vision as he headed for an alley.

As the two beat cops moved through the scattering crowd, one of the gamblers stepped in front of the officers. Jake allowed himself to turn his head slightly to see what was going on. The gambler gestured wildly and pointed to another man walking away from the gathering. The patrolman raised his arm and pushed the man aside at the shoulder.

Jake kept walking as he watched. The alley, only twenty feet ahead, offered a heavy cloak of darkness.

Just what he needed. No time to get entangled with the local law enforcement, he thought.

Before he reached the turn between the buildings, he saw the desperate gambler make the wrong move. The man lurched back toward the officer that had pushed him aside. He grabbed the patrolman by the collar with both hands. Jake heard the man's plea, echoing down the street.

Bad bet's about to become a bad night.

Jake's prediction came true as the second officer clenched his shock stick, yanked it from the hook on his belt, and brought it down on the gambler. The flicker from the charge was unmistakable. Jake could see it clearly, even half a block away. He shook his head in pity as he ducked into the alley.

His eyes adjusted after a few steps blindly into the shadows. He walked the alley and empty shadows revealed their secrets. Most of the dark hideaways weren't as empty as they seemed.

"Need a place to stay?" The sultry voice breathed out of recess in the wall to his right. The face it belonged to appeared. The woman leaned forward enough to catch a soft fan of dim light.

She wore a long angelic dress, but Jake knew she would appear any way a man wanted if he paid the going rate.

"I have a place here," she said, "if you need it, even if it's only for the hour."

Jake said nothing and kept walking.

He reached the end of the alley, but found a turn into another and took it.

More shadows. He stepped through a few puddles trying not to think what the liquid might be. The sounds of the busy streets of Eon were muffled by the buildings, blurring the silence, into a steady background murmur.

Somehow the alley felt colder. Maybe the darkness, he thought.

Some of the city light came from the signs and the lights on the buildings, and from within them. But Eon had a sky glow. That's what they called it. Made the place more like people expected it to be, like a city… on a planet. Not some cluster of stacked and welded buildings and superstructure drifting in uncharted space.

But the alleys didn't get the sky glow. The towering cityscape created slivers of darkness, black veins that ran throughout the metropolis. And they ran dirty and cold.

He knew these were the places he needed to look to get what he came for.

Trouble was, with thousands of such shadowed corridors, knowing which to search proved tricky.

He walked on, taking a few more turns.

"Not your neighborhood, is it?"

Jake stopped and gazed at the filthy man crouched on the ground beside the back wall of a building that, no doubt, appeared much brighter and welcoming on the street side. "Whose neighborhood is it, then?"

The man fidgeted his hands together, giggling in as distasteful a manner as Jake thought possible before answering. "If you don't know that," he giggled some more before finishing his response, "then you are in the wrong place."

"I'm looking to buy something," Jake said. "Who would I talk to?"

"Women? Juices?" The man pushed his sleeve up and held his arm out for Jake to see. It bore marks, from wrist to elbow.

"No." Jake turned and moved his hand near his blaster, drawing the man's attention to the threat.

The man withdrew against the wall. "No trouble. No trouble here."

Jake relaxed his hand away from his blaster. "I'm looking for some hard-to-get items. Stuff you can't find on the streets."

"Oh, I see. You want to talk to Baron Vos."

"Where can I find him?"

The man raised his arm. It shook as he pointed down the alley. "Keep going. If you make it the next five blocks, then you may find him."

"If I make it?"

The man shrugged and began giggling again. Then he curled up and ducked his head down. He mumbled and continued to giggle between unintelligible mutterings.

Jake shook his head at the wretched condition of the man. Then he left him to his choices and continued down the dark alley until he could hear the insane giggling no more.

He walked through the alleys for three more blocks without seeing another person. As he passed each adjoining alley the most persistent rays of light from the streets made their way across his path, but only slightly. The signs hanging from the buildings, affixed at the edge of the street-facing sides, blocked much of the light. A dumpster in the first intersecting alley and piles of trash stacked way too high in the next two held back a good bit of the glow from the street. It seemed to Jake that the street dwellers preferred the obstructions between them and the darkness of the back alleys. The fact that so many people busied themselves in the street and hardly anyone ventured where Jake now walked heightened his sense that he was heading into trouble.

He heard a whirring sound overhead and looked up. He let his eyes adjust for a second to peer into the long shadow from the building on his right to the one on his left. Once they did, he spotted the source of the noise. Forty feet off the ground hovered a drone. It was about the size of his hand. He figured it had at least six blades. They were spinning too fast to see them clearly, but he could see the black lines of the framework that extended out to six points. He caught a reflection from what he figured to be a lens suspended below the center of the craft. He watched the drone, and it seemed to be watching him.

He stood for several seconds, waiting it out. The drone stayed above him. He placed his hand on his blaster. The drone lifted higher. Then it flew off around the side of the building.

A guy can't walk dark alleys in a crime-infested city without being spied on. What's the galaxy coming to?

FORCED VENGEANCE, CHAPTER THREE

Tiffin sat against the wall of the long-vacated room on the twenty-sixth floor of a mixed-use tower. The bottom two floors were various stores, some open, some shuttered, all the open stores selling stuff below and in some cases over the counter that would have the owners locked up, or worse in any other place. Above those, a storage company took up the next ten floors. Half the remaining floors were rental units, living quarters mostly, but a few offices as well. The apartment she was in, along with the rest of the floor, hadn't been officially occupied in over a year.

She wasn't the only squatter on the floor. Three other people each claimed one of the two-room apartments, but all of them took a corner unit. They had an unspoken agreement to keep to their own part of the building, each separated by six similar apartments.

Hers was the best unit on the floor. Most of the wall dividing her two rooms was already collapsed when she laid claim to the space six months ago. She knocked the rest of the framing and panels down her first week there. The open space was more to her liking, and she liked the cross breeze it created. She had grown quite fond of the large room. Much better than huddling behind a dumpster in an alley. The room only had two windows busted out, one on each outside wall. With just one floor above her and no adjacent buildings quite as tall, she had a penthouse view of the grimy city she'd known since birth.

The wind blew in through the south-facing broken window and out the west-facing one constantly, but she had grown used to it. North had been fixed to City Hall when Eon outgrew its trading post status and became a city. She slept near one of the interior walls to avoid the gray polluted mist she and most city-dwellers called rain. Her bed was the tattered couch she'd pulled from behind her former residence, a dumpster five blocks away. It was a bitch hauling it up the stairwells, took her two days. It was worth it, though. All the springs had worn out in just the right places. She couldn't sleep on anything else now. She knew that meant she was spoiled, but hey, if she didn't look out for herself, who would, she thought.

She maneuvered the two joysticks on the controller to her favorite drone, Birdy. Watching the view Birdy's cameras beamed to the screen on her controller, she guided the craft away from the stranger below it. She flew it higher and then around the corner of her building.

She looked up from the screen of the controller in her lap, her legs stretched out in front of her on the floor. She wore long green shorts with cargo pockets on the thighs. She had her ankles crossed, one clunky brown lace-up boot resting across the other. Peering over the tips of her boots, she spotted her drone outside the glassless window. She moved the toggle stick on the controller box and Birdy flew into the room, settling to a hover a few feet in front of her.

She heard the patter of tiny feet to her right. "Oh, did that startle you, Squeakers?" She looked over at the mouse peering out a hole at the end of a doubled-over scrap of carpet on the floor. Leaving the drone controller on her lap, she reached into the pocket of the tan vest she wore over her brown t-shirt and pulled out a tiny chunk of cheese. "Here ya go." She tossed it across the room toward the mouse. The crumb settled a few inches in front of the loose carpet. Squeakers twitched his nose. He scampered out of his hiding spot and plucked the cheese from the ground before scurrying back under the carpet. She watched him nibble the morsel. Then she took another piece from her shirt pocket and popped it into her mouth. She rolled it around with her tongue for a moment before chomping it up and swallowing it. "You're right. Not bad."

She glanced around the room, taking a second to admire the torn poster tacked into the crumbling plaster on the wall to her left. It was an advertisement for some place called Erith. She liked the picture, even if she had no idea where Erith was. There were oversized greeners, more than a hundred, she figured. They weren't the two-foot-high ones that grew in the air-making factories. They were so much bigger. She knew the picture was probably a fake. No place made greeners that size. Still, she thought, wouldn't it be cool if they weren't fake. What if she could go there someday? What if she could actually leave Eon, she thought. Deep down she knew she'd never see it. She knew it wasn't possible. She was born on Eon and would die on Eon. But looking at the image, she often allowed herself to imagine she had plans to go there soon.

"I'll take you too, Squeakers. I'm sure there's lots of cheese."

She drew in a deep breath and sighed. "Right. Let's see what else is going on out there today."

She placed her thumbs onto the two toggle sticks on her drone controller and flew Birdy back out the south-facing window.

The sky was dim, most of the light came from signage on hers and the other buildings, but much farther down than her floor. The other glow, the sky glow as she knew it, shone from halfway across the city, an area she'd only been to a few times. The glow was always in the sky, but it didn't do much to light up her neighborhood.

She guided Birdy by the view on her controller's screen. She knew the neighborhood well. She could've flown the drone around every building within ten blocks without more than an occasional glance at the screen. But she watched the image Birdy's camera sent back.

Scouting—knowing what's going on in the streets and alleys below—is how she stayed alive on her own for as long as she could remember. She did it on foot, or hands and knees really, hiding and scampering like Squeakers until she was nine.

That's when she ran into a lady she came to call Nan. She spent six months living with her. She liked it. She'd heard about family. It was good while it lasted. Nan showed her how to take things apart and how to make things. She got good at turning scraps and broken bits into gadgets and tools. That's what Nan did. They had a lot of fun creating gizmos and mechanical tricks.

One night Nan went out looking for scraps. She told Tiffin she was going to bring her some good parts, and they'd make something great together. Tiffin waited three days before she realized Nan wasn't coming back. The next week, after she'd gathered up the best bits and scraps from the small place Nan rented in a line of two-story buildings made into apartments, Tiffin moved out and went looking for her own place. That was eight years ago.

She flew Birdy along the street that ran in front of her building, and down past the next four buildings. Then she backtracked, guiding the drone past her place again and the street the other direction, about the same distance. Nothing looked out of place. Dozens of people, this race and that. Scaled. Hairy. Tall. Short. Four arms. Two arms. Making deals. Heading places. Causing trouble, but not enough to draw the attention of the checkered hats. The usual traffic, she decided.

"Let's check on that alley guy, Squeakers."

She ran the controls with an effortless touch, guiding her drone down the alley on the opposite side of her building than she'd taken it before, hoping to watch from behind the man that stared her drone down earlier. She didn't like how he'd threatened to shoot Birdy the last time.

Her screen dimmed for a moment before Birdy's auto-correcting lens kicked in, compensating for the darkness of the alley. She kept Birdy a little higher than before, but nudged the slider between the two toggles to zoom the camera focus. She had a good view down the alley, from the edge of her building on past the next two towers. Beyond that, it was too dark too see.

She didn't see the man from before, but there was another figure below. He looked a little bigger than the other guy, not a race she'd seen before. "Probably passing through." *Wonder where they go from here. Or where they come from.*

She saw the thick-set guy lift a palm-sized device near his mouth. He looked like he was talking into it. Tiffin pressed a button on the controller.

"He's here," the man said. "I think I know what he's after."

"Who?" Tiffin said to herself, listening to the audio coming through her drone controller.

Birdy's directional microphone picked up more. "I'm going to take care of him, but I'm going to enjoy it too. He won't get off Eon. Just leave it to me."

Tiffin turned to the carpet where Squeakers had been hiding. "Oh, that's interesting, huh?"

18133178R00206

Printed in Poland
by Amazon Fulfillment
Poland Sp. z o.o., Wrocław